Silent Winds, Dry Seas

Silent Winds, Dry Seas

A NOVEL

Vinod Busjeet

Doubleday

New York

This is a work of fiction. Names, characters, places, and incidents either are the product of the author's imagination or are used fictitiously. Any resemblance to actual persons, living or dead, events, or locales is entirely coincidental.

Book design by Maria Carella
Jacket photograph: Mauritius, Le Mouchoir Rouge
© Ellen Rooney/Robert Harding; boat © stocknshares/iStock/
Getty; lace based on an illustration by Norb_KM/Shutterstock
Jacket design by Emily Mahon

Library of Congress Cataloging-in-Publication Data
Names: Busjeet, Vinod, author.
Title: Silent winds, dry seas : a novel / Vinod Busjeet.
Description: First edition. | New York : Doubleday, [2021]
Identifiers: LCCN 2020052001 (print) | LCCN 2020052002 (ebook) |
ISBN 9780385547024 (hardcover) | ISBN 9780385547055 (ebook)
Classification: LCC PS3602.U444 S55 2021 (print) |
LCC PS3602.U444 (ebook) | DDC 813/.6—dc23
LC record available at https://lccn.loc.gov/2020052001
LC ebook record available at https://lccn.loc.gov/2020052002

MANUFACTURED IN CANADA

1 3 5 7 9 10 8 6 4 2

First edition

In loving memory of

Gita Beker-Busjeet

a daughter who taught us the meaning of courage, dedication,

and service to others

From one citizen you gather the idea that
Mauritius was made first, and then heaven; and
that heaven was copied after Mauritius. Another
one tells you that this is an exaggeration . . .

—MARK TWAIN, *FOLLOWING THE EQUATOR*

Contents

Silent Winds, Dry Seas

I

A Haircut on the Beach

"Before I married your father, I was engaged to his younger brother Amar," my mother said.

I had heard rumors about Mama's engagement. It was a family secret that the adults acknowledged but didn't want to talk about. All these years, I had somehow been made to understand by the Bhushan clan that it is not a subject to be brought up. Papa certainly never talked about it. This time, however, I sensed that Mama wanted to tell me more about Amar.

We were in my parents' house in Mahébourg, on the southeast coast of Mauritius, in the Indian Ocean. The first Bhushan, who arrived from India in 1853, moved to this predominantly Creole town after completing his five years of indentured labor on Ferney Sugar Estate. I had flown over to the island from the United States, two oceans and nine time zones away, after hearing of my father's deteriorating condition. He was asleep in the bedroom next door, a week after the surgeons had cut open his chest to insert a pacemaker. They had advised sedation, given his feisty behavior at the hospital. The doctors and nurses had humored him, since the hospital superintendent had been his student in primary school and held him in high regard.

In the three decades I'd been away, the beat and

rhythm of the Mauritian countryside had changed. The
friendly cadence of bicycles, interrupted every now and
then by lorries carrying sugar, had given way to the rattle
of smoke-spewing buses and cars. The hospital where my
father was operated on had also undergone transformation:
fresh paint on the buildings, pruned shrubbery and flower
beds adorned with gladiolus, chrysanthemum, and bird-
of-paradise, and a well-equipped ICU, a far cry from the
hospital of my childhood where Grandma died—untended
garden, rusty corrugated iron buildings, with verandas
where dogs lay panting in the heat. After the doctors' reas-
surances, the anxiety I had felt during my stopover in Paris
had given way to optimism about my father's prospects. I
felt tranquil and listened eagerly to my mother.

"Six months after our engagement, Amar enrolled in
the British colonial army. Soon after, they shipped him to
Palestine. A famous hotel had been blown up in Jerusalem
and many British officials had died."

I realized she was referring to the King David Hotel.

"Why did he sign up? Didn't he ask for your opinion?"
I said.

"Service in the colonial army offered him the promised
land. It was not only the money. He was fed up having to
obey his elder brothers. First it was Kapil. When Kapil died,
it was Ram. If you live under their roof, you have to listen
to them. The situation was much better when Devnarain,
the eldest brother, was still alive and head of the Bhushans."

"He could have rented a house on his own," I said.

"He was jobless. When the Bhushans got together to
discuss the wedding expenses, Uncle Ram and your father
refused to contribute any money. So Amar signed up for

the army, thinking he wouldn't be called, that he would stay in the barracks in Mauritius and draw a salary."

"Didn't you dissuade him?"

"How could I when Grandma, too, became unreasonable? She insisted on the Bhushans' buying me gold jewelry; for her, gold was protection against poverty."

My mother got up and retrieved a document from her armoire. She handed it to me, and a postcard. The document, bearing the letterhead ON HIS MAJESTY'S SERVICE, stated: "We regret to inform you that No. MAUR/18023627 Private Amar Bhushan of the Royal Pioneer Corps, 2051 Company, Nathania Camp, died of wounds on April 24th, 1947 at the Bir Ya'Acov British Military Hospital."

Mama lingered on the postcard, black-and-white, now yellowish. It depicted an orange grove in Jaffa. "He wrote in simple French because he knew I had only three years of primary school and didn't understand English. He kept sending me postcards and romantic letters. I can't find them now. I must have mislaid them in the upheaval following his death."

I held Mama's hands, wondering if Papa or Uncle Ram had anything to do with their disappearance, until I recalled finding, in the debris left by Cyclone Carol in 1960, a few ruined black-and-white postcards—Port Said, Haifa, the Church of the Nativity—and throwing them away. I blushed.

It was hard for me to understand how my mother could so easily accept whatever her mother and future in-laws decided for her. I wanted to tell her my thoughts, then I realized that she was only sixteen when she got engaged, and decided to keep quiet.

"I think Amar had a breakdown around the time he enlisted. *So l'esprit tine fatigué.* We both knew the Bhushan family was in bad shape. The older generation had wasted all their savings on rum. The younger Bhushans had just sold the ancestral home in Mahébourg to pay off creditors and they borrowed money to buy sugarcane land from which to earn a living," she said. "When the news that Amar was leaving Mauritius was out, Uncle Ram pressured him into selling his share of the land to him."

Little did Uncle Ram know that his action would, more than twenty years later, shortly after his death, set in motion a court case that would consume the Bhushan clan, tear it apart and drain it of thousands of rupees. Papa would sue for annulment of the land sale and distribution of the land to Amar's "rightful heirs."

Hanging on the wall was a photo of the Bhushan brothers and sisters: Papa, Uncles Ram, Mohan, and Neeraj, and their two sisters; at the center, Amar in his British army uniform. Everyone smiled and beamed with pride. In addition to Papa, only Uncles Mohan and Neeraj were still alive. Mama looked at it and turned to me. "I'm not sure if Amar was given the proper rites by the Bhushans when he died."

"You could have done that," I said.

"Not when he had brothers who were still alive to perform the ritual. Everyone in the community would blame me and Grandma if I did something."

My mother walked back to the armoire and opened the window, letting in the sea breeze.

"After your uncle died—I don't remember whether it was six months later, or a year—the neighbors told us what they heard on the radio: the British were leaving Palestine and a new country was being created. Israel."

She wrapped the document and postcard in white linen, and paused.

"That was a different era. I was considered a widow, a poor widow. No young Hindu man would think of marrying me.

"Grandma asked relatives and close friends if they knew anyone who would be interested in marrying me. Two widowers came—a policeman and a laborer. Each had children. Each looked at our hut, asked Grandma what jewelry and furniture she was going to provide, and was never heard from again."

"I bet you that laborer lived in a thatched hut," I said.

"Everyone has the right to advance in life. Laborers, too. I don't blame him," Mama said.

She patted me on the shoulder. "The reputation of my family was at stake. Your father realized that the reputation of the Bhushan clan would also be tarnished. To save our honor, your father married me. He felt it was his responsibility."

"Did you love him?" I said.

"I couldn't afford to think that way, Vishnu. I said to myself that love can always come later. It grows."

"Did Papa tell you if he felt anything for you?"

"He must have thought the same way I did—love comes later."

I shook my head as I thought of the romantic entanglements in my life, the pleasure and the heartache that love had brought, and that led me sometimes to wonder if romantic love was overrated.

"We married in a religious ceremony on December 15, 1948."

Mama reminded me that in those days, most Hindu and Muslim couples didn't have a civil marriage—the one recognized by law—until a year after the religious wedding.

"I moved to Mapou, where your father and other Bhushans lived with Uncle Ram. I cooked for the whole clan—Uncle Ram, Uncle Mohan, and young Uncle Neeraj—washed their clothes, and cleaned the house. On top of that, I was expected to teach your father's two sisters embroidery, to enhance their marriage prospects."

"Didn't the sisters help you with the chores?" I said.

"They were young. Their parents had died while they were infants. Here I was, eighteen years old, in a huge house, being a maid for everyone, and a mother to two girls close to puberty and left idle by their elder brothers. After three months, I wanted to leave."

She paused.

"But I couldn't."

Though my mother was now in her seventies and her worried look and wrinkles were familiar, her face betrayed the dilemma confronting her so soon after her wedding. Her mother, who visited every Sunday, advised her to stay with her husband and his extended family and "sweat it out."

No. Grandma admonished her: it was her duty to stay.

Grandma had problems of her own. Grandpa had owned and operated a bus, a sign of some wealth, especially in the countryside. Afflicted by a mysterious illness when Mama was thirteen, he sold it to pay mounting medical bills. When he died, Grandma borrowed money from her

brothers-in-law to buy a few acres of land and move to the
thatched house. Looking back at the situation, my mother
asked aloud, "God! What were they thinking when they
married me to a Bhushan? An alliance of two bankrupt
families, the Bhushans and the Gopals?"

Six more months went by and my mother toiled without protest. "Papa liked being taken care of," she said.
He took her side loudly and publicly when Uncle Mohan
grouched about the sticky rice dish he was served. " 'She
made a very good biryani. Cook it yourself next time.' "

One day, Mama asked the two sisters to help rake the
piles of leaves blown into the yard by a particularly windy
anticyclone. That evening at the dinner table, both Uncles
Ram and Mohan lectured her.

"How will they find suitable husbands if they turn dark
laboring in the sun?" said one of them, Mama wasn't sure
who.

"You know what your father did? He banged on the
table and told them, 'What's wrong in being dark? I'm not
fair or brown like you; my skin is black. Black as chicken
shit.' "

"Your uncles were shocked," Mama continued. "They
couldn't believe a primary school teacher would use such
language."

"Then, after a moment of reflection, your father told
them, 'My wife toils in the sun for you all, and she's still
fair.' "

When Mama learnt that Uncle Mohan was getting
married, she was elated. Another woman would join the
household and, as her junior, she would surely be assigned
her share of household chores. My mother was soon to

be disappointed. Uncle Ram asked Mohan and his bride to move out, as the government-owned house was getting overcrowded. He told them he was concerned that the authorities would investigate.

"No one believed that," my mother said. "Uncle Ram was concerned about additional mouths to feed. Mohan had just been fired from the police force for insulting his English boss while drunk."

"One morning, not long after Uncle Mohan and his wife had left, I was in the kitchen boiling tea when your father came in, glum, holding a shirt. 'You expect me to wear this?' he said. He shoved the collar to my face. I told him I could do a much better job ironing his clothes if I didn't have to slave for his brothers and sisters. His eyes turned wild. 'We help each other here. Don't you see, we survived bankruptcy because of our joint family.'

"'No one helped Amar when he was in need,' I told him.

"To this day, I don't understand how I let these words escape from my mouth!" she said to me.

"He looked around, picked up a frying pan, and flung it at me. I ducked. It missed and crashed on the floor. By the time Uncle Ram and young Uncle Neeraj arrived, I had run to the bedroom and locked it. I asked to be taken home, back to Mon Désert."

Listening to my mother, I could not fathom my father's behavior. He had taken my mother's side against the clan and then, for a stupid shirt, got physically abusive with her! I was disappointed, torn between anger and sadness.

"She better go!" Uncle Ram, as the eldest brother, decided. "We can't tolerate this kind of behavior."

"After I packed—I made sure to take my gold jewelry—Uncle Ram instructed Uncle Neeraj to take me to the bus stop. As I stood on the threshold, Uncle Neeraj spoke. His voice was soft: 'Why not say you're sorry, and stay?'"

MAMA GOT UP, caressed my hair for a few seconds, and proceeded with her story. "The first time I felt you move was in that bus, as we left Port Louis. I pressed my hand on my belly. I looked at the noisy secondary school boys and girls around me, and I wanted my child to be like them when it grows up—healthy and educated. By the time I reached Mon Désert, I had taken a decision—to buy a sewing machine. Uncle Neeraj had given me fashion magazines, and I was determined to earn my living as a modiste."

My mother's hand embroidery was already well known throughout the Grand Port District, beyond the confines of the village. The sewing machine would consolidate her reputation as a seamstress. Soon she was doing well financially. She sewed women's dresses, blouses, and skirts, and men's shirts, and that provided for the basic necessities. The embroidery was for a higher-end clientele who paid enough for her to afford little luxuries like Yardley soap from England and georgette saris.

Mama's narration stirred my memory. I must have been three or four when a young mulatto woman came to get her dress fitted. It was the first time I saw a woman wearing a hat, the kind the wealthy sport at the horse races. "She wasn't rich," Mama said when I asked about her. "She was the concubine of a *kolom* in the sugar estate—

you know, the ti blanc who supervises the laborers in the cane fields." I had forgotten that expression, *ti blanc,* the white at the lower echelon of white society, comfortable but not wealthy or blue-blooded enough to belong to the Dodo Club. Other recollections followed: girls from the neighborhood or poorer relatives coming to learn to sew and embroider from Mama. "Like your father's sisters, they needed a métier that would make it easier for them to get a good husband."

She continued, "Let me get back to your birth, Vishnu. One day I was nauseous and I vomited over the dress I was working on. I hadn't foreseen such complications from my pregnancy. Grandma pleaded with Dr. Maurice Curé to help."

"Dr. Curé, the founder of the Labour Party?" I said, with more than a tinge of pride that my birth was helped along by such a famous person.

"He treated me for free and prescribed rest. Grandma informed your father about your premature birth, but he and the Bhushans said that I had disgraced them."

The hooting of a bicycle horn on the street interrupted us. It was the cake seller peddling his fresh-out-of-the-oven delicacies: *"Gateau coco! Feuilleté! Macatia chaud chaud!"* I leaned over the window and waved to him, "Not today."

Mama carried on. "Dr. Curé had said that your underweight body needed special attention. You had no energy to suck my breast and swallow; I soaked wicks in the milk and squeezed them in your mouth. I bathed you in rice water and Grandma massaged you with coconut oil. You were a great baby; you didn't cry. Over the next few months,

I worked constantly. I wanted to show Grandma and the world I could make it. Until the day I walked to the public water fountain, about a year after your birth."

Having grown up in the vicinity, my mother knew all the neighbors. That day, she felt uncomfortable as she collected water in her bucket. Before she got married, the men sitting around the fountain to exchange news and gossip and play dominoes greeted her with a simple "Namasté" or "Salaam." Now they leered at her. It was known in her part of the village that her child was not acknowledged by the father.

"Arey, who's the father?" someone said.

Another followed with a wolf whistle.

When one guy tried to grope her, she threw the bucketful of water on him and ran home. Within an hour, Mama's uncles beat up the groper and told Grandma not to send Mama to the fountain.

"Your father and the Bhushans talked about *their* disgrace. These men saw *me* as the disgraced one, the discarded woman," Mama said.

I saw the pain on my mother's face as she recounted her story, and my body shook with rage—rage at the way the Bhushans and the village men behaved. Why had she waited that long to tell me about all this hurt? Only the thought of my father recuperating in the bedroom next door tempered my rage.

Mama continued. "At least if your father acknowledged you as his son, I could face these men. I decided to fight for that."

My mother was aware of the Bhushans' attachment to their ancestral traditions. Shaving a child's birth hair, especially a boy's, was an important rite of purification for them; hair from birth bears negative experiences and attitudes from past lives that must be shorn. "If I can somehow arrange to have your mundan ceremony performed at the Bhushans' by their priest, I would have achieved recognition for you."

Uncle Mohan's wife had given birth to a boy. "I went to see her early morning, when her husband was out cutting cane in the fields. I brought her baby clothes I had embroidered and a set of monogrammed pillows and bedsheets. She was thankful, and I told her how much I would appreciate an invitation to her child's mundan." My mother planned to take me along and ask the Bhushans to include me in the ceremony. "How can they refuse in front of their pandit?"

She waited in vain for that invitation.

"I had to do something that would force the Bhushans to pay attention," Mama said.

She consulted an aunt who was the mistress of a Brahman. "Nothing prevents you from hiring a pandit to perform the rite in public. Shame them," said the aunt. "Can you do it the Bhushan way? They are of the sheep farmers' caste and offer a lamb in sacrifice. They invite the whole clan and half the village and serve rum. Can you afford that?"

"Who says the Bhushan way of lamb and rum is the right way? Our ancestors left India a hundred years ago. Who really knows how they did things in the old country? Each family in Mauritius has its own pandit, and every pandit does his own thing," said my mother.

The aunt arranged a ceremony on the beach in Mahébourg. Even though the Bhushans no longer lived there in the 1950s, everyone in town knew them. They were the first descendants of Indian coolies who had owned horse carriages in the south—and many Hindus commented on the way they flaunted them throughout the district. "Aping the whites," they said. A thriving jewelry shop had further enhanced the Bhushans' position as "a prominent family." Many still remembered because they were stunned by the Bhushans' subsequent bankruptcy, which drove them away from Mahébourg.

Mama continued. "My aunt and I chose a Monday, market day, the busiest day of the week. Grandma invited your maternal uncles and aunts, and my Catholic friends from childhood came. Your screams made the barber's task difficult. After he shaved your head, my aunt walked me waist-deep into the sea, facing the sun. As the pandit recited the prayer to Surya Devta, the sun god, I released the tufts of your hair in the ocean."

No lamb's head was chopped and no rum was served. Only the sea breeze blowing the scents of camphor, sandalwood, and incense through the filao trees was there to be relished.

Mama continued. "It was a feeling most strange. As the waves ebbed and flowed around me, I remembered what my great-grandmother, my ancestor from India, had told me: 'Thousands of miles under the sea, there is a holy canal linking this sea to the Ganga River in India.' For a second, I saw myself in Banaras praying on the banks of the Ganga. Banaras, the city founded by the god Shiva."

Mama closed her eyes.

Like most Mauritians, she had never been to the land of

her ancestors, and her vision of Banaras derived from calendars depicting holy festivals and Hindu gods in all their
splendor.

How the Bhushans learnt about the seaside ceremony
wasn't clear. Creole fishermen hauling fish from their boats
and Indian planters carrying their vegetables to the bazaar
stopped to look. "Up the slope from the beach," Mama
added, "the servants of Monsieur Le Juge de Segrais, the
Franco-Mauritian aristocrat, were watching from the vast
veranda of his mansion. The green roof and gables sparkled
that day."

"Maybe the Creoles thought of their Catholic bap-
tism," I said.

"A week later your father and Uncle Ram were at our
doorstep."

Mama paused for a second.

"Let me check on Papa in the bedroom," she said.

I RELIVED MY earliest childhood memory. I was playing by the public water fountain with the other boys in
the neighborhood. We were watching an airplane fly into
the clouds after it grazed the treetops at the far end of the
road. So it seemed to us at the time. The island's airport
was nearby, but I didn't know that yet. I was around three
years old. As I took the path leading home, the sugar factory siren blared, announcing the end of the workday, and
Grandma appeared, a huge bunch of sugarcane leaves bal-
anced on her head, a sickle by her waist. We walked to
the cowshed and Grandma fed the leaves to her two cows.
Behind the cowshed there grew fruits—pineapple, mango,

bananas, and lychee—and a curry leaf tree and betel plant, and there were steps that led to a stream where my mother washed clothes and chatted with other women while I entertained myself by clinging to a fallen tree trunk floating in the river.

"Vishnu!" my mother said.

I ran to our thatched house. Mama was bent over a pail, mixing water, mud, and cow dung into a paste.

"Pour me some water," she said. I can't recall how long she took—minutes or hours—but I watched her apply that paste on the soil. Once dry, that was our floor.

That evening, I heard my mother moan, "Be careful, Ma, don't burn me."

I parted the drapes that separated the kitchen from the bedroom and saw her on the bed, flat on her belly, Grandma by her side. On her naked back, a flame was burning under a glass. Mama's fair skin was a glowing red. In the darkness, the flame cast shadows that flickered on the newspapers decorating the walls, made of dried sugarcane leaves. The play of light and shade frightened me, and I closed the drapes.

Later, much later, my mother explained that Grandma was using an ancient Indian therapy called ventouse, or cupping: the vacuum created by heat in a glass eases knots in the body and reduces aches and pains.

While Mama was with my father next door, other childhood memories came back, all populated with relatives. The noisy wedding where I saw a gramophone for the first time and was allowed to touch it. Glued onto the wooden base was a photograph of a sweet dog listening to the music coming out of the trumpet, and a label I couldn't

read at the time: HIS MASTER'S VOICE. A religious ceremony where the kids giggled when the dhoti-clad pandit
chanted "Om Swaha, Om Swaha, Om" over the holy fire.
My first trip to the cinema: the enormous moon laughing
at me, the shaky wooden frame of the bus with its blinking
headlights, the conductor handing passengers tickets from
his wooden dispenser, the curved staircase at the Salle des
Fêtes Cinema, the hero on a galloping horse who sang in a
language I didn't yet understand:

> Chal chal re musaafir chal
> (Let's go traveler, let's go.)

On all these occasions, my mother and maternal grand-
mother figured prominently, holding my hands, twist-
ing my ear to shut me up, buying me grilled peanuts and
gâteaux piments.

My father, however, was absent. I don't remember seeing him in that thatched house in Mon Désert.

"WHAT DID YOU do when Papa and Uncle Ram showed
up?" I asked Mama when she returned.

"My sewing machine had to go with me. I didn't want
to be totally dependent on your father."

Her words took me back to the first memory of my
father, Shiv Bhushan. It was a bus ride when I was around
the age of five or six. He sat next to Mama, with me across
the aisle, next to Uncle Ram. The passengers were gawking at us. I'm not sure whether it was because Uncle Ram

and Papa wore smart, well-ironed suits that made them the best dressed on the bus, or because of the incongruity of Uncle Ram carrying a Singer sewing machine on his lap.

At our destination, Mapou, forty miles north of Mon Désert and three bus changes away (including one in the island's capital, Port Louis), Papa and Uncle Ram brought us to a very different dwelling. A solid house, not rich, but definitely more comfortable: a roof with shingles, shiny wood floors, walls adorned with painted oranges, lemons, and flower patterns. Instead of the candles and oil lamps at Mon Désert, electric bulbs hung from the ceiling. There were books on shelves, and even some magazines hidden under a bed. Later, when I shared the bedroom with him, I found out that these were magazines belonging to young Uncle Neeraj, then learning the tailor's trade and not yet a dandy and a counterfeiter. The house had a living room and three bedrooms.

The outdoor stone kitchen, which was as large as the house in Mon Désert, stood next to a huge banyan tree from whose tresses I remember swinging to and fro. The fruits in Mapou were different. Split pomegranates and their red seeds blanketed the backyard, and formed a mantle around a lone cotton tree. A road lined with grapefruit trees ran in front of the house, and across were the railway station and rail tracks. About a hundred yards away was a hangar where locomotives were parked and metal pipes, coal, and timber were stored. It soon became a playground for me and the neighbor boys and girls.

Mama and I had moved to a house provided by the Railways Department to the railway stationmaster, Uncle

Ram. The steam whistles of the trains puffing to a halt or leaving the station fascinated me. It was a world far removed from the oxcarts and the few lorries that passed by our thatched house in Mon Désert, on their way to the factory with their loads of sugarcane. The clatter of oxen hooves and cart wheels was gone; the thunder of locomotive engines now filled my ears.

I liked Uncle Ram. He often took me down the road to Ah-Kam's and, while smoking and savoring drinks with his friends at the bar—it was hidden at the back of the shop owned by the Chinese family—he spoilt me with sweets. Sometimes he brought me to the Mapou District Court, two minutes' walk from Ah-Kam's. The barristers walking around in their black robes and stiff white collars and the disheveled, unshaven men in handcuffs escorted in and out of black vans marked HIS MAJESTY'S PRISONS awed me. And on many Saturdays, we traveled by bus to Port Louis to enjoy the horse races at the Champ de Mars. Papa and Mama stayed home.

"Why had Uncle Ram been so harsh with you and yet always spoiled me with sweets and gifts?" I asked my mother.

"You were the son he never had," Mama said. "Do you remember his planter's chair—the rattan armchair with the extended arm serving as a leg rest?"

"Oh, yes! He used to boast that it was made by craftsmen from Pondicherry in the style of the Compagnie des Indes. He admired French colonial furniture."

"You were the only one allowed to relax in it apart from him," Mama said. "None of his brothers dared touch it in his presence."

I recalled Uncle Ram relaxing on that armchair. "Vishnu, the big white man used to sit here and look over his plantations, extending far into the horizon," he said, pointing to the Belle Vue and Labourdonnais sugar estates in the distance with a sweep of his arm, as if they belonged to him.

At the same time, I couldn't forget Papa convalescing next door in the bedroom. At eighty-eight, he had outlived all his classmates and friends. On January 1, 2000, when I had called him to wish him a Happy Millennium New Year, he confided his secret for longevity: "I have a special mantra which I recite every night." I suspected he got it from the Tamil mystic who had been his father's friend and spiritual guide. I asked Papa to share it. "It's a secret; and you have to earn it through tapasya. You never cared for this Hindu practice of austerities and spiritual purification, Vishnu."

In his long life, did he ever tell Mama he was sorry for what happened in Mapou and for his abandonment of her?

Before I could ask Mama that question, she went on: "Do you remember your original birth certificate?"

"Original?"

"Yes, the handwritten one, not the one that comes from the computer."

From her armoire, Mama pulled out a plastic folder that smelled of mothballs. Inside it was a legal-size stamped paper embossed with a wax seal, the kind one sees in colonial museums throughout the Commonwealth, from London to Delhi, from Canberra to Cape Town. Under the printed column headings were specimens of fine penmanship from another era, in black ink.

Date of Birth: July 31st, 1949
Name/Surname: Vishnu Gopal
Natural or Legitimate: Natural, acknowledged by
    the mother.
Name/Surname of Father and Mother: Seeta
    Gopal, no calling, of Mon Désert.

Running horizontally across the page on the bottom
half, in equally fine penmanship, in red ink:

Acknowledged by Shiv Bhushan as his natural
child—October 1, 1955
    Legitimated by Marriage—September 20, 1956.

II

Questions

1956

Grandma, harvesting watermelons,
collapsed in the sunny field.

The nurse shouted at Mama:
"No visitors after four o'clock!"
Mama knocked on the door of the head nurse:
"Against regulations."
The doctor's secretary:
"Do you have an appointment?"

"Where is my mother?" she cried.

That evening, Papa dropped me at Cousin Shankar's.
All the children were there, sitting on bales of
    potatoes,
drumming on pots and pans.
"How dare you?" Uncle shouted.

Next morning Auntie took me to Grandma.
She was wearing red, her wedding sari.
I thought of the toys she gave me at Christmas
and the shirts, chocolate bars, Pepsi.

My uncles and Papa lifted the coffin.
Mama clung to it, wouldn't let it go.

When the procession passed the village fountain,
I asked Mama, "Why can't we go with them?"

III

All the Same Sauce

1957

When the ambulance arrived, I was standing in the middle of the room, the screaming baby boy in my arms, his excrement dripping all over my white shirt and elbow. My mother was rubbing cologne on the face of Mrs. Kajal Desai, the baby's mother, who lay silent on the brass bed, shivering, her blouse soaked with perspiration, her sari in a mess. For more than ten minutes she had been writhing like an angry serpent on that bed, her mouth and throat struggling to tell Mama something. The two paramedics rushed her into the ambulance. Mama took the baby out of my arms, asked old Madame Joseph, our Creole neighbor who had just walked in, to take care of me, and ran into the ambulance, which sped off. I was eight years old.

Madame Joseph grabbed the hurricane lantern from the veranda and led me to the dark bathroom—a shack in the backyard, some six feet by six feet, with a water pipe hanging from the ceiling, no showerhead. She let the water run full force over me, asked me to wait for her, and left.

I stood shivering in the darkness. Through the holes in the rusty corrugated iron roof I could glimpse a few stars and the moon.

We had moved to the Desais' house in Rose Belle vil-

lage a year earlier, in 1956, when Papa, recently confirmed
in his primary school teacher's job, was transferred there
by the Mauritius Ministry of Education. During the day,
buses plying the Route Royale, which linked Port Louis to
Mahébourg, drove by the house every half hour. Bus passengers and those in the much rarer taxis and private cars
could not miss the hand-painted advertising board nailed
to the huge mango tree in the front yard:

Desai Printers
Wedding Invitations
Rubber Stamps etc

My parents were renting two rooms from Mr. Desai,
whose family occupied the six other rooms in the house;
our two families shared the veranda and the kitchen. I
remember clearly the Desais' furniture, luxurious compared with ours: carved wooden chairs decorated with
flowers and birds and, Papa told me, imported from India
and Yugoslavia; velvet sofas; and a German tube radio—
a Grundig, in a rich brown wooden cabinet. The walls separating the rooms were made of thin wood planks, so we
heard the radio music and the news, and didn't complain.
We had four simple plywood chairs, a dining table where
I did my homework and Papa prepared his teaching notes,
a cupboard, and two beds. Even their gods were richer:
the Desais' elephant god Ganesh, in shiny metal, shared
an entire room with Lakshmi, the curvaceous goddess of
wealth—a room with drapes and rugs. Our Ganesh, made
of wood, stood solitary on a shelf in a corner of my parents'
room.

Madame Joseph returned with a scrap of torn skirt
with which she vigorously dried me, then took me to her
place. Modest as our rented rooms were, Madame Joseph's
dwelling was poorer. Sitting on the plot of land adjacent
to the Desai house, it consisted of one room that served as
kitchen, bedroom, and living room. She also rented from
Mr. Desai, who owned three other properties in Rose Belle
and villages nearby.

Madame Joseph handed me a huge shirt that must have
belonged to Mr. Joseph before he died. While I was trying
to prevent the ample sleeves from sliding down my thin
arms, she busied herself in the kitchen corner of the room.
"Vishnu, have some warm milk with honey," she said when
she came back. She sat me on the bed, poured herself two
pegs from a bottle labeled AI RHUM DE PRESTIGE, and we
quietly sipped our drinks. The southeast trade winds were
blowing in the scents of mango, lychee, and zamalac, and
the moon cast its light on the floor. Like everyone else,
Madame Joseph left her window open in the summer.

Madame Joseph improvised a mattress for herself by
piling some jute gunnysacks on the floor. She kissed the
Jesus Christ on her necklace good night, and soon she was
snoring. I was restless. I stared at the ceiling, covered my
face with the pillow, turned left and right as I pictured Mrs.
Desai and Mama in the ambulance. I was half asleep when
a lizard darted across the wall and landed on the window-
sill. I didn't want it to jump on me, and got up to chase
it. Against the faint light in the Desai bedroom window,
some twenty-five feet away, I thought I saw silhouettes.
Silhouettes of two people bending and picking something.
I rubbed my eyes and looked again and they were gone. I

looked at Madame Joseph: her mouth was open; her night-gown had moved up her hips, revealing scaly skin and calluses on her soles and toes. Two cockroaches were navigating around the gunnysacks.

WHEN MAMA WOKE me up, dawn was breaking. The backyard cocks crowed and the neighborhood stray dogs barked. Madame Joseph was in the kitchen corner. I asked Mama what had happened to Mrs. Desai. "She is dead." She turned to Madame Joseph and added, "The doctor told us she swallowed acid."

Handing Mama a cup of tea, Madame Joseph said, "Mr. Desai uses acid in his business. I saw him bring them special bags last week."

While they talked, an image from Grandma's funeral, six months earlier, crossed my mind—Mama pounding on her mother's coffin and futilely clinging to it as my uncles and my father carried it out of the house. It occurred to me then that Kajal had left me forever, and tears filled my eyes.

"The police drove us back from the hospital around five, me and Vishnu's father." Like many women of her generation on the island, when addressing others Mama referred to Papa not by his name, Shiv, but as "Vishnu's father." "I couldn't wake you until they had left. They searched the whole house, even our rooms."

"What did the police ask Mr. Desai?" Madame Joseph said.

"You know Mr. Desai. He is gentleman. The police believed everything he said." Mama, whose only act of literacy was signing her name on official documents, knew about ten words in English. She spoke Kreol Morisien, a mostly French dialect. To her, the word *gentleman* (always without the indefinite article *a*) meant a dandy with the gift of the gab who used educated speech to get what he wanted—an apt, if incomplete, description of Mr. Desai.

Madame Joseph sighed. "He'll probably buy the police a case of Chivas Regal."

Mama told Madame Joseph that the police were mostly concerned with the whereabouts of everyone that evening. Mr. Desai explained to them that he had gone shopping for supplies in Port Louis, twenty-three miles away, and was driving back home when his wife was taken to the hospital. Anil, his son from his first marriage, was at his grandma's. Papa had gone to the parents-teachers meeting at the school, then straight to the hospital when he heard about the ambulance at the house.

"Did they ask you anything, Mama?"

"Of course, and Papa too."

Mama took me in her arms and continued. "Papa warned me in Bhojpuri not to say anything bad about Mr. Desai. The two policemen were Creoles; they don't understand our Indian language."

"Men: all the same sauce," Madame Joseph said, shaking her head.

PAPA, WHO TAUGHT the sixth graders, and I, a pupil in the fourth grade, walked together to school every morning, about a mile. The day my parents came back from the hospital in the police car, Papa and I didn't leave for school until noon. On the way, Papa tried to make conversation, but I was too sad. I don't remember tears; I just felt empty. A friend had left me. She was such a friend that one day I had called her by her name, Kajal, and Mama scolded me and told me to show proper respect by addressing her henceforth as Mrs. Desai.

Slim, with rosy cheeks and long black hair, Kajal was petite; the biggest girl in sixth grade was the same size. She had arrived in Rose Belle shortly after we moved there and looked much younger than her husband. Years later, when I was in secondary school, Mama told me that Kajal was seventeen when she died, and Mr. Desai at least forty. Mama told Papa about the wedding gifts Mr. Desai lavished on Kajal:

"You should see her gold mangalsutra; it's perfect on her long neck."

Craning her neck and collaring it with her fingers, Mama said, "I'm still waiting for mine."

"Your mother should have married you off to a Bombai," Papa said.

The Desais were "Bombai," Mauritians whose ancestors hailed from Bombay. To my parents, that implied a few differences from the majority Biharis on the island, who were mostly laborers or small planters, hence rustic. Bombais were mostly in small business or the refined crafts such as goldsmithing, and Biharis viewed them as having a certain degree of sophistication associated with the city. Moreover, being generally more fair-skinned than Biharis, they were more highly prized in the marriage market. Mr. Desai was one of the few Bombais who lived in the countryside. I heard Madame Joseph tell Mama that he didn't like to mingle and hated the noise in the city.

In the first few weeks after her arrival in Rose Belle, Kajal wanted to play with me and read books under the zamalac tree. When I came back from school in the afternoon, and on the weekends, she read me French novels I didn't always understand—Françoise Sagan's *Bonjour Tristesse,* Marcel Priollet's *Reine de Tango.* Words like *femme fatale, faire l'amour, débauche,* and *entrelacée* cropped up. She taught me swear words used in the city: *cul, pute.* We plucked the bell-shaped pink fruits from the zamalac tree and gorged ourselves. Kajal was beautiful and was opening my eyes to a new and lovely world.

She was so unlike Mama, who always kept busy—if she was not cooking or cleaning the house or ironing clothes, Mama was making lace embroidery that people had ordered for special occasions like weddings and baptisms.

I spent much more time with Kajal than with Mr. Desai's son, Anil, who was thirteen and in Form III in secondary school. The veranda was equipped with a Ping-Pong table. A few times, I asked him to teach me to play, but he got irritated and complained to Mama, who warned me to stay out of the veranda when Anil was there. I thought then that he disliked me because I had once called him a girl after I surprised him admiring himself in a handheld mirror.

Mr. Desai, who conducted his business from two rooms in the house, would sometimes come out and tell Kajal that she should be cooking and cleaning instead of playing with a kid. She would then run to the kitchen and ask my mother to help her.

After a month or so had passed, at dinnertime, across

the thin wood walls, we heard Mr. Desai shout, "Is that all you can prepare? Omelets day in and day out! Bland sandwiches and salads!" The noise of dishes slamming against wood followed. Then the sound of slaps on the face. A thud.

"You good-for-nothing imbecile! I'll tell your mother and brothers about this. I bet you were too snobbish to learn some decent cooking."

We heard cries and sobs. I could still hear them when I went to bed and fell asleep.

The next day, when I returned from school, Kajal and Mama were in the kitchen. Kajal's lips were swollen. A few minutes later, Mr. Desai walked in, wearing a double-breasted jacket adorned with a red pocket handkerchief. He offered Kajal roses and a box of chocolates. She stormed out.

"Mrs. Bhushan, I am at a loss," he said. "I don't know what to do with her. Please, I implore you, teach her how to cook what men like your husband and I eat—curries and vindaloos, rougaille creole." He stepped to the door, stood there for a few seconds, then walked back. "I'll be grateful, really. Tell Mr. Bhushan he need not worry about a rent increase this year."

Over the next months, I saw Mama a few times in the kitchen teaching Kajal the mixing and blending of spices, the amount of time different dishes should be sautéed, fried, or simmered, and the pairing of sauces with meats and fish. Kajal seemed indifferent. She was more interested in reading, and her taste was shifting to crime stories. When Mr. Desai saw her with a copy of the French version of Caryl

Chessman's *Cell 2455, Death Row,* he slapped her in front of me.

The violence increased. One morning when Madame Joseph and Mama were in the backyard slicing mangoes for pickling, I sneaked into the kitchen to help myself to a little bit of the French pastry meant for afternoon tea. I had barely snatched a slice of the Napolitain cake when I saw Kajal walk towards them. I watched with apprehension and horror as she lifted her blouse and showed Mama and Madame Joseph the darkening wheals and scars on her back and on her belly. "He did this with his leather belt," she said. When she lowered her blouse, I stepped forward, took her hand, and squeezed it.

Mama asked Kajal, "Why don't you put your mind on the cooking?"

"I don't want to cook for that repulsive man. He hits me, then wants sex. His flesh sags."

Madame Joseph said, "Men: all the same sauce."

After Kajal left, Mama and Madame Joseph spoke about how her belly had gotten bigger.

"Vishnu, go do your homework. Madame Joseph and I have to talk."

A few weeks later, Kajal explained to me in some detail how babies are made. Mama was aghast when I told her what I had learnt. "Vishnu, you're too young to hear all this. Now, don't tell Papa. Okay?" And to Kajal she said, "How can you expect me to help you when you behave in this manner?"

I remember Mama knitting baby socks and embroidering tiny pillowcases that Kajal brought to her. But I don't remember how many weeks went by before Kajal gave birth to a baby boy whom they named Dayal; it was such a long time ago.

After Dayal's birth, there was a period of quiet, and even joy. Mr. Desai bought toys and distributed sweets to us and the neighbors. Kajal's mother and two brothers came to visit, but Mama remarked with surprise that they had not stayed long. She and Madame Joseph talked about how their mothers had lived with them for weeks after the birth of their babies to help them with the chores of mothering.

Soon, though, Mr. Desai began complaining about how Kajal was feeding, cleaning, and clothing Dayal. As with the cooking, Mama helped. She taught her the proper way to wash cloth diapers and how to insert the pins so as not to hurt the baby when changing them. I felt sorry for Kajal and played with the baby on most days, until Papa told me to stop; he wanted me to read the books he brought from the library instead.

It was impossible for Kajal to please Mr. Desai. Again dinnertime became beating and sobbing time. Anil, Dayal's half brother, spent more afternoons and weekends at his grandma's; he told me that he couldn't study in peace with all the noise. Until Dayal's arrival, Anil studied and read on the veranda.

One day when the beating and crying were particularly intense, Mama told Papa over dinner, "We must move out of here. It's not healthy for Vishnu to be exposed to this."

"We have to wait for this year's crop, and see how much we can save," said Papa, referring to the two acres of sugarcane fields he had inherited, which he tended on the weekends.

We got a respite from the beating and crying when we spent a weekend in Mahébourg at the wedding of one of Mama's nieces. On our return, Sunday evening, Kajal's face was in such a condition—black eyes that were half-shut, swollen lips, bruised temples—that even Papa felt compelled to act.

"She's going to run away if you continue like this," he said to Mr. Desai. "She'll go to the police."

Mr. Desai shrugged his shoulders. "Your wife isn't here for two days to help her, and she can't function."

I wished I were big enough to smash Mr. Desai's face. The sadness I felt seeing Kajal's expression gave way to anger.

"Why are you looking at me like a bulldog?" Mr. Desai said to me.

"Leave Vishnu out of this, Mr. Desai. He's a child," said Mama.

In the kitchen, Mama asked Kajal what had happened.

"He was pestering me so much about the way I take care of Dayal, I mistook salt for sugar and put it in his tea. He got mad and said I did it on purpose. I told him he was an asshole."

Mama recoiled at the word: "Kajal, you shouldn't use this kind of language in front of Vishnu."

"Auntie, you have to help me. I want to get out of here."

Unlike Kajal, who was totally dependent on her husband, Mama earned some money from her embroidery. On Monday morning, she gave Madame Joseph bus fare and lunch money and sent her to deliver an urgent message to Kajal's mother.

Kajal's mother and two brothers did not come until the following Sunday. I remember the day of the week vividly, because when they arrived, I was sitting on the stone steps leading to the veranda, chewing sugarcane and watching the brightly dressed Creole families walk to Sunday Mass. Mr. Desai wasn't home, and Papa was away working in his sugarcane field. They sat on the veranda with Kajal, whose bruises, black eyes, and swollen lips were still visible. She held Dayal in her lap. Mama and I were in our front room behind the veranda, me pretending to do my homework and Mama doing her embroidery. We could hear them clearly through the thin walls. Kajal's mother and brothers repeated what Mr. Desai had told them about Kajal's failings, and Kajal cried and called Mama, who went out on the veranda. I followed her.

"It's none of my business to tell you what to do, but I think you should take her home with you," Mama said to them. "Most men hit their wives, but like Mr. Desai I haven't seen or heard before; Mr. Desai, he is Bluebeard."

I smiled, with a little bit of pride: I had read her the children's version of how the wealthy French aristocrat murdered his wives.

Mama went on. "The neighbors say Anil's mother died mysteriously and his second wife left him."

"Rumors spread by envious people," one of the brothers said.

Kajal's mother spoke: "Her husband says she does not obey. She's always been a disobedient child. Oh, God, I don't know what I've done in my previous life to deserve such a daughter!" She raised her voice: "I warned her father—too much education is not good for girls; they lose respect for our traditions. Kajal was reading all that rubbish about love."

Suddenly Madame Joseph appeared. "Ma'am, you talk like you just got off that bloody boat from India. You forget that boat hit our shores more than a hundred years ago. Look what he's done to your daughter's face. How can you leave her here?"

I was unhappy that Kajal would no longer play with me, but I silently agreed with Madame Joseph.

Kajal's mother looked at Madame Joseph's bare feet and worn-out clothes and frowned. "She needs someone like Mr. Desai to discipline her," she said.

"Ma, take me with you. Please. Look at your beautiful grandchild; he'll make you happy."

"A married woman belongs with her husband," said Kajal's mother.

After Kajal's folk left, Mama and Madame Joseph drank tea. They wondered aloud whether Kajal had had a boyfriend in the city, a sweetheart from secondary school.

"Her mother couldn't allow that," said Mama. "Girls from respectable Hindu families don't have boyfriends before marriage."

"Maybe he was poor or had no job," Madame Joseph said.

Days later, maybe two to three weeks, Mama was kneading flour for my favorite Indian bread, dal puri, when I went into the kitchen. "Vishnu, Dayal has been screaming for more than ten minutes. Mrs. Desai hasn't come to make dinner. Go check if she needs something." I went through three rooms and saw no sign of Kajal or baby Dayal; I ventured into the bedroom. On the bed, Kajal lay foaming at the mouth, tearing her hair, her body coiling and contort-ing. Baby Dayal, who stopped crying when I came in, was at the foot of the bed. He had no diapers on.

WHEN KAJAL'S BELONGINGS were disposed of, I got to keep the books in which she had inscribed her name. Mama and I shared her perfume. Occasionally, I would open the flacon and inhale the fragrance.

Three months after Kajal's death, an investigating magistrate heard testimony in the Judges' Chambers at the Mahébourg District Court. As I walked to school that day, I saw Mr. Desai leaving home in his car, dressed in his very best. My parents had left for the court earlier, by bus. The magistrate classified the case as a suicide.

The following year, Papa got a raise and had a bumper sugarcane harvest. We moved to Mahébourg, and in 1960 I was admitted to the Royal College Curepipe secondary school. When the bus to school passed the house where we had lived in Rose Belle, I always looked out, hoping to catch a glimpse of what became of Baby Dayal and Anil and Mr. Desai—for I could see the veranda from the bus. But there was never anyone there. And one day, in my sec-ond year of secondary school, I noticed that the advertising sign for Desai Printers was gone.

Kajal and Mr. Desai were slowly fading from memory. Women from the movies now occupied my thoughts and imagination. Baby Dayal, however, still haunted me. At a neighbor's funeral wake in 1962, we ran into Anil, who was now eighteen and about to complete his secondary school studies; I was thirteen. He was playing with a baby when

Mama asked him to help her serve tea to the mourners. As he walked towards me with the baby, I pulled back.

"It will shit on me," I said.

"Vishnu, that's not nice," said Mama.

The following year, when I turned fourteen, Kajal came back to me. Chemistry lab class did it. I learnt that aluminum plates used in manufacturing rubber stamps were bathed in diluted acid to enable the designs to be etched and raised. Now that I had read *Romeo and Juliet,* I imagined Kajal bringing the bottle of diluted acid to her lips, but, unlike with Juliet, the acid ate away her delicate stomach. If only I had gotten to the bedroom earlier! When I asked the chemistry teacher if he knew of people committing suicide with acid, he said, "I don't know anyone personally. But if they want to, cyanide is the best—the corpse exudes an aroma of almonds." That led me into deeper reverie. I had seen a photo of a painting of Ophelia drowning, surrounded by flowers; I now pictured Kajal floating in the river, perfuming the air. I must have been in love with Kajal, I thought.

Two years later, when I was slowly outgrowing my teenage fantasies, I learnt that the smell from cyanide is of *bitter* almonds.

Around that time, we had a visitor.

"Madame Joseph!" said Mama as she opened the door.

Madame Joseph had changed: she now leaned on a cane and wore shoes.

Mama's eyes were moist. It was time for afternoon tea, and after we sat down, she served cakes. "What brings you here?" Mama said.

"The pig is dead," said Madame Joseph.

Mama furrowed her brow.

"Mr. Desai. He died a painful death . . . throat cancer."
Madame Joseph's face showed no emotion; her voice was
resonant but calm.

I said nothing. I was still angry at the way Mr. Desai
had treated Kajal.

"How is Dayal?" Mama said.

"He is growing into a fine boy. His grandma looks after
him."

"And Anil?" I said.

"Vishnu, I don't know what to tell you. After Kajal's
death, Anil and his father fought constantly. Mr. Desai sold
his business and Anil left home to live in Beau Bassin,"
Madame Joseph said. "His grandma says he's going to
change his name."

"I would do the same if I were Anil," I said.

Mama looked at me in a way only she could, showing
approval and concern at the same time. I wondered, then
and many times since, if she sensed that Mr. Desai's death
unsettled me, that it brought back images of Kajal's suffering: her bruises and black eyes, her pleading in vain to
return home to her mother, her final agonizing moments
on her bed.

I continued: "Madame Joseph, can I ask you something? Did you ever find out what really happened to Kajal
that night?"

"Mr. Desai shipped Anil to his grandma that day. He
told everyone he was in Port Louis for supplies; but I know
he had already made his monthly trip for supplies the week
before," Madame Joseph said.

Mama turned to me. "Mr. Desai warned Papa that he would kick us out of the house if we gave too many details to the magistrate. Earlier that day, Kajal had complained of stomachache. Oh, my God, when I think back, I was so naive then."

"I overheard Mr. Desai's brothers when they were visiting—you know, the two who stay together in Curepipe," Madame Joseph said. "They were drunk and babbled about how they went to the house that night and took some bottles. They threw them down the latrine in their outhouse."

Shaking her head, she added, "Men: all the same sauce."

I remembered the silhouettes in the Desais' bedroom, and related what I had seen to Mama and Madame Joseph. "I should have told you and the police the day you came back from the hospital. It's terrible."

"Son, you were eight years old. The police wouldn't have believed you."

"Mama, I never tried to help Kajal."

"How could you? You were a kid," said Mama. Her face turned somber. She paused. "That was a very dark period of my life. I feel so guilty I didn't do more for her."

Madame Joseph and I moved close to her and held her hands.

THROUGHOUT MY SECONDARY school years, Mama asked me to read the daily newspaper to her. It was only four pages, in French, with legal notices in English. A few days after Madame Joseph's visit, I saw this:

NOTICE OF CHANGE OF NAME
ANIL Desai residing at Beau Bassin hereby petitions the Master
and Registrar of the Supreme Court for change of his name to
JAMES OLIVER MORGAN . . . etc.

Mama said nothing when I translated it for her, but her face showed distress. She mentioned it to Papa at dinner.

"I saw the notice. He thinks an English name fits his skin color better," he said.

Some three months after publication of the legal notice, there was a knock on the door.

"Anil," said Mama as she opened it.

"Auntie Seeta, I am James now. James Oliver Morgan. But you can call me Anil. You and some older relatives can."

Mama's eyes were moist. "Oh, Anil, you're so handsome in that suit." She touched his gold cuff links lovingly. "You've got style—gentleman, like your father! How are you doing? You've got a job?"

"I'm now active in the Protestant Church; they have taught me so many things, Auntie."

"Son, why did you have to convert?"

"How could I remain a Hindu after all that my father did? To my mother, to Kajal, to me. The way Hindus treat women—it's a disgrace."

"Anil, it's not a Hindu thing; it's a man thing. Look around here—the Creole fishermen go to Mass on Sunday morning, get drunk at the bar at noon, and come home and beat up their women."

"It's not the same, Auntie. The fisherfolk are illiterate; my father was educated."

"Anil, even the white people—you don't know what goes on in their mansions. They walk hand in hand and kiss on the beach, but remember what Madame Joseph used to say—'Men: all the same sauce.'"

"Auntie, I'll be different. They're grooming me to be Deacon; you and Uncle Shiv should come hear me in church. The parishioners love me. The Reverend says I know how to bring out the poetry when I read the Psalms. Vishnu, come too, you'll enjoy it."

A MONTH BEFORE I left Mauritius for university study, Madame Joseph died and I went to her funeral. As the Catholic priest left and mourners started shoveling soil over her coffin, I walked to the Hindu section of the cemetery and found Kajal's grave. I cleared the leaves, rooted out the weeds, stood and contemplated her name on the headstone. For how long, I couldn't tell.

Papa spotted me and called, "It's time to go."

A part of me did not want to leave.

IV

For a Fistful of Rupees

I

How come you're all eating ice cream?
The teacher stares at Sundar's shoeless feet,
pricks Murday's torn shorts with his cane.
Did your fathers give you pocket money?

My friends say nothing.
Raymond, who eats ice cream every day,
points to me.
The ice cream man bicycles away.

The teacher takes me to Papa's classroom.
Papa digs into his jacket pockets,
counts.
Dear colleague, you have my permission.

II

Children, what is the Seventh Commandment?
Raymond raises his hand, writes it on the blackboard.

Sundar, hold his arms down firmly.
The teacher adjusts my buttocks against his desk.

Murday, the right cheek. One. Stronger. Two. Three. Change places with Sundar.

Sundar, the left cheek. One. Stronger. Two. Three. Six scoops, six lashes.

V

Silent Winds, Dry Seas

1960

The Class 1 warning for Cyclone Carol had been broadcast on the Mauritius radio before Uncle Ram and I boarded the bus at ten in the morning. The previous day, his wife, Auntie Ranee, their baby, and Mama had left for Coromandel village, about twenty-eight miles north, to help Auntie's parents prepare for the yaj. Class 1 warnings weren't much to worry about; in the cyclone season, we get quite a few of them. Besides, the yaj is not just any religious service. It is the highest form of prayer, one that Auntie told me would last the entire day, from sunrise to sunset. According to the priest, that day, February 26, 1960, was particularly auspicious for a yaj in the Hindu astrological chart, the Panchang.

Uncle Ram, who had little if any religion, was keen on meeting the many relatives who were expected to show up. Papa stayed home. Though a devout Hindu, he shunned public displays of devotion like the annual Maha Shivratri pilgrimage to the holy lake of Grand Bassin, and wasn't the gregarious kind. Since the yaj was organized by his sister-in-law's clan, not by the Bhushans, Papa felt no obligation to attend. When we left home, he told Uncle Ram, "Please don't forget to show Vishnu the secondary school. It's as important as the yaj."

Six months earlier, our family had moved from Rose Belle to Mahébourg, where we shared a house near the Pointe des Régates beach with Uncle Ram and his family. I had always enjoyed visiting Uncle Ram in his various postings as railway stationmaster throughout the island. He was always jovial and would show me around the stations, let me wander in the train compartments, introduce me to the postmaster next door, and demonstrate how the telegraph and the semaphore signals worked. Now that he had retired and we were living in the same house, with a wood partition separating the two brothers' families, he intrigued me. During the day, he walked to the district court to listen to witnesses' testimonies and lawyers' pleadings, and in the evening he visited bars with other retirees, and quite often came home drunk. He remained his cheerful self at all times, whereas Papa, who was younger by eleven years, always looked serious and rarely smiled. The two brothers seemed to have only one thing in common: every day they both dressed up in suit and tie, winter or summer.

Uncle Ram beckoned me to sit next to him at the back of the bus. Through the rear windows the turquoise ocean had turned darker and the waves rougher, but I had seen that before and was not alarmed. None of the passengers looked worried. The wind, however, reminded me of an incident at the bazaar two days earlier, when a Creole fishmonger accosted me: "Vishnu, half of Mahébourg heard your uncle's invocation last night. You're by the sea, and with that voice of his and the strong wind, his words travel far. 'Hawa baand, samoondar soukarey,' he roared all night. What does he mean? Is he a prophet?"

Indeed, the last words Uncle Ram uttered every evening, in a thunderous and imperative voice, were "Hawa baand, samoondar soukarey," never "Good night." I had until then thought these were meaningless words from a tipsy man. When I told Mama about the fishmonger's question, she said with a benevolent smile, "Uncle Ram likes to puzzle and challenge. Those Hindi words mean 'Halt the winds, dry out the seas!'" She added, for reasons unclear to me at the time, that at both his weddings, Uncle Ram had scandalized the Bhushan clan and the Hindu community with his behavior. This was the first time I heard he had married twice. When I asked Mama to explain, she told me, "It's better you ask him. I don't want to be part of any gossip."

As our bus left the terminal, Uncle Ram pointed to a man running towards a taxi. His elegant turban, the ashen marks on his forehead, the saffron-colored string garland on his neck, and his dhoti indicated he was a pandit, a Hindu priest.

"Look at his loincloth flapping in the wind. Do you see between his legs?"

I thought Uncle Ram's question strange, but nodded in agreement.

"You see the pandit's eggplant dangling?"

I laughed. "No. I understand what you mean, though."

"That's what the dhoti does: everything hangs. That's what they wanted me to wear at my wedding. Can you believe that?" Uncle Ram said, caressing his jacket lapels.

"All the bridegrooms wear that at our weddings," I said.

"That's what the clan wants you to wear. They flock to you when you have a secure job. They live in your house for two years, eat your food, and then they have the nerve to dictate what you should wear at your wedding."

"They lived with you when you married Auntie Ranee?"

"I'm talking before Auntie Ranee's time. My first wife."

"You had a wife before Auntie Ranee? What did you do . . . I mean about the dhoti?"

"I flung it on the floor and threatened to walk out of the wedding if I couldn't keep my suit on."

I was shocked. I had never imagined jovial Uncle Ram could be so defiant.

"You have guts!" I said.

Uncle Ram shook his head but avoided my eyes. He looked out the window. The branches of trees lining the road were swaying. He put his arm round my shoulder and squeezed me tight. "You'll show your guts one day by leaving this place. Emigrate," he said.

But I wanted to talk about his first wife. "Did you love her as much as Auntie Ranee?"

"Vishnu, you're only ten. You know about love?"

The old Creole couple in front of us turned their heads, peered at my skinny legs and shorts, and said to each other, "Today's kids!"

Uncle Ram punched my upper arm. "We should travel together more often. We'll have plenty of time to talk about love," he said.

As the bus puffed uphill towards the High Central Plateau, I could feel the wind steadily growing stronger: the moment I opened the window for fresh air, I had to close it. On the road, sari-clad women carrying dry wood on their heads for their stoves were straining to balance their loads.

Bulls towing carts were slowing as the wind blew in their
eyes. When we got off the bus in Curepipe, the sophisticated town where foreigners and many wealthy Mauritians
lived, it was fun watching the women struggle to cover
their underwear as the wind blew up their skirts. Uncle
Ram was looking, too, and he winked at me.

TEN MINUTES LATER, we stood in front of a massive
two-story stone building with wrought iron fence and
gates, and windows the size of doors. The manicured front
lawn and the central facade supported by columns gave it
the allure of a small palace. This was the Royal College
Curepipe secondary school. With the cyclone warning, the
students had the day off. Uncle Ram pointed to the statue
of two soldiers on a huge pedestal at the entrance and said,
"Every July 14, the police band plays 'La Marseillaise' here,
and on November 11 they celebrate the Armistice. The
governor and the big shots salute." I didn't understand what
he was talking about. I found it strange that the soldiers
held a laurel in one hand, pointing skywards, and a gun
with bayonet in the other hand. I kept quiet, not wanting
to sound stupid. Uncle Ram carried on: "The building is
modeled on Buckingham Palace." That I understood. He
went inside and after a few minutes came back with the
caretaker. For the next thirty minutes, they showed me
facilities I never imagined existed in a school—basketball
and volleyball courts, a gym with contraptions whose
purpose I couldn't figure out. And what a library! Ebony
bookshelves, mahogany reading tables, etched glass panes,
first editions of Dickens novels and Charles Darwin's *On*

the Origin of Species on display. I hadn't heard of Darwin. "A revolutionary book that Catholic priests and pandits should read," said Uncle Ram.

He told the caretaker, "Let's take the boy to the Grand Hall." I was ushered into what looked like a huge theater, except that on the walls were big wooden panels with lists of names going back to the 1800s. "Ça banne lauréats, banne grand bougres," the Creole caretaker told me in the local patois: laureates, bigwigs, the school's top students who made it to Oxbridge and the Sorbonne. The island's academic hall of fame. The names on the panels until the 1950s were mostly French, a few with the nobility-denoting particle *de*—de Chazal, de Commarmond. Uncle Ram made me read a few names aloud. "You get your name there, Vishnu, and that will be your ticket to leave the island. You can then tell the pandits and the clan to go to hell."

Uncle Ram thanked the caretaker with five rupees for the unofficial tour.

MAMA WAS RIGHT, I thought as I took my seat on the bus from Curepipe to Coromandel. Uncle Ram does like to challenge and puzzle.

"Uncle, why are you telling me to emigrate? Most of these laureates came back. I read about them in the newspaper."

He sighed. "We'll talk about that later. Let's have your name on that wooden panel first."

"And how am I going to get admitted to that fancy place?"

"We all expect you to win the scholarship entrance."

"No one from Mahébourg Primary has ever done that."

"That's why your father is cramming your head with all those books they don't teach you at Mahébourg Primary."

"I don't know about that."

"Of course you know." He gently pinched my nose and pulled it. "You've jumped over two grades; at ten, you're already in sixth grade. You're ambitious without even knowing it."

We arrived in Coromandel at one in the afternoon. As we walked to the house of Auntie Ranee's parents, I could smell the burnt offerings of fragrant sandalwood, grains, nuts, spices, and aromatic medicinal herbs and hear the chanted mantra "Om swaha, Om swaha." Garlands of marigolds decorated the porch, swaying left and right in the wind. On the open veranda, two priests, the family, and adult relatives sat on the floor cross-legged, in yoga-like lotus posture. Auntie Ranee and her two sisters, whom everyone referred to as the Regal Sisters because of their statuesque features and royal deportment, sat in a semicircle around the pandits. In the two rooms behind were kids and those too old and frail to sit cross-legged. Each time the Regal Sisters poured the offerings into the copper receptacle for the sacrificial fire, the priests added ghee, using the sacred betel leaf as a spoon. The flames rose high, the dry twigs in the receptacle crackled, and a smell of simmering butter filled the room. When the gusts of wind blew in harder, it was spooky: the flames shot up dangerously, almost touching the wooden frames of the house. But the priests' dexterity was astounding. With a 180-degree sweep of their arms and hands, they calmed the flames and the kids at the back clapped.

About fifteen minutes later, Uncle Ram sneezed. He addressed the priests: "Panditji, how many more hours?"

The older pandit looked at his watch and replied, "About three."

"Three more hours of swaha, swaha?"

The pandit frowned. "In India, a yaj can last months, even years."

Auntie Ranee and her two sisters turned and shot Uncle Ram a look that could qualify as a royal reprimand. Mama looked at me and smiled. Some of the men snickered. Uncle Ram took me by the arm, turned towards the porch, and motioned these men to follow him. Papa had made me read *The Pied Piper of Hamelin,* and Uncle Ram looked very much like the Piper except that he was leading a dozen grown men, not children, out of the house and into the street. As I walked out, I turned my head and saw my cousins in the back room: bored by Sanskrit prayers they couldn't understand, they watched my departure with envious eyes.

"Let's go to la boutique Dokter," said Uncle Ram.

The "Doctor's Shop" was an establishment whose business license was prominently summarized on a hand-painted black tin plate above the door:

Aman Lim
General Retailer and Dry Goods
Liquor On & Off

Known throughout the Mauritian countryside, the village bar was a special room in a general retailer store, often owned by a Chinese family who lived in the back rooms

of the building. Aman Lim's bar was full. Creole fishermen who couldn't venture to sea because of the weather
and Indian laborers back from the fields kept Aman busy.
He called his wife, and after they exchanged a few words
of the southern Chinese language of Hakka, she led us to
their back garden. She brought out two kitchen tables and a
few chairs and arranged them under a flamboyant tree. She
handed me a sardine-and-tomato sandwich and a Pepsi.
Her two children continued playing in the garden as she
opened two bottles of rum.

Uncle Neeraj, the younger uncle who emulated Bombay film stars, sprinkled a few drops from each bottle on
the ground before Aman served the drink. Then everyone
sprinkled two drops from their glass.

"Why do you do that?" I asked.

"It's for God. He gets thirsty, too," said Uncle Neeraj.

"God is a shriveled eggplant," said Uncle Ram. "I do it
to quench the thirst of those who loved me."

"Big words today, Ram! You need to pour the whole
glass!" exclaimed the others.

Aman Lim brought in plates of curried mutton, steam-
ing with the aromas of cardamom and coriander.

"We Hindus aren't supposed to eat meat on prayer days,
not even eggs or fish," said one of the men as he plunged his
fingers into the choicest piece.

"Maja karo," said Uncle Neeraj, showing off his limited Hindi. "As the English proverb says, eat, drink, and be
merry, for tomorrow we die."

The others laughed and attacked the food with delight.

The men talked a lot. They talked about the horses
that would win the following week's races, about how their

wives wasted their hard-earned money on pandits and religious ceremonies, even about apartheid in South Africa and
the capture of Adolf Eichmann by Israel's Mossad. They
were arguing about Mauritian politics when the wind blew
a papaya at Uncle Neeraj's feet, its seeds and pink flesh
splashing on his shiny two-toned shoes.

Uncle Ram reacted: "It looks like Carol is serious. I
hope she changes course."

"If it comes, we can say good-bye to our sugar crop,"
Uncle Neeraj replied as he wiped his shoes with his cologne-
soaked handkerchief. "We already lost twenty percent of
the cane after Cyclone Alix six weeks ago."

A third bottle was ordered and consumed. Uncle
Neeraj reminded everyone that Mauritius had had a long
streak of good fortune—no cyclone from 1946 to 1959. The
men argued about cyclones with the passion and energy of
schoolchildren fighting over Mauritian and English football teams.

"The 1892 cyclone was the worst in Mauritian history.
Winds of 135 miles an hour at a time when most houses
were huts of thatched cane leaves," said Uncle Neeraj.
"Even the *Illustrated London News* wrote a whole page about
the devastation."

Uncle Ram's face reddened. Since he had the lightest
complexion of all the Bhushan men, I thought it was from
too much rum flowing to his face. But then he abruptly
grew somber, in a way I had never seen.

"Nineteen forty-five was the worst," he said. "It was
the year of three cyclones. Three."

He banged the table with his fists with such force that
the younger Chinese child began crying and ran inside the

shop. There was complete silence. We could hear the wind and feel its warmth on our faces.

Uncle Neeraj lowered his voice: "Ram, we all know you're the most educated and best-informed one here. But I've read that the strongest of the 1945 cyclones was only ninety-seven miles an hour."

Uncle Ram slapped at his watch. "It's four o'clock; let's go back to the yaj."

Uncle Neeraj attempted to lighten the atmosphere: "We better get there while there's still some ganja and bhang left." Ganja was the marijuana our ancestors had brought from India as a meditative herb, and bhang was a concoction of marijuana, milk, and spices served at Hindu weddings and other festivities in the rural areas.

The sky had changed to red. A strange, dark, menacing red.

As we came out through the shop, the rum drinkers were now outnumbered by customers seeking plywood, nails, canned food, and candles. Aman, now helped by a white-haired Chinese woman counting on an abacus, told us that a Class 2 cyclone warning had just been issued. "Do you want to take a bottle home? If we get a Class 3 warning tomorrow, shops will be closed." Uncle Ram ordered one. "Let the boy carry it, sir," said Aman. He had noticed Uncle Ram's unsteady walk.

When we reached the yaj, the ceremony was winding down. The guests were gently throwing flowers on one another—a gesture of benediction—and singing the concluding mantra of peace and harmony, "Om Shantee Shantee Shantee."

Uncle Ram had a final question for the priests before

Auntie Ranee could say "You're stinking of rum" and drag him away:

"Panditji, what does the Panchang say about Carol? Will she swerve to Madagascar?"

THAT EVENING, UNCLE NEERAJ and his wife gave Mama, Auntie Ranee, and her baby a ride back home in their brand-new Morris Minor. Uncle Ram and I hopped on a bus. On the first leg of the return journey, Uncle Ram took a nap. "For the rum to wear off," he said. The bus windows shook and rattled. Sometimes the wind gusts suddenly changed direction and it felt like the bodywork would fly apart. But the Bedford bus, with its prominent MADE IN ENGLAND insignia, stood its ground. The younger passengers were thrilled, and the driver was eager to demonstrate his superior driving skills. At each bus stop, we could hear the whistling of the wind.

On the Curepipe–Mahébourg leg of the journey, Uncle Ram stayed awake. The road ran downhill all the way, and the bus suspension system wasn't working properly. At times it felt as though we were on a soft-bounce trampoline. I was fascinated by the sky, which now resembled a red dome rimmed by dark clouds, but I was also perturbed by the argument between Uncles Neeraj and Ram at Aman's bar.

"Uncle, why did you insist the 1945 cyclones were the worst?"

Uncle Ram clenched his right fist and looked at me. His knit brow made me wonder if I had asked a disturbing question. Slowly he unclenched the fist; I could hear him breathe out before he spoke. "All Uncle Neeraj and the others know and care about is their sugar and their money, and their prayers. They know nothing about cyclones, real cyclones."

Real cyclones? Were there unreal ones? Mama did say Uncle Ram liked to puzzle and challenge.

"My geography book says . . ."

"Vishnu, keep your geography book for your exams. In 1945, I buried my two women. That's the cyclone they know but prefer to forget."

Earlier that morning, Uncle Ram had asked me what a kid like me knew about love, and now he was talking about his two women.

"You . . . you had two women before Auntie Ranee?"

Out of the corner of my eye I saw the young woman on my left stretching her neck to eavesdrop.

"My first wife I married to fulfill my duty. It was an arranged marriage. She was a very good woman. But I kept loving another."

"Why didn't you marry the one you loved?"

"She was a Creole. The Bhushans said she would make our blood impure. The local pandit warned that she had performed black magic on me."

"Why didn't you go live with her?"

"You're a nice boy, Vishnu," he said, patting my shoulder. "Her folks wanted me to get baptized in the Catholic Church and become Thomas Bhushan."

I laughed. "Uncle Thomas Bhushan! That's funny."

"Her brothers threatened to chop off my eggplant. They said I dirtied their family honor."

As the bus windows clattered in the wind, Uncle Ram repeated, in a bitter voice, "Dirtied their family honor."

"Your wife let you see her?"

"I tried to treat both equally. I rented a house for the Creole woman."

Uncle Ram's jovial self was gone. He wasn't sad, exactly. He was more like a wounded bird, trying to fly but helpless.

"How did they die?"

"You're a curious kid. I told you you're ahead for your age. You'll win that entrance scholarship."

He looked out. The leaves on the trees lining the road were scattering all around. The dark rim round the red sky had grown wider.

"My wife died giving birth a week after the first 1945 cyclone. My beautiful Creole died of malaria a month later, three weeks after the second 1945 cyclone. And your uncles were angry that I paid for her funeral."

At the age of ten, I'm not sure I grasped the import of all that Uncle Ram had revealed. Nonetheless, I could see the pent-up rage in him. And I realized, vaguely, that he wanted me to avoid a similar fate.

I turned to my left and saw the eavesdropping woman dabbing her eyes with her sleeve.

We both dozed off until we got close to Mahébourg. When Uncle Ram woke up, he leaned against me and raised his left buttock cheek.

"Hiroshima!" he shouted as a sonorous fart trumpeted out.

The older passengers pretended not to hear. The younger ones goaded him: "Another one, Uncle."

"Nagasaki," said Uncle Ram, lifting his right buttock cheek for an even richer fart. "Mesdames, messieurs, I have an important announcement: the Americans will use atomic power to blow out cyclones." He then intoned,

Hawa baand, samoondar soukarey

THE MAHÉBOURG BUS terminal was five minutes' walk from the Pointe des Régates beach. By the sea, one senses the power of an incoming cyclone through the skin, the ears, the nose. We heard the waves lashing the shore. The wind was no longer blowing through the leaves; it was groaning and howling. The fishermen and the sand diggers had moved their boats to higher ground. No one was on the road. A police car drove through town, alerting everyone through a loudspeaker that a Class 3 warning was now in effect.

When we reached home a few minutes later, Papa was putting tools away. He had secured the windows with shutters, battens, and crossbars.

"Great job, Shiv," said Uncle Ram as he went around the house. "You've even trimmed the tree branches."

"If you had come a bit earlier, you could have helped. You know my rheumatism has been acting up."

Uncle Ram took the bottle of rum purchased in Coromandel from my hands.

"Shiv, no need for you to get worked up. This house is made to last. It would have been okay if you had just relaxed."

Uncle Ram had bought the house with the lump sum he received upon his retirement, a year earlier. For his more than thirty years as railway stationmaster, he had stayed in sturdy and elegant colonial-style houses provided by the British colonial government. His Mahébourg home matched these houses: built with the best wood from Indonesia, it was admired by many in this coastal town, the more so since it had a large yard with fruit trees—guava, avocado, custard apple, pomegranate. And the house had withstood the 120-mile-per-hour winds of Cyclone Alix earlier in the year.

Papa had just changed into his pajamas when Uncle Ram shouted from his side of the house, "Shiv, you missed a great yaj. You should have seen the women seated round the two pandits with their fluttering dhotis. They could not stop gawking at their eggplants. The Regal Sisters had the best view." Papa caught me smiling at Uncle's words and admonished me with his index finger.

AFTER A NIGHT of howling winds and buffeting rain, we spent February 27, 1960, indoors, like most Mauritians. In the morning, a police car announced by loudspeaker that a Class 4 warning—the highest level of alert—had been issued. Cyclone Carol had swept Saint Brandon Island, three hundred miles northeast of Mauritius, and winds of at least 120 miles per hour would hit our island.

We were all anxious. All the precautions that could be taken had been taken. Throughout the day, the winds grew more violent and the rain more intense.

At dinnertime, Uncle Ram opened the bottle bought at la boutique Dokter. At eight thirty, the electricity went off. At around nine, he thundered, "Shiv, did you ask Vishnu what he thought of the Royal College?"

"He told me he liked it," Papa replied.

"That boy is destined for England," said Uncle Ram. "You wait and see: he'll come back with an Englishwoman."

Mama looked at Papa in a way that clearly signaled that he should respond firmly to this.

"Don't talk like that. He is only ten," Papa said.

"He has the brain of a fourteen-year-old."

Auntie Ranee interjected: "Stop drinking and talking rubbish. People are worried about the cyclone."

"Worried about the cyclone? The Bhushans and the community are worried about their purity. Vishnu, I have a better idea. Englishwomen are too boring for you—bring back a European. Brigitte Bardot or Sophia Loren. Shiv, did you hear what I said? That will improve the Bhushan stock *and* defile it."

No one responded. The subdued light of the candles and hurricane lamps produced the mood of a vigil for Cyclone Carol, not one conducive to confrontation.

That evening, and for the first time since I lived in that house, Uncle Ram did not say his usual "Hawa baand, samoondar soukarey." The last words he uttered as he went to bed were:

1945   1945   1945.

I don't know if Auntee Ranee or Mama or Papa detected the same sentiment, or even paid attention, but I thought his voice was sorrowful. I went to bed feeling sad for him.

Outside, Cyclone Carol's ire was turning to rage. I was afraid.

. . .

THE NEXT MORNING, February 28, 1960, at around 8:30, we heard a loud bang. It sounded like a huge sheet of metal hitting our house. This was followed by many more such bangs, of wood beams and shingles flying in the air and crashing on the road or against the neighbors' houses. There was the eerie sound of trees being uprooted and crashing to the earth.

Suddenly Uncle Ram shouted, "Shiv, come here. I need your help."

I followed Papa to Uncle's living room. The front door was open and the cyclonic wind was pummeling with such force that Uncle and Papa couldn't push the door shut. They couldn't even reach the doorknob. Mama, Auntie, and I stood behind them, hoping that the human barrier thus created would prevent, or at least reduce, the wind whipping in. We looked at each other: we were sure Uncle Ram had forgotten to close the door when he went to bed. We remembered his drunkenness.

A loud creaking noise from above tore through my ears. I looked up. The wind blowing in through the open door was battering the gable roof from the inside. Planks were detaching from the beams.

Uncle Ram was exhausted. It was clear we were going to lose the front roof. As rain poured into the living room, Papa, Mama, and Auntie began to move an armoire to a room at the back, which had its own gable roof. On the mirrored doors of the armoire, I caught a shadowy glimpse of Lion Mountain. I turned my head: a window had flung open, revealing the mountain on the horizon. It looked

like it never had before—desolate, dreary, no longer con-
juring up the stately lion of sunny days.

"Run to the back," Papa said.

I felt his hands grab my shoulder, then I spotted Uncle
Ram's stationmaster's cap on the floor. It was his treasured
possession, one he proudly displayed on the wall. I wrig-
gled free, made a dash for it, and picked it up.

Another great bang sounded and the front roof was
gone. Somehow it did not fall on the floor—Papa and I
would have been crushed to death. It flew away from the
house.

We huddled in the back. With the wind now bang-
ing inside the house, we saw and felt its fury—we were
inside its fury, we were almost part of it. Papa yelled that
Cyclone Alix, six weeks earlier, looked like a trial run. He
and Uncle Ram decided we should lock the back and run
to the neighbor across the road, the Prem family, who had
just built a new house. Papa, being the strongest, would
hold Auntie Ranee's baby; Mama and Auntie Ranee would
carry the jewelry and valuables; Uncle Ram would carry
legal and bank documents; and I would run ahead of them
so they could keep an eye on me.

We massed near the door, waiting. Papa felt a lull and
told me to run, and the next thing I knew I had landed
like lead under the custard apple tree. I tried to move, but
I felt nailed to the ground. The velocity of the wind was
such that the rain was moving horizontally. Like a mad
magic carpet, a corrugated iron sheet from a neighbor's
roof swirled over my head, nearly decapitating me. I was
terrified. Mama looked distraught. Papa shouted at me to
wait. Uncle and Auntie were speechless. Then there was

a true lull, and we all ran to the Prem family. The whole neighborhood, some thirty people spread across five rooms, had sought refuge there, nervously drinking tea and listening to the wind.

BY 11 A.M. it was over. Sunshine and calm settled in, the brutality of nature, its random malevolence surrendering to beauty. So radiant was the sun that day that I think of it whenever I hear Rimsky-Korsakov's *Russian Easter Overture*. The rays of the morning light conveyed by the violin, the joys of the spring expressed by the flute, and the jubilant fanfare in the trumpets transport me back to that glorious sun.

I walked to the thicket of tangled ferns next to the custard apple tree. There I used to spend a few minutes every afternoon admiring chameleons—the ease with which they swelled their bodies and throats, and turned their eyes in opposite directions. To the young kid that I was, they seemed, with their turquoise, yellow, green, and red colors, to be cousins of the bewitching snakes Uncle Ram had taken me to see at the circus. They now lay lifeless, severed and scattered under the badamier, the tropical almond tree. I felt I had lost some friends.

Strewn around the small bodies were a few postcards. The ink had washed away, the written messages a smudge. I could read the printed captions—Port Said, Haifa, Church of the Nativity—but the photos were unrecognizable. I threw them in the trash heap.

I could hear nails and hammers everywhere; the neighbors had gone back home to salvage what they could.

Papa and Uncle helped Mama and Auntie Ranee move the soaked mattresses and bedsheets out into the sun. Papa brought out our books to dry.

"Ram, a miracle. The Ramayana and the Mahabharata are intact," said Papa. He was proud to own these Hindu religious epics brought by our Bhushan ancestor when he arrived from India as a coolie. Then, raising a book to eye level for Uncle Ram to see, he added, "Louis Segond's French Bible . . . wet but in reasonable shape."

Uncle Ram shrugged his shoulders and continued moving furniture into the yard to dry.

I searched for my collection of soccer cards, which I had culled over the years from Uncle Ram's cigarette packs. It was the envy of my classmates. The wind had dispersed the cards throughout the house, the veranda, and the front yard. They were so soggy that I could barely discern the photos on the two I prized most—Bobby Charlton of Manchester United and Jimmy Greaves, England's top scorer. Uncle Ram must have seen the sadness on my face. "I'll get you new ones," he said.

Not long after, I heard Papa. "Ram, look at Devnarain's copy of *Histoire de France*. It survived the fire, but now it has to be discarded. The only memento we have of him." Papa was close to tears. He was referring to the fire that engulfed their house when they lived in the nearby village of Ferney. Devnarain was the eldest brother, who died at the young age of twenty-eight, the one looked upon by the Bhushans as the supreme example of self-sacrifice for the uplift of family and clan, the one whose salary as a schoolteacher supported his seven siblings in hard times. A brother who was the standard to live by.

"Are you sure it can't be retrieved?" Uncle Ram said as he tried to disentangle the pages. "Let's check if his name is still visible, or his notes in the margin." After a minute or two, he shook his head. "You're right, Shiv. No trace of his exquisite penmanship."

Uncle Ram took a deep breath, looked at Papa, and wrapped his arms around him.

The hug lasted more than a few moments.

WHEN THEY HAD completed the salvage work, Uncle Ram took my hand, nodded to Papa, and said, "He needs to see the world," and off we went to the bus terminal.

An unlicensed bus had just arrived, with the entrepreneurial driver offering a ride "as far as we can go, since many roads are obstructed by fallen trees." Uncle Ram and a dozen or so people took the offer and the bus meandered for a mile, until we reached the Beau Vallon tennis court. Some white boys and girls from the sugar estate were straddling the trunk of a flamboyant tree that had landed there. Tree trunks were scattered all around; we could no longer advance. Along the way, practically everything was leveled: the shops, the bakery, the car mechanic's workshop—all human habitations except those built of concrete or stone. The top floor of the Salle des Fêtes, the cinema where I saw my first film, had crumbled. Uncle Ram said, "We're lucky. Our back roof and the structure still stand."

On the way back, Uncle Ram took me to a spot midway between the Catholic church and the Hindu temple, both of which had lost part of their roof. When we got there, his face registered the greatest shock of the day. He pointed to a flattened building. "This is the house I really wanted to buy when I retired. Our ancestral home where your father and I grew up. Our parents owned a coach and horses then." He showed me where his parents' bedroom had been, the room he and Papa shared, as well as the kitchen and the barn.

"Why did you move from this house?"

"Your grandpa owed money he couldn't pay back, and the house, the coach, and the horses all were seized. That's when the family went back to Ferney, first home of our ancestor from India."

He stood motionless for a few minutes, looking at the rubble, then we headed back.

THE SUNSHINE LASTED four hours. Five years later, at the Royal College Curepipe secondary school, I learnt that the eye of the storm, forty miles in diameter, gave us that perfect weather as it hovered over Mauritius. At three in the afternoon, Carol returned. In the morning, the wind had blown southeasterly; the afternoon round brought winds from the northwest, a sequence that inflicted maximum destruction. Once again, we locked the back part of the house and ran to the Prem family. While Carol wreaked havoc all afternoon and night, I thought of Uncle Ram's devastated ancestral home that he couldn't buy back with his retirement lump sum. I thought of the two women he had lost in 1945. And, as I was a believer in God in those days, I prayed for his house next door to survive.

VI

The Incident at Madame Lolo

On the morning of Monday February 29, 1960, the radio announced that Cyclone Carol had left Mauritius, and described the aftermath of the 155-to-180-mile-per-hour winds: eighty thousand homeless among a population of six hundred and twenty-five thousand; seventy thousand buildings destroyed; sugarcane and vegetable crops wiped out; thirty-nine dead. For the chief meteorologist of Mauritius, an Englishman reminiscing years later about his career in the far-flung outposts of the British Empire, Carol was an experience "worth a life time of back-room service and study." For me, it was a new world. Many of my primary school classmates, sons of fishermen and sugarcane laborers, now lived in tired camping tents set up in soccer fields. The colonial government distributed rations of rice and oil. India donated blankets and cooking utensils. A year went by during which all we saw and heard was masons pouring concrete and carpenters hammering and nailing timber. By mid-1961, sturdy buildings dotted the island; thatched houses had all but disappeared, except for those sheltering cows and goats. Uncle Ram and Auntie Ranee's wooden house in Mahébourg, which they shared with us, boasted a new roof with Malaysian shingles and a veranda floor with faux marble.

Down the street from us, on the corner of the road

leading to the main bus terminal and the beach, a concrete
house replaced the wooden dwelling that Carol had razed.
A middle-aged lady and two younger women, probably her
daughters, moved in. Over the next few weeks, we noticed
that their visitors were all male, well dressed, and traveling
by car. I knew some of them were Franco-Mauritians living
in the posh areas of Blue Bay, three miles away. I overheard
bits of conversation between Uncle Ram and my father
about how odd it was for the landlord, who was reputed
to be a religious man, to allow something immoral on his
property, and in our neighborhood. One day, I was on my
way to the bazaar to buy vegetables for Mama and Auntie
when the lady asked me if I could mail her letters at the post
office. I can still summon her perfume, a blend of lavender
and rose. She offered me English biscuits, a luxury in those
days. For quite some time, until my mother found out and
forbade me, I combined errands for home with errands for
the women, and was invited in for tea and confectionery
that came in tin boxes decorated with red double-decker
buses. There was a regular visitor, someone I took for a
decorated veteran. He entertained me with stories of how
he fought in North Africa alongside Englishmen, Sikhs,
and Gurkhas under Marshal Montgomery's command
against Rommel and the Germans at the decisive Battle of
El Alamein. The lady later told me that he was a deranged
man who had never left Mauritius and that the military
medals on his jacket and cap were fake.

"Don't always believe what you see or hear," she said.

In that year of lavender-and-rose perfume and English
biscuits, I won a scholarship to attend the elite Royal College Curepipe secondary school, seventeen miles away, and

for the first time, classmates were calling me "fat." One of the kinder kids, who later became the school's boxing champion, showed me a Charles Atlas advertisement for a program to "build a sculpted body in 15 minutes a day" and advised me to order its twelve lessons by mail. He was surprised to hear that I couldn't afford it. Pimples erupted all over my face, and across the thin wooden wall separating the kitchen from the dining room I heard Auntie Ranee and my mother discuss a cure.

"Tell Vishnu to rub his soiled underwear on his face every morning."

"He's too young to secrete that fluid in his sleep," my mother said. She was mistaken, and I wondered whether she'd forgotten I had turned eleven.

At home, Mama and Auntie hummed melodies from the Hindi movie *Chaudhvin Ka Chand,* while the Creole neighbor and his new bride played the romantic instrumental "Stranger on the Shore" loud enough for us to hear it every evening. On my first day at secondary school, the pink-faced English rector, stern in his black academic gown, told us that we were being groomed for "leadership" and that we should consider ourselves in the same league as the boys at Eton and Harrow. The next day, two of the senior boys, both from the big city, came to blows arguing about which was the better song, Cliff Richard's "The Young Ones" or Elvis Presley's "Can't Help Falling in Love."

A FEW DAYS after her pimple cure conversation, Mama asked me, "Do you still remember how to get to Madame Lolo? Auntie Ranee needs you to take her there."

When we lived in Rose Belle five years earlier, my father would sometimes take me with him to the adjoining village of Madame Lolo. There he would try to persuade recalcitrant parents to send their kids to primary school, where he taught, instead of putting them to work in the fields. In Auntie Ranee's presence, my mother made me swear to keep the trip a secret from my father and Uncle Ram. On a Saturday, after Papa and Uncle had left to tend their respective sugarcane fields, we boarded the bus at the main terminal, close to the shore. The sea was tranquil, the leaves on the trees motionless.

The bus was festive, crowded with merry people going to the capital to watch the horse races at the Champ de Mars. As always happened when Auntie Ranee moved among a group or entered a room, the standing passengers made way for her. She had an aristocratic gait, a regal air that commanded respect. A young couple gave us their seats. Some passengers were exchanging hot tips about the horses to bet on; Student Prince seemed to be the favorite that day. I envied them, but I was stuck with Auntie Ranee for the eight-mile journey. I asked her the reason for the trip and learnt that Karan, her adopted younger brother, had run away from home and fled to Madame Lolo, not long after their mother had died.

"Why didn't you ask the police to find him?" I said.

"The police? He's run away with a woman."

The passengers close to us became still. They stared, their ears keen for more details. Auntie shot one of them a nasty glare and they turned their heads away.

Auntie Ranee asked me about school and we talked about the new subjects I was studying.

When we got off at Rose Belle, I was eager to learn more about the woman.

"I've never met her. She's probably a négresse," she said. When Auntie used that pejorative word, it didn't necessarily mean a woman of African origin; she meant any woman, Hindu, Muslim, Creole, or white, who liked to parade her beauty and have too much fun.

"What are you going to do?" I said.

"Teach them a lesson."

"How?" I said.

She didn't answer, and her steely face didn't encourage me to press on.

As I led her past the Roman Catholic convent and the railway station and we crossed the rail tracks, I felt very proud to be her guide. I was now a big boy.

After walking about half a mile of dirt road, with fields of watermelon on each side, we arrived at Madame Lolo. It flanked a river and a rudimentary wooden bridge. I had forgotten what it looked like, how different it was from Mahébourg, where I had spent the last few years. I had a village in my mind; what I saw was a hamlet. We came across no cars or buses, only two bullock carts. There was no village store and no bar or tavern. Many of the men were dhoti-clad, the older ones wore turbans, and quite a few were squatting on their doorsteps. In Mahébourg, a largely Creole community, most men, including Hindus and Muslims, wore jackets, trousers, or suits. It was as if we had entered the rural India depicted in the old movies. The triangular red flag of Hanuman, the monkey god, flew in front of every house, proclaiming we were in the Hindu heartland.

No one smiled, and no one pressed palms to greet us

with the traditional Indian namasté gesture. The arrival of a tall woman with all the trappings of the city—georgette sari, gold necklace, short sleeves—aroused suspicion. I could hear my shoes and Auntie's sandals tread the ground.

"Straighten your shoulders," she told me as she walked to the person who appeared to be the eldest in the village.

Auntie Ranee joined her palms, introduced herself as Karan's eldest sister, and asked to be taken to his house.

KARAN RESPONDED IMMEDIATELY when the village elder called him, and asked Auntie and me to come in. His front yard was adorned with trees laden with pomegranates ripening in the sun, in various shades of red. From the outside his house looked modest: corrugated iron roof and sidings, and at most two rooms and a kitchen. We sat on the veranda and Karan offered tea and lemonade. I was dying of thirst, but Auntie spoke for me: "Not for us, not now."

Karan looked out of place in Madame Lolo, with his Western clothes and Elvis haircut, which he must have seen in the film *Jailhouse Rock* or *King Creole*.

Auntie wasted no time. "Karan, you know that after Mama's death, I'm head of the family. I'm the eldest, older than our two sisters, and older than you."

Karan acquiesced with a nod. He kept his eyes on the floor.

"You're my responsibility now," she said. Her tone was gentle, motherly. "We all make mistakes, and we learn from them."

Auntie paused and waited for a reaction. Karan raised his head but put it down immediately.

"I hear you've got yourself a rundee. Couldn't you wait for us to find you a virtuous woman?"

"She's not a rundee, she's a good woman."

"That's not what I heard. She sold her body for a living."

"Stop listening to gossip, Ranee-bahen." Karan addressed Auntie with the respectful suffix due to an elder sister. His voice was meek, at least next to Auntie's.

"Do you know how many she's slept with before you?" Auntie said.

The cries of a baby inside the house pierced the air.

"Oh, my God!" Auntie beat her forehead with her hands. "A baby! You're only nineteen! She's trapped you!"

Karan sprang from his chair, probably to run to the baby and quiet it, but as he reached the door, Auntie shouted, "Ask your vesya to come out." Auntie had uttered another Hindi epithet for "whore," except this time it was cruder.

Karan's woman was on the veranda with the baby in her arms before Karan had time to pop his head inside the house. She was striking, like Auntie, as beautiful but in a different way. Whereas Auntie was so fair that people referred to her as "the Kashmiri," Karan's woman was dark, like my father, with South Indian features.

"You barge in here calling me names. But you don't know what Karan and I have between us. You can't understand love."

The baby continued to cry.

Karan's woman, still standing, unbuttoned her blouse and brought the baby to her breast.

"Aren't you ashamed to parade your breasts in front of this boy?" Auntie said, pointing to me.

Karan's woman raised her breast to insert the nipple

inside the baby's mouth. As the baby sucked the big black breast, my eyes savored its roundness. This was breathing and moving—it was different from the breasts my classmates and I drooled over in the magazines at Renaissance Bookshop.

To my relief, Auntie asked Karan for a lemonade. Auntie drank hers; I gulped mine down.

Auntie charged again. "Where did you pick up that piece of garbage?" she said to Karan.

The violence of Auntie's words hit Karan. His face and ears turned red. I was shocked, too. I had never imagined she could speak that way. Karan's woman, however, didn't lose her composure. She sat down on the chair left vacant when Karan went to fetch the lemonade. Maybe my memory has been warped by the spell she cast on me that day, but I remember her taking her seat with elegance and grace.

I looked around me. A group had gathered, about half a dozen men, squatting in a semicircle in the front yard. They were close enough to hear the argument on the veranda. I don't know if Auntie was aware of them at that moment. If she was, she showed no sign of it.

No one interfered. They just listened.

"Can you tell me about your family background? Who are your parents? What is your khandaan?" Auntie said.

"My clan or bloodline is not important. We have a child together, that's what matters."

Auntie got up and shook Karan's shoulders. "Can't you see how shameless she is? Addressing me with such effrontery! Leave that rundee and go home to Coromandel. You have two sisters waiting there who care for you."

When Auntie turned, she scanned the semicircle of men. She paused before she spoke.

"Don't you have anything to say?"

The semicircle was impassive. She might as well have addressed a heap of stones.

She motioned for me to get up. She said good-bye to Karan, glanced at his woman, and walked to the person who had taken us to Karan's house. "You must be a respected elder here. Please keep an eye on my younger brother."

"Don't worry about them," the man said. "She's one of ours, and she'll learn to take care of her man and child. We'll have a wedding when the right time comes."

All the men bowed, joined their palms, and said, "Namasté."

As we walked away, some women came out of their homes and joined palms likewise.

ON THE WAY back to the bus stop, I saw that Auntie's face was red and there were sweat stains on her blouse. My young mind was perplexed: no one in Madame Lolo had challenged or questioned what she said, and yet in the end they supported Karan and his woman.

As we crossed the railway tracks, I told Auntie that surely someone must have told her the woman's name. "You have relatives and friends everywhere," I added.

"Who cares what her name is?" she said.

On the bus, we dozed off, worn out by the day's drama.

When we reached home, Mama asked Auntie, "How is she?"

"They have a child," Auntie said.

.   .   .

IN 1962, WE moved out of Uncle Ram's house, but
I continued visiting every Saturday. In mid-1963, Uncle
Ram, who also had a story of forbidden love in his past,
died of liver cirrhosis, the result of drinking too much rum.
On a Saturday visit six months later, two years after the
confrontation at Madame Lolo, I saw Auntie Ranee bent
at the fountain in the yard, washing clothes. A child was at
her side.

"Vishnu, isn't she beautiful?" Auntie said.

"Oh, yes! Whose child is she?" I said.

"Karan's. Her name is Sapna. Her mother died last
month."

It took me a few seconds before I muttered something.
The December heat was oppressive, and Auntie's diaph-
anous blouse of pink chiffon stirred in me memories of
the many nights I had fantasized about Karan's nameless
woman, her breasts, her defiant demeanor.

"How come you didn't tell us so we could come to the
funeral?" I said.

"There was no need to make a fuss about the poor
woman," Auntie said.

She told me that Karan was too depressed to care for
Sapna and that she was going to take the child in and raise
her. When I asked the cause of death, Auntie said, "The
doctors don't know." A few weeks later, when a cousin
whispered "gonorrhea," Auntie summoned her to her
house, took her to task, and warned that she would make
her a family pariah if she didn't quash that rumor.

It was disconcerting. Why was Auntie defending the

memory of the woman she despised? Was it because she wanted no stain on the family's honor? That couldn't be, since she had made sure to distance herself and the family from the "rundee." Was it because she wanted Sapna to grow up free of any stigma? Was she going to love Sapna? I was too young then to entertain the possibility that she was, like many of us, a bundle of contradictions—her maternal instinct driving her to love Sapna, and her sense of social respectability leading her to withhold love from those who didn't live up to her standards.

I WISH I could explain why, in my adolescent years, I gradually forgot Karan's nameless woman and her daughter. Sure, competition for a scholarship for studies abroad was intense and left us little time for anything else but study. Every Monday morning (so it seemed) at assembly in the courtyard, the English rector kept reminding us that our school expected "the highest level of performance." And I wanted to thrive, not merely survive, among the children of the elite.

Events in Mauritius and in the world were also engrossing: the Indian-Chinese conflict over Tibet, the Profumo affair, the May 1968 French student riots, local elections in 1967 followed by independence in 1968. All this was true, but it was also true that screen goddesses had replaced Karan's woman in my fantasies: Natalie Wood and, unknown to my friends who dismissed her as a B-grade actress, Belinda Lee, the wife of Potiphar in *Joseph Sold by His Brethren*.

By the time I started graduate school in the United

States, Karan's woman and her daughter Sapna had become a distant memory. Until one day in the late seventies, while browsing in a secondhand record store in Greenwich Village, I came across the psychedelic album cover of Carlos Santana's *Abraxas*. On the left was a crimson angel, tattooed and bestriding a flying conga drum, pointing to a Hebrew aleph symbol in the blue sky. At the center, surrounded by sunflower, lilies, and violets, watermelon and bursting pomegranates, sat a tall Black woman with majestic breasts, naked and radiant. A white dove stood between her legs, which were spread wide apart. It was a breathtaking but incomprehensible juxtaposition of the sacred and the carnal. I turned to the album's back cover to look for an explanation and found an excerpt from Hermann Hesse's *Demian:*

> We stood before it and began to freeze inside from the exertion. We questioned the painting, berated it, made love to it, prayed to it: We called it mother, called it whore and slut, called it our beloved, called it Abraxas. . . .

Mother, whore, slut, beloved: these words took me back to Madame Lolo. Given the time difference, I telephoned my mother in the evening. She told me that Sapna had committed suicide three months earlier. A cold sweat ran throughout my body.

"Sapna killed herself and you didn't think it necessary to tell me right away?" I said.

"You never asked about her before!" my mother said. "I didn't know she meant that much to you."

Mama's words stung. I took a deep breath.

"She was only fifteen or sixteen. Why did she do it?" I said.

"When Auntie Ranee died two years ago, Sapna lost her anchor," my mother said. "She didn't have the strength to go on."

"Did Auntie Ranee really love her? Did they have a fight?"

"Vishnu, stop talking rubbish," said my mother. "Of course she loved her. You're nine thousand miles away, and you don't know what goes on here. She fought all those people who taunted Sapna about her mother. If you called more often, you would have been better informed."

After I hung up the phone, I paced back and forth in my tiny room, restless. I called a cousin in London who had stayed in touch with Karan. He said something about Sapna having inherited her mother's genes. "Sinful genes," he said.

I needed fresh air. As I walked out of my graduate student hostel towards the solid solemnity of Grant's Tomb, on Riverside Drive, I pondered Mama's three-month silence on Sapna's death. It dawned on me that I had never told her what I saw and heard at Madame Lolo. And I hadn't behaved in a manner that indicated I had felt anything for the mother and the child. Had I repressed the memory of Karan's nameless woman and their daughter in my attempt to move on? I felt ashamed, guilty.

A year or so later, Karan passed away. Liver cirrhosis, just like Uncle Ram.

I have since thought intermittently about the incident at Madame Lolo and Auntie Ranee's words and actions. As I look back on my pubescent fixation on Karan's woman, I ask the family questions about her. They avoid the subject and view me with suspicion. They apprehend that lurking in my mind is the hope or wish that Auntie's "rundee" and "vesya" were just figures of speech she used to scare her adopted brother Karan back to the fold, not epithets based on fact.

Last year, after more than forty years, I returned to Madame Lolo. Cousin Shankar had told me that the place had changed so much that it was worth a visit. It has now grown into a full-fledged village with signs of increasing affluence. The Hanuman flags are bigger, glitzier, and most are hoisted on top of miniature concrete temples in the front yards, no longer on bamboo poles. No one squats on the road; most people are gainfully employed. The fields of watermelon have disappeared, the dirt path has been transformed to an asphalted road, and there is parking space near the bridge, which is new and made of shiny metal. Most important, Karan's dwelling and the pomegranate trees in the yard are gone.

As I said good-bye to Karan, to his nameless woman and their daughter, and to the Madame Lolo of my adolescence, I felt sad. But I also understood that I can't remain steeped in nostalgia. I felt no sense of loss at the disappearance of the old world. The river has been consecrated, and on its banks a holy shrine has been erected. Some years ago, local sadhus elevated the status of the river in Madame Lolo to that of Ganga Yamuna Dhaam, a pilgrimage destination. An officiating priest told me, "The site has a Facebook page. You can find a film on the Madame Lolo shrine on YouTube."

I clicked on the YouTube film, expecting a Hindu devotional hymn as background music. The soundtrack was from Santana's *Abraxas*.

VII

Truants

I

While Uncle Neeraj is away,
I forage under his bed.
Among his forbidden magazines
I discover a puzzling cover:
at the foot of a volcano spewing flames and lava,
a woman, hair disheveled, is locked in a kiss.
Stromboli erupts: *Ingrid Bergman's affair heats up the*
    film set!

At dinner, over fiery eggplant vindaloo,
Papa says Stromboli is inactive at the moment
and that I'm too young to understand "affairs."
Mama's face darkens.

II

Five or six years later, on a day
that smells of lychee and mango
and the Mascarene paradise flycatcher
flaunts its chestnut plumage,
a friend and I skip school after the lunch bell rings
and walk uphill to the Trou aux Cerfs,
a lovers' lair which gushed volcanic ash millennia ago.

Down the slope of the crater,
where aromatic trees hide secrets,
we stumble
on our teacher of revolutions
agrarian, industrial, American, and French.
She's riding the brute who made us conjugate
amo, amas, amat, amamus.

She glares at us
like the virgin goddess Diana
spied bathing in the spring.

VIII

A Massage for the Holy Man

1963

Earlier in the afternoon, with Auntie Ranee and other members of the Bhushan clan, I had stood by Uncle Ram's bedside, his breathing labored and his eyes glassy. Auntie hoped Uncle would at least utter the word Krishna or Bhagwan or any other of God's names before departing this world. He only said "Ma." Auntie's face shrank, the dark circles under her red eyes grew bigger.

Soon, out of nowhere, Uncle's drinking buddies appeared and were holding his corpse while my father washed him in the yard, by the custard apple tree. Within a few hours, coffee, tea, biscuits, and snacks were laid out on the veranda, on tables brought by the neighbors. It was in 1963, during the August school holidays. I was fourteen and couldn't understand how people were going about with so much energy on a such a sad occasion. Some were playing cards, others chatting. I tried to control my tears. My mother charged me with keeping an eye on the food and drinks, to let her know when to replenish. By seven in the evening, the veranda was overflowing with people, noisy from the rum some had brought as an offering to the departed, and from the applause and jeers directed at a young man just returned from overseas. He had chal-

lenged a local pandit on God's existence and proclaimed
how proud he was that Uncle Ram had introduced him
to atheism. His supporters, a minority, heckled the pandit,
who warned them, "You will pay for this in your next life."

Just as Uncle Ram's wake threatened to turn into pan-
demonium, Cousin Shankar and his father, Uncle Roshan,
walked in.

Uncle Roshan was of average build and height. But he
had a reputation for being fierce and for standing up for his
rights. Mama had told me that in his youth, his bearing and
blue eyes had earned him the nickname Maréchal Rommel
among the Franco-Mauritian girls on the sugar estate. Some
in the village even claimed that one day, as the girls bicycled
by the weighing station, they were awestruck by the sight of
Uncle Roshan holding the white weighman by the throat;
angry at the weighman for understating the amount of sugarcane he had delivered, he challenged the accuracy of the
scales and accused him of cheating. At weddings, funerals,
wakes, young people enjoyed hearing him argue against the
Puranic pandits, the orthodox Brahman priests. They jostled
to sit close to him and clapped their hands whenever he, a
non-Brahman, cut down his opponents. Mama, proud of
her brother's rhetorical prowess, had also told me that many
elders marveled at Uncle Roshan's superior knowledge of the
Scriptures but refrained from adopting his strict, monotheis-
tic views; they were afraid of punishment by a deity, or bad
karma—they might be reincarnated as a crawling animal.

Uncle Roshan's entrance silenced everyone. The pandit,
a Puranic, got up and went inside, where Auntie Ranee was
talking to my parents. Uncle said, "Panditji, are you running
away from a vigorous debate?" He took the pandit's chair,

and I handed him a cup of tea. He turned his sharp, angular face, maintaining eye contact with those on his right for the duration of a sip. Turning his head to the left, he said, "No doubt strong-willed Ranee will ignore her husband's wishes and indulge in all sorts of Puranic rituals. Wait for the milk-drinking ceremony next week: the priest will rub his Adam's apple and claim that the milk Ranee offers him isn't flowing down his throat. 'Ram's soul is strangling me; it is demanding Ram's felt hat,' he will say, and Ranee will give him the hat. A more vigorous rub at his Adam's apple, the soul craves for Ram's clothes; then it will be Ram's silver watch, and by the time Ram's soul is appeased and ready to transmigrate to a new body, Auntie will have given the priest more than a few of Ram's favorite possessions."

To a teenager like me, the milk ceremony sounded hilarious, something to look forward to. My cousin Shankar, three years my senior, elbowed me and whispered in my ear, "They don't know my father. He is full of bullshit."

Before Shankar could continue, his father focused his intense eyes on me. "Vishnu, I saw you laugh. This is no joke. Did your mother ever tell you why I'm not Puranic like the Bhushans?"

Uncle Roshan didn't wait for a response. "Years ago, after the saffron ceremony on the eve of a wedding, the pandit said, 'Fellow Brahmans, join me in the dining room for dinner.' I asked the pandit, 'What about the other guests?' He told me they have to wait till the Brahmans have finished. I had just turned twenty-one. I stood up and told the guests, 'There are empty seats at the table. Let's eat with the Brahmans!' My father lifted his hand, ready to slap me, but controlled himself; instead he cursed me in front of everyone. I walked to the dining room. No one followed me. That's when I decided to join the Vedic Sabha; they don't believe in the caste system. And they worship only one God!"

I was relieved when my mother called me to help her. Shankar followed me inside and said again, "My father is full of bullshit."

Shankar and I had gotten closer since our family moved, about six months earlier, to Mon Désert, my birthplace, where Uncle Roshan lived. A few days after the wake, when I went to see him, his father opened the door. "Come in, Vishnu, I want you to meet Swami Ananda. A learned holy man from India."

I knew that swamis from India, orthodox or not, had a certain cachet among the Hindu community on the island, much like a visiting prelate from the Vatican among the Catholics. They were supposed to know more than the local swamis and priests; I imagined they came to train the local priests.

"They love Mauritius because of the higher standard of living and social standing they enjoy here, whereas in India they are a dime a dozen," Papa used to say. I had heard that Uncle Roshan hosted some of the Vedic Sabha swamis. So I wasn't surprised to see, in the living room, a portly middle-aged man in a saffron robe reclining in an armchair, with a book in his hands.

Seated on the floor, Shankar was massaging the swami's feet. He looked at me with a grimace, embarrassed to be caught.

All the same sauce, I thought, recalling how Madame Joseph expressed her cynical view of men. A Vedic Sabha swami likes to be pampered just the same as an orthodox, Puranic one.

"I came by to see if Shankar can go to the beach with me," I told Uncle Roshan.

The swami's face turned sullen.

I quickly added, "Maybe in an hour or two? I'll run some errands in the meantime."

"Shankar is going to Swamiji's sermon this afternoon," Uncle said.

The swami beamed a benevolent smile. "Shankar is a good son. Filial duty is divine duty," he said.

"Why don't you join us, Vishnu?" Uncle Roshan asked. "Swamiji will speak on 'Spirituality and Youth.'"

"Papa will be upset; you know he's Puranic." And I turned to the swami and said, "He worships all the gods—Shiva, Vishnu, Krishna, Ram, Sita, Hanuman," taking mischievous pleasure in slowly enunciating every name. "I'll come by another time."

I lied. Papa was orthodox, but he didn't care if his family or relatives listened to Vedic Hindus or Catholics or atheists. He even brought me copies of the *Watchtower* magazine that Jehovah's Witnesses handed him on the street every now and then. From me, he only expected that I participate in the annual pinda ceremony at home, a Hindu ritual of remembrance and worship of our ancestors. My sole obligation: offering the dumpling of rice and sesame seeds destined for those of our forebears who are "unknown or forgotten." Religion was one area where Papa wasn't strict or authoritarian.

I felt sorry that Shankar couldn't do fun things like his friends. Not only could he not be at the beach that day. On weekdays, he had to rise early and bicycle with his father to the sugarcane and tomato fields, where he worked from six to eight before going to school and from five to six in the evening after school. Not that Uncle was poor and needed the help; he owned enough land to be able to hire additional laborers and overseers. Shankar was the dutiful son destined to till the soil, while his younger brother and other siblings didn't even know where the fields were. His weekends, brightened by occasional family gatherings, were spent in the fields or on "devotional duties," such as attending sermons and massaging holy men.

"Why don't you tell Uncle that you have lots of homework and that you need time?" I said to Shankar.

"I've told him. He is okay if I just pass; he doesn't expect the highest grades. So long as he can tell his friends and neighbors I've got my Cambridge School Certificate, that's fine with him."

FOUR YEARS WENT by. Uncle Roshan hosted more swamis, whose feet were massaged by Shankar, who continued working in the fields every morning and late afternoon. Papa spared me field labor as I strove for the top marks needed to win a coveted laureate scholarship for university studies abroad.

"To hell with all the sermons on abstinence!" Shankar said to me one day. "I've decided to have some fun." The meager pocket money doled out by his father, he started spending at Rekha's, a brothel in Mahébourg. He went there every two weeks or so, seizing the opportunity when Uncle Roshan traveled to Curepipe for all-day meetings at

Vedic Sabha headquarters. Having a girlfriend was not an option in conservative Mauritius, unless you belonged to the upper reaches of society.

After he obtained his Certificate, he asked his father to pay him regular wages for his labor.

"Son, you're not working for me. You're investing in your future. As long as you stay in this house and eat my food, you shouldn't expect any payment," his father said.

Shankar spoke to his mother about the matter. She told him she had enough to worry about with her four daughters—having to marry them off being the main worry—and didn't want an ugly confrontation with Uncle Roshan.

Many of Shankar's classmates, some from less well-to do families, went to study overseas and wrote to him about life in the big cities—London, Paris, Bombay. He received post-cards with photos of Big Ben, the Arc de Triomphe, the Taj Mahal. The nightclubs in Soho and Pigalle. That reminded us of the orphan from Mahébourg who had impersonated the Maharajah of Baroda and forged his signature on his checks, lavishly living it up in London: dining at the Savoy and showing up in a Rolls-Royce at Soho nightclubs, with a brunette on his left arm, a blonde on his right. He was condemned to only six months in jail by the judge at the Old Bailey. Mahébourg was proud of its poor son sodding it to the rich, of the colonized son of a milkmaid fooling the English. We didn't feel sorry for the real Maharajah, either. We had relished the accounts in the local newspapers.

Shankar dreamed of escape: escape from his father, from the swamis, from field work. Sugarcane hell, he called it. Uncle Roshan constantly drilled in his ears stories of their ancestors' sacrifices and resilience, how they worked their way from indentured coolie to independent planter. But Shankar had made up his mind to go abroad. He was fed up with handling manure and fertilizer. The smell of molasses nauseated him.

His level and grades, however, were not good enough for him to earn admission to university, let alone a scholarship. But nursing in the United Kingdom was an option. The newspapers carried articles about how the English (most of us didn't know or care about the distinction between English, Welsh, and Scots) no longer wanted to be nurses. Nursing was dirty manual work best performed by immigrants from the colonies. Shankar's Cambridge certificate would get him into a nursing course, and, better still, he would draw a salary.

We had heard of letters of admission from British hospitals torn to shreds and thrown in the dustbin by parents worried that their children would never come back. I told Shankar to use our address, since he usually wasn't home when the postman came on his daily rounds.

"I can't do that. I have to be honest with Pa. I'll tell him what I intend to do, even if it leads to a fight," Shankar said.

The swamis have trained Shankar well, I said to myself. The swamis and his father.

Later, Shankar gave me a detailed account of what happened.

"Papa, do you remember what you said at Uncle Ram's funeral wake?"

"I said many things that day. What do you want to talk about?"

"You told us how your father cursed you, and how you forged your own way. I want to do the same. I want to find my way, I want to fend for myself."

"Forge your way, fend for yourself. Sophisticated words! What's your plan?"

Next morning, Uncle Roshan told Shankar that his plan had kept him awake all night. He had thought deep and hard about his own youth, and the prospect of his elder son leaving for England disturbed him. He needed time to think and asked Shankar to do the same.

"Think? Present him with a fait accompli," I told Shankar. "Apply and see what he does. He won't look good with friends and family if he doesn't let you go. He's always carrying on about how Hindus should not trail the other communities in education."

After a month, Shankar received a few letters of rejection. Not long after, he received two letters of acceptance, and he settled on Hammersmith Hospital, in London, where two of his classmates had already started their studies. He used his pocket money to pay for his passport, which he proudly showed me. He made travel reservations—part of the fait accompli scheme.

We decided that I should accompany him when he went to Uncle Roshan with the big news. Uncle was reclining on the same armchair where the swamis got their massages. His face turned red. "So you're ready to go now, Shankar," he said.

"I have all the papers and the traveler's checks to cover my initial expenses. I need your help with the airfare," Shankar said.

"You've made all these arrangements without asking me?"

"I didn't want to miss admission deadlines," Shankar said.

"How dare you? I asked you to think about it, not act behind my back. You take yourself for a big man now? Too big to stay around here?"

I was mortified at the turn of events.

"Uncle, I told him to do it," I said.

Uncle ignored me and addressed Shankar. "Your ambition has dwarfed the respect you owe to your parents!"

He resumed his Maréchal Rommel bearing, and we understood it was time to leave the room.

"Why don't you ask my father to help you?" I ventured.

At home, I realized that my suggestion was a risky bet. "What gives you the right to conspire with Shankar against his father?" Papa said. "You know I don't like Uncle Roshan to meddle in my business. Now you want me to give him a reason to do so?"

The last time Uncle Roshan had dropped by, unannounced, my mother was rubbing an ointment on Papa's muscular calves and feet. Next to her was the heavy bucket of hot water she always brought. I thought my father could perform that daily footbath-and-ointment ritual himself, and had told him so a few times. Uncle Roshan couldn't control himself. "My sister has been your wife three hundred percent all these years," he said. "Though she's half your size, she's taken care of you with the devotion of three women. Show her some gratitude by taking her to the cinema once in a while."

With that incident in mind, I told Papa, "He wouldn't meddle so much if you treated Mama right."

He looked vexed, then had a faint smile. He called Mama.

"Look at how your brother is treating his son. He talks big about education, and he doesn't want to spend money to send Shankar abroad. I bet he boils his banknotes and drinks the broth." He welcomed this opportunity to trash his brother-in-law.

He agreed to pay Shankar's airfare, but Mama counseled Shankar to enlist the support of his paternal uncles, too. "It's not just the money. Your father needs to be persuaded that going to England is the best thing. He's probably afraid you'll return with an Englishwoman, like your cousin in Port Louis."

Shankar's paternal uncles were excited when they heard of his admission to nursing school, but they didn't want to get involved. "You can't talk with a man who thinks he knows everything," said one. "Roshan will turn the conversation into a religious argument," said the other.

When Shankar went to inform his father that he had secured the money for his airfare, Uncle Roshan was in his orchard at the back of his house, lounging on a rattan armchair with a cup of tea. To me, he looked strangely serene, as if the birdsong, the pink bougainvillea flowers, and the murmur of the wind had soothed and pacified him.

"Shankar, you've been the best son I could have hoped for. All the swamis said that about you. Now you want to leave. Who'll take care of me when you're gone?"

"Mama is here. The other children."

"What can they do? You've done everything right. Your brother and sisters know nothing about sugarcane, nothing about growing tomatoes."

Uncle Roshan inhaled the tea's aroma.

"They can learn, Pa. As I did," said Shankar.

"With all that land, you can earn a good living right here."

"I want to travel."

"For more than a hundred years the family has proudly tilled this land, and now you're going to clean the Englishman's dirty bottom! How can you touch the intimate parts of those bastards who raped and looted India? You should have more pride than that!"

"Your best friend's son is in Manchester doing nursing. There's nothing wrong in that."

"I'm getting old, Shankar. Rheumatism in my bones."

"I'll visit often," said Shankar.

Uncle rose from the armchair, grasped Shankar's hands, and pressed them between the palms of his hands.

"How many who leave come back? In Mahébourg, in Mon Désert, I don't know anyone who's come back."

Uncle Roshan turned to me. "Vishnu, do you know anyone?"

I didn't know anyone who'd returned, and I didn't answer. On the bus, at the barbershop and the bazaar, one couldn't avoid hearing about the young who fled unemployment by emigrating. Or who looked for the good life overseas.

I saw that Shankar's eyes were moist.

"I love you, Pa. I'll stay."

Uncle Roshan paused for a second, drew his arms around his son, and held him tight.

I was disappointed with Shankar for not having the guts to stand up to his father, and angry at Uncle Roshan and the swamis for elevating obedience as the supreme virtue. I was even upset with my mother: she had been meek and had not made an effort to convince her brother to let Shankar go. Over the next few years, however, maybe because I read too many Chekhovian tales in secondary school, I shifted the blame. Or, rather, I widened the net: the tyranny of family and the lack of gumption of the clan were responsible for what happened. I resolved to stand up to my father if he were to oppose my going abroad.

Later, much later, events unfolded that made me realize how little I knew about the mysterious bonds that tie father and son.

IN DECEMBER 1990, more than two decades after he capitulated to his father's wishes, Shankar visited me in Boston. In the intervening years, I had completed secondary school in Mauritius and college and graduate school in the United States, and was on the fast track in my international finance career. Unlike his classmates and friends, Shankar did not marry. Through his letters and phone calls, I learnt that he planted new varieties of sugarcane that dramatically increased the yield on his father's land. But he was not reaping the benefits. His father maintained a tight grip on finances. Shankar also informed me that two sisters had gone overseas to study and that his younger brother had eloped with a Muslim girl; Uncle Roshan felt that this act of rebellion sullied his reputation, especially within the Hindu community.

Shankar's trip to America was his first abroad. Unlike most visitors from the tropics who prefer to visit in the spring or summer, he chose winter because he wanted to see, touch, and walk in the snow. He'd seen it on Christmas cards sent to him by his friends abroad, on glossy calendars, and in films like *Doctor Zhivago*. And he wished to visit a nursing school. Harvard, the Boston Museum of Fine Arts, Faneuil Hall, and other monuments associated with the American War of Independence were further down on his list.

On a snowy day, a friend of mine who taught at the nursing school of Mass General gave him a tour and arranged for him to have lunch with some of his students. In the evening, I took him to a pub in Harvard Square to warm up with Irish coffee. He was surprised at the ID checks that the students went through: no one back home had ever heard of drinking age limits. Once we got over discussing the fifteen- or twenty-year age gap between us and most of the pub's patrons, I asked him what he thought of the nursing school.

"Being Pa's nurse, my life's not very different from those of the nurses here, except for all that technology."

Loud cheers erupted in a corner booth. Shankar stretched his neck to look. Wistful, he added, "And I never experienced that."

I was afraid he might form an overly rosy picture of student life. "Not all students can afford this, Shankar. This is a privileged few. Many are boiling pasta or eating pizza in their apartment," I said.

I knew from Mama that Uncle Roshan was bedridden and Shankar's mom was too weak to care for him. Shankar told me that neither his sisters and their husbands nor his brother and his woman had any interest in sharing the caregiver tasks, and that he bathed and shaved his father.

"I remember as a child I used to watch him shave. He would whip shaving soap into a white lather that shone, and work it into his stubble in circles with a brush. His technique in handling that old-fashioned double-edged razor fascinated me: the blade just glided across his face. It was a show," he said. With a sigh he added, "I can't give him such a close and smooth shave."

When Shankar was not emptying and cleaning chamber pots or bathing his father, he was supervising the laborers in Uncle Roshan's fields. He confided that he would have liked to spend more time on this trip and visit London, Paris, and Amsterdam, but he couldn't get a nurse's aide for such a long period and his sisters were unwilling to help out for a week or two.

"I hope Uncle leaves you the major part of his estate," I said.

"My friends tell me the same thing," he said.

"There's no need to be sheepish about it," I told him.

"My sisters want to put Pa in a nursing home," he said. "I can't do that to the old man."

"He hasn't been fair to you in the past. I would hope he shows some gratitude now."

"You've been in the West for too long, Vishnu. If I don't take care of him, who will?" Shankar said.

He rose and surveyed the room. There was something troubling about the abrupt way he did it. On the surface, he was soaking in the pub ambience, the background music, the boisterousness, the smoky atmosphere. But when I looked at him, he avoided eye contact. I pulled his hand.

"There's something you're not telling me," I said.

He hesitated for a few seconds, then sighed. "Pa doesn't trust anybody. He takes his checkbook and his bank statements with him to the bathroom," Shankar said.

"He fears you're stealing from him," I said. "And yet you're the one who's there for him, always."

When we reached my rented townhouse, close to midnight, my mother called and asked for Shankar. As he put down the phone, he screamed a series of expletives at his sisters and brothers-in-law. They were moving Uncle Roshan to a nursing home and had done Mama the courtesy of informing her beforehand, earlier in the day. Shankar was extended no such courtesy. Nor was he consulted.

"What makes them believe the nursing home will take better care of Pa than I can? I love him."

"But you're not there now," I said.

Shankar insisted that the nurse's aide would have taken good care of Uncle Roshan until his return and that the sisters were heartless. "We can afford two nurse's aides, if that's what it takes to keep him home."

"Why don't you look at it positively? They've freed you from a heavy burden. You can now visit Europe."

"He wanted to die in his bed, at home. No one bothers about his wishes," Shankar said.

I suspect he didn't sleep that night.

Shankar advanced his return and left for home two days later. The District Court rejected his petition to have his father nursed at home. Over the next three months, Uncle

Roshan's health deteriorated fast ("His fate was sealed when they dumped him in that damn facility," said Shankar) and I rushed to Mauritius, mostly to give support to my mother and to Shankar.

I was greeted at the nursing home by quotes from the Bhagavad Gita, the Hindu sacred text, posted on a pillar in the lobby. One caught my eye, the gist of which is "Even God cannot forgive one's transgressions, for the laws of karma are immutable and inescapable." As I went up the staircase, I thought of an interview Elie Wiesel gave on the Nazi perpetrators of the Holocaust. "It's not for me to forgive; only God can," he had said. I thought that was stark, but the message at the nursing home was much starker. It was grim.

Upstairs in his room, Maréchal Rommel was now lying in a fetal position, trembling. It was not a shiver occasioned by feeling cold or from poor blood circulation. It was a tremor triggered by the fear of death. "Don't let me die, Shankar. I'm counting on you." He was ninety-one years old.

As Shankar massaged him, Uncle Roshan grew still and chanted "Om" (ॐ).

IT IS TRUE, Shankar was trained by his father to be the person who was going to work for him, take care of him in his old age. But that alone could not explain what I witnessed. Shankar loved his father; it was in his nature to love his father that way. When Uncle Roshan died, Shankar asked me to oversee the wake. We took his body to the orchard where father and son had confronted each other years ago, and we washed him while prayers were chanted. His wake was subdued compared with Uncle Ram's. Rum was notable by its absence, and the group that gathered was reverential, not rambunctious. In other respects it was a grander affair. I arranged for a huge tent to be set up to welcome the expected crowd and for coffee, tea, biscuits, and snacks to be delivered by a caterer. At the wake and at the funeral the following day, people praised Uncle Roshan's contributions to society—defending the rights of small planters against the sugar estate, promoting girls' education, electoral canvassing for the Labour Party. Even Puranic priests, his theological foes, came to pay their last respects. "Sri Roshan set high moral standards for the Hindu community," eulogized a swami whose feet Shankar had massaged in his teenage years.

After the funeral, Shankar discovered that his father had transferred ownership of the ancestral home and the choicest land to his younger brother, the one who challenged and dishonored him by eloping with a Muslim woman; the one who, according to a servant, had hit Uncle Roshan when the latter had complained about his care. His father also held joint bank accounts with the other siblings. When Shankar told me this, I thought back on how, almost three decades earlier, the Bhushan family had been torn apart by the court case over Uncle Ram's inheritance. I wondered if we were going to see a similar fracas in Shankar's family.

"I don't understand why my beloved brother has acted so unfairly," Mama said. "Those children must have pressured him into signing away his property to them while Shankar was away in America."

I felt that Uncle Roshan had known what he was doing,

that he respected people who dared challenge him. Shankar's younger brother had stood up to him, and though this behavior may have upset him initially, it reminded him of his younger days. "In his youth, Uncle challenged the Puranic priests and his father. He challenged the sugar estate management. He accumulated authority through acts of rebellion," I told Mama.

"You've read too many books, Vishnu," Mama said.

A week after the final funeral rites, I bade good-bye to Shankar and encouraged him to visit me again in the United States.

In the months that followed, the thought that I had been too harsh in my judgment of Shankar nagged at me. In many respects he had done right, being there for his father all those years. I, however, stayed overseas, pursuing my dreams, leaving my parents behind. A feeling of being selfish crept up on me, and I phoned my mother and told her so. "You shouldn't feel that way. Your father and I are happy the way things happened. Look at all the Bhushans who are in America because of you. Counting their families, around twenty. You financed the education of some, housed them, helped them adjust."

Two or three years later, I watched the movie *The Crying Game*. It has an anecdote taken from the fables of Aesop and Persia that reminded me of Shankar and his father. A scorpion convinced a frog to let him ride on his back as the latter swam across a river. The scorpion stung the frog before they could reach the other shore. The frog asked the scorpion why he had done something that would drown them both. The scorpion replied that he couldn't help it. It was in his nature.

IX

Saturday Ritual

That evening, Papa skipped his favorite meal.
Mama said, "I'm too weak today to deplume the
    rooster and cut its throat."
Papa walked out to the backyard towards the chopping
    block.
"Meanwhile, I'll blend the spices and prepare the
    curry paste."

Mama said, "I'm too weak today to deplume the
    rooster and cut its throat."
She beckoned me, pointed to the coop.
"Meanwhile, I'll blend the spices and prepare the
    curry paste."
I grabbed the fattest rooster with the proudest red-
    crested head.

Mama beckoned me, pointed to the coop.
Gripping the rooster's legs, I pinned it down on the
    wooden block.
I grabbed the fattest rooster with the proudest red-
    crested head.
Mama handed Papa a sharp knife. "Chop it off with
    one stroke."

Gripping the rooster's legs, I pinned it down on the wooden block.

Papa raised the knife, took aim at the neck, the rooster's eyelids fluttered.

Mama handed Papa a sharp knife. "Chop it off with one stroke."

Sweat dotted Papa's brow, his hand shook. "I can't do this."

Papa raised the knife, took aim at the neck, the rooster's eyelids fluttered.

Mama wrested the knife from him. "It will escape if we wait too long."

Sweat dotted Papa's brow, his hand shook. "I can't do this."

Mama put the knife in my right hand, fourteen years old.

Mama wrested the knife from him. "It will escape if we wait too long."

Wielding that knife for the first time, I delivered a clean blow.

Mama put the knife in my right hand, fourteen years old.

The rooster's body twitched, blood spattered.

Wielding that knife for the first time, I delivered a clean blow.

"Papa, do you realize how strong Mama is?"

The rooster's body twitched, blood spattered.

"She's done it all these years. And she's vegetarian."

"Papa, do you realize how strong Mama is?
She raises our chickens, chops and cooks them.
She's done it all these years. And she's vegetarian."
That evening, Papa skipped his favorite meal.

X

Conclave of Goons

1964

"I went to an attorney today," Papa said. "He insists that Ram's land should now revert to me, not to his widow. Ram was not my brother but my cousin, and so was never entitled to any part of my parents' property."

He pulled out an envelope from his jacket pocket.

Six months had elapsed since Uncle Ram's death.

"All these years you've said he's your brother," I said.

We had almost finished dinner. Mama had plunged her spoon into the halwah dessert but left it there. Blood rushed to her ears and cheeks.

"Birth certificates don't lie," my father continued as he opened the envelope. "Vishnu, read this to Mama."

I was stunned. The names of Uncle Ram's parents were those of Papa's paternal uncle and aunt.

Mama rose from the table. "Vishnu doesn't have to read me anything. You know, and all the family elders know, that your uncle and aunt were childless. They begged your parents to have themselves named as Ram's parents on his birth certificate, and your parents agreed as a goodwill gesture to them."

"The attorney has filed a case in court," Papa said. "It's time to correct an injustice."

"How can you have a clear conscience when you're depriving Auntie Ranee and their daughters of their livelihood?" I said.

"They'll have enough to live on," Papa replied, cold and matter-of-fact. "They have Uncle Ram's pension and a beautiful house in a quiet neighborhood."

I had grown close to Uncle Ram: he was the one who took me to the horse races and regattas where I caught a glimpse of the island's high society; to weddings and fairs. I loved my books and aspired to be a laureate, and my father's intellectual guidance was inestimable. But now girls interested me as well—if only I had the guts to approach them. I saw in Uncle Ram my favorite Shakespearean character—a Falstaff who could help me get rid of my shyness. On more than one occasion, gregarious Uncle Ram had taken me for lunch at his favorite tavern and gotten the barmaid to befriend me. When he died, a month after he had last taken me to the bar, it was a tragedy.

The following Saturday, while my father was away in his sugarcane fields and I was doing my homework, a group of Bhushan elders showed up. In those days, much more so than now, relatives and friends just dropped in unannounced and uninvited. As it was an hour before lunchtime, Mama abandoned her embroidery work to prepare a large meal.

After the usual compliments on her hospitality and cooking, one of them asked, "Isn't Shiv ashamed of not acknowledging a blood brother as a brother, whatever the birth certificate states?"

"You should go ask him that yourself," Mama said.

The elders frowned, not pleased with what they viewed as Mama's disrespectful tone.

"Beti, you should try harder to persuade Shiv that he is wrong. Once this case is heard in court, with the public watching, the honor of the Bhushans will be in shreds," a second elder said.

To emphasize the gravity of the matter, another elder rephrased these words in a mix of Hindi and Kreol: "Ghar ke izzat bahot important hai." Then he turned to me: "As you proceed in life, we hope you also understand the importance of our family's honor."

When Papa returned in the evening, Mama complained that she was fed up with cooking for all his relatives only to be blamed by them for his behavior.

"These are emissaries sent by Ram's wife. She thinks I'll change my mind simply out of respect for their old age. The law is the law."

"Whatever the law says, you're wrong," I said.

"Vishnu, let the adults deal with this," Mama said.

Three or four more visits from the elders took place in the following two or three weeks while I was at second-ary school and Papa was teaching in his primary school. When it was clear that my father would not budge, Auntie Ranee asked Mama's help in arranging a meeting of the Bhushans at our house—all the adults, male and female, not just the elders. Mama agreed. She knew that not every-one invited would show up for a confrontation where sides had to be taken. She hoped this meeting would stop the steady onslaught of emissaries. Feeding them and clean-ing up after them were taking a toll on her, and taking her away from her embroidery and lace making. After each emissary visit, a bitter fight erupted between her and Papa, father insisting on his legal rights and Mama talking about moral obligations.

Mama ensured that my father stayed home one Saturday by reminding him of work that had to be done around the house. She asked me and Cousin Shankar, who lived some two hundred yards away, to be on the veranda to welcome the relatives. When Shankar arrived, my father was uprooting weeds in the small mango and lychee orchard at the back of the house—weeds whose evocative English names he enjoyed repeating to Shankar and to himself: blue panic grass, black nightshade, purple nutsedge, and pigweed. He had no idea what was brewing.

The first to show up, around 10 a.m., were two couples, the Parsads and the Lokhuns, hardworking proprietors of small plots of land on which they grew sugarcane and vegetables. Shrunk small by age and battered by years of manual labor, Uncles Lokhun and Parsad sported distinctive mustaches. Uncle Parsad's was a long, waxed handlebar mustache that earned him the ironic nickname Lord Kitchener of Khartoum—for he had none of the military bearing of the British marshal. Uncle Lokhun had a toothbrush mustache, Charlie Chaplin style. On the weekends they worked as traveling barbers, a vanishing breed, serving the Franco-Mauritian managers living on the sugar estates. They were the "keepers of the faith," the repository of ancient traditions from India. The Bhushan clan looked to them for guidance on rituals to be observed or performed at births, weddings, funerals, and other life-cycle events. To Shankar and me, the westernized younger generation, the Parsads and Lokhuns looked like they had just arrived from the village in Bihar that our ancestors left in the 1800s to come work as indentured laborers on the island. They dressed clumsily in Western suits, their wives in the plainest mono-chromatic saris. Though they were devout Hindus, their clothes, their gait, their demeanor, and their voices led us to believe they had heard and heeded Jesus's message that the meek shall inherit the earth. Vishnu and I couldn't see them changing the mind of my strong-willed father.

The couple that walked in about fifteen minutes later couldn't have been more different. Emulating Bombay stars of the era, Uncle Neeraj favored sunglasses, white jacket, pleated pants, and two-toned shoes. Whenever he visited, he surreptitiously handed me magazines with titles like *Intimité* and *Volupté,* featuring half-naked women and sto-ries of torrid love affairs. His wife had a trendy dress sense that made us teenagers salivate. She draped her sari hipster style: starting low on her hips, tight fit, with a short cling-ing blouse, midriff and navel bared. She knew the other uncles called her "vulgar" behind her back, but she didn't care. Shankar and I had previously heard the older uncles comment in Bhojpuri: "Gaand mein sharam nahin." She has no shame in her ass. The younger uncles expressed their ambivalence—admiration of her beauty, disapproval of her flaunting it—in Kreol: "Li content montrer so bazaar Bom-bay!" She loves to trot out her Bombay wares!

The Neerajs were the only Bhushans who owned a car and lived in a two-story concrete house with fridge and electric stove. Uncle Neeraj always traveled with the latest and most professional photographic equipment. He was a tailor. At the time, we didn't know he moonlighted as a dollar counterfeiter, though everyone wondered how he could afford his lifestyle. True to his occupations, Neeraj was jovial and keen on offending no one, and it was hard for me and Shankar to imagine him taking a position, much less trying to persuade my father to change course.

When my father came out onto the veranda, he was greeted warmly by the visitors. He sat down, calm and courteous. If he was surprised, he didn't let it show. While the women were with Mama in the kitchen, the men exchanged notes on the sugarcane harvest—average tonnage of cane per acre, the sucrose content, the price paid to planters by the sugar estate. As usual, Papa encouraged Shankar and me to sit in on adult conversations: he believed we could learn life lessons.

The ambience changed drastically with the arrival of Uncle Mohan. At six foot four and with a martial bearing, he occupied the veranda. Shankar and I had heard of his reputation. My mother had told us that as one of the very few Hindus recruited into the colonial police force after World War II, Uncle Mohan had an excellent chance of making it to the top of the force, in a country with a majority Hindu population. One night he turned up drunk at the police station and insulted the English Inspector of Police in front of the constables. The Inspector asked him to apologize in the police barracks quadrangle in the presence of everyone, but he was too proud to do so and was fired. Uncle Mohan preferred to switch to the backbreaking work of cutting and transporting sugarcane in the tropical sun. He was known for not backing down whenever he clashed with his neighbors, and that earned him the grudging respect of the other uncles. The uncles sometimes called on him to show up when a threat of physical force was called for in their disputes with neighbors.

Uncle Mohan's swagger as he entered and the stench of liquor on his breath suggested that he was itching for a fight. His namasté greeting to my father looked perfunctory, not the respectful namasté to which the head of the clan is entitled.

Papa rose and went towards the kitchen, perhaps to ask Mama if she had anything to do with what was going on. I looked at him, then at Uncle Mohan, and felt uneasy.

"Your father is a greedy coolie whose education has gone to his head," Uncle Mohan said.

"You shouldn't talk like that to teenagers; it makes them disrespect their parents," Uncles Parsad and Lokhun told him in unison.

Uncle Mohan ignored them. I felt beads of sweat wetting my brow.

Mama had just begun serving snacks and tea when Auntie Ranee arrived—not alone, as everyone had expected, but accompanied by Uncle Surya. This was a major coup engineered by Auntie Ranee, I thought. Uncle Surya was in a different league in the eyes of the Bhushan clan: he worked for the British Admiralty; his eldest son was in medical school in Scotland; his eldest daughter was an acclaimed actress, the first Hindu girl on the island to perform on the stage; and he owned more land than everybody else in the room combined. He was of the clan but beyond its norms.

Uncle Surya, the urban sophisticate living in the Plateau, and my father, the primary school teacher, liked and respected each other. Papa enjoyed visiting him, for he was the only relative with whom he could have an intellectual conversation, and that, too, over a glass of the finest Scotch bought duty-free at the Admiralty store. They were close. The fact that Surya's mother and Papa's father were siblings was not lost on those on the veranda. Was Auntie Ranee going to drive a wedge between the two?

Uncle Surya proposed a deal: that the land under dispute be divided equally between Auntie Ranee and my father. Auntie Ranee nodded her assent. Dad responded that he had no time for negotiations and he would take whatever the law gave him.

Uncle Mohan thundered: "Shiv, you dirty pig, you're using your education and knowledge of law to deprive an illiterate woman and your nieces of their due!"

Uncle Mohan lunged towards my father.

I sprang between them.

Uncle Mohan went on: "Who do you think you are? Richard the Third? Dispatching Ram's kids to the tower?"

"Mohan, you've got your Shakespeare right but your history wrong," my father said. "A little learning is a dangerous thing."

The exchange was lost on the uncles and aunts, except for Uncle Surya, who struggled to hide his smirk. Uncle Mohan was disarmed.

Uncle Neeraj adjusted his sunglasses. "I don't understand this fight. Why are you at each other's throats for a few miserable acres of barren soil that the white sugar barons dumped on Indian coolies at a good price?"

"Neeraj, all you can see is dirt and stones. You just confirmed what Surya and I agree on: small islands breed small minds," Papa said. He looked over the room and addressed everyone: "Ten years ago, the sugar estate dug an irrigation canal through that land. Were we compensated for that? Ram sat on his fat ass, instead of standing up to the white man. We can't even use the water that flows through. I'll sue the sugar estate for damages once I get ownership of the land."

"Papa, what about Auntie Ranee's rights? The fairness you talk about? All that stuff about the Bhagavad Gita and Mahatma Gandhi?"

My father raised his voice: "Vishnu, how do you hope to achieve your dreams of attending Oxford or Cambridge? On my monthly five hundred rupees' salary?"

"I don't understand you. You dish out banknotes to every beggar who knocks on our door, and you don't give a damn for Auntie Ranee and her children!" By this time, my shirt was damp with perspiration.

Uncles Parsad and Lokhun muttered about clan unity, and how it had helped the Bhushans progress from coolies living like slaves on the sugar estate to being small independent planters. No one was paying attention.

My mother's voice exploded: "You domineering man. You want to control everyone, just as you've controlled me all these years."

There was a collective gasp among the women.

This was the first time I had heard Mama raise her voice with my father.

Uncles Neeraj and Surya looked at each other, stupefied.

The traveling barbers shook their heads. In a rare moment of un-meekness, Lord Kitchener of Khartoum exclaimed, "That's what happens when the new generation doesn't heed the lessons of our Scriptures. In the house of

Ram there now is come the Mahabharata, the epic war. We now face our own battle of Kurukshetra and the annihilation of the Bhushans. Prepare for the Kali Yuga, the age of evil."

Papa looked at my mother. "So," he said, "you organized this goonda sabha!"

He shouted at the others. "That's what you are: a bunch of goondas. A conclave of goons. Get out of my house."

WITHIN MINUTES THE veranda was empty. I went to my bedroom and slumped against the headboard. Shankar came in, a look of concern on his face. "This brawl over land is exhausting," I said. "All this going and coming, when will it end?"

I reached out for my history textbook and opened it. "Shankar, I read two pages of this and I can't continue. Concentration gone. I'm tired."

"The solution is simple: you need sex. You're old enough now. You need a good fuck. There are two new girls at Rekha's. Come with me tomorrow."

"And catch syphilis—"

I had barely completed the word when we heard shattering glass.

We returned to the veranda. Uncle Mohan was back. He had thrown a stone at the windows and was challenging my father to come out and fight like a man.

My father emerged from the kitchen with a machete and, with an agility that astounded us, he ran outside, ready for Uncle Mohan.

By then a small crowd of neighbors and passersby had

gathered on the street. The spectacle of a quiet school-teacher wielding a machete was a once-in-a-lifetime event, and there was no doubt where their sympathies lay: Papa had taught many of them and, with his average build, he was the underdog.

"Give it to him!" the crowd shouted. I hoped that my father would control himself: he was no match for Uncle Mohan.

Suddenly Io, a tall neighbor with a massive frame, who in his youth had spent some years in jail, emerged from the crowd, walked calmly to Uncle Mohan, and asked him to cool it. A few years earlier, Papa had helped Io get a grounds maintenance job at the local primary school.

Mama pulled my father back inside.

THE CROWD QUICKLY dispersed. It was midday. I needed fresh air. I asked Shankar to accompany me to the public fountain near the house, under the sprawling shade of a flamboyant tree. At the time I was born here, fifteen years earlier, this fountain had been the main source of drinking water for the neighborhood. Now that everyone had running water at home, it had become a meeting place for relaxation, a game of dominoes or cards, or for gossip. As I leaned against the tree, I sensed that a circular band clamp squeezed my skull tighter and tighter. My brain alternately throbbing, pounding, splitting. I felt the pain behind my forehead, on the left side, on the right, in the back, around the eyes.

My headache was the kind for which an American doctor today would immediately order an MRI or CT scan.

But this was 1964, in the middle of summer, and medical options in those days were limited in the village of Mon Désert, to which my parents had returned after living in various places on the island. On the veranda, my mother touched my brow to feel my temperature—no fever—and gave me two aspirin tablets.

"He's never complained of headaches before," she told Shankar, and asked him to help me to my bed while she went to fetch some Tiger Balm ointment. That's when I lost consciousness.

What happened over the next few months is a blur, the events confused in my memory. Over the years, most of my recollections have been confirmed by Shankar; a few have been contradicted.

When Mama returns with the Tiger Balm, I'm crooning, "I've just kissed a girl named Maria." Natalie Wood hovers over the bed and sings, "One Hand, One Heart." I press a pillow to my chest and we launch into the West Side Story *duet. Natalie comes closer, grabs my pillow, and throws it on the floor.*

Mama wears a faint smile.

"Mocking me, aren't you, Mama? And you too, Shankar, you son of a bitch? Jealous?"

I start crying, I beg for pardon. I'm ashamed I swore in front of my mother.

Natalie floats away.

My books are scattered on the floor. Who threw them there?

I hear my mother, almost as an echo: "Shankar, bring Uncle Shiv here. Take the bicycle and go get a taxi."

A taxi? That's expensive. We must be going to Hollywood to meet my beloved Natalie. Papa is in his trademark suit, tie, and felt hat. Mama and Shankar come along for the ride.

The car levitates to its destination. The Department of Public Works must have read my letters of complaint to the newspapers: the potholes and bumps have disappeared.

The airplane overhead roars its approval. I shout, "It sucks away our sins."

We reach Natalie Wood's Beverly Hills mansion.

Dr. Maurice Curé's nurse assistant opens the door, takes me down a corridor. It's the exam room.

"Where's Natalie?"

"Vishnu, you've come in for a chat," the doctor says.

On the walls, a diploma from the Sorbonne Faculty of Medicine. "Doctor, I thought you studied at Trinity College in Dublin. That's what you told me last time we spoke about your student days in Europe."

Whispers. Papa and Dr. Curé leave the room.

"Doctor, you must renew that medical certificate exempting me from Mr. Steele's physical education class. That martinet thinks he's still in the Royal Navy."

Papa returns with another doctor. The Labour Party leader who won the hearts of Creoles, Hindus, Muslims, and Chinese alike has been transformed: he's shorter, his white skin has turned brown. He is Dr. Seegobin, Papa's doctor.

"Are you prescribing suppositories for my father's constipation?"

The doctor extends his hand. "How's your headache?" His posture is upright, his tone avuncular.

"*Headache? What headache?*"

I walk up to the wall behind him and examine the anatomical chart. I can't figure it out. I pick up the model skull on his desk.

"*You love* Hamlet?" *the doctor says.*

"*I prefer* Othello."

The doctor smiles. "*At your age, I enjoyed* As You Like It."

Your dad took you to both Doctors Curé and Seegobin during your illness, but not on the same day. He said your topsy-turvy brain was making a biryani out of Shakespeare. You mouthed stuff like "The arithmetic of memory is smooth as monumental alabaster, and equals the sum of the seven ages of man."

The doctor sits me down and presses his stethoscope to my chest. I knock it away.

"*I'm tired, Doctor.*"

"*Don't cry. Have you been studying a lot?*"

"*Of course not.*"

"*Girlfriend problem?*"

"*He's too young to have a girlfriend,*" *someone says.*

"*Along with the tablets I've prescribed, he'll need a complete rest at home for a month . . . maybe more,*" *the doctor says.* "*Here's a medical certificate for the school.*"

The doctor and Papa lower their voices. I hear "*Brown Sequard.*" *Brown Sequard . . . where they administer electric shocks to patients and put them in straitjackets.*

"*Are you sending me to the lunatic asylum? I don't want to see Dr. Raman, dokter fou, Dr. Madman.*"

Papa shows me the medical certificate. Acute pneumonia.

.   .   .

Stuck at home. As the days go by, the church bells sound louder, the calls to prayer from the mosque more frequent.

The hues of the evening pervade the house.

Shankar comes by.

I fling books out the window. He runs outside, brings them back.

Mama serves me crab curry—"your favorite," she says—but I'm not hungry.

Knocks on the front door. I hear school friends. Someone answers the door. No one comes in. Do they think I have a contagious disease? Is that what Mama told them? Or Papa?

The olive white-eye bird trills on the window ledge.

I want to go outside. I'm not coughing or sneezing.

"Mama, I don't have pneumonia."

Mama's kitchen beckons.

I open the glass and mason jars: the spices never looked so colorful.

I sprinkle yellow turmeric on paper, some red chili powder, and brown cinnamon and smear them all over.

"Vishnu, are you making masala? Let me to show you."

"I'm making art, Mama, art."

"Is that a mountain?"

"Modern art, Mama. Ultramodern."
"Why are you tossing the jars in the sink?"
Mama beats her forehead.
"My God, what have you done?"

I open the newspaper. "Shankar, look what's playing—Splendor in the Grass, *with Natalie Wood."*

Papa walks in. I turn the page. "Dad, look what Hindi movies are playing—Junglee, Pyaar Ka Saagar." *I thrust it in his hand:* "Come on. Read it."

He is baffled. I smile: I don't have to lie to him anymore about going to the cinema. "Cinema is a vice. All about robbing banks, murder, and adultery," *he always said. Now I won't have to tell him there's a play at school—Shakespeare, Molière, Racine, or Marivaux.* "No, Papa, I've been going to the movies. Isn't that right, Shankar?"

Cousin Shankar blushes. He's the one who introduced me to cinema.

It wasn't a newspaper. You took out a handkerchief from your trouser pocket and read from it as if it was a newspaper.

I rub my eyes and feel drops of water on my cheeks. An artist stands next to my bed: long hair, gold earrings and necklace, saffron scarf, loose white pants, barefoot. He moves his hands over my body in circular motions, clockwise and counterclockwise, closes his eyes, takes a deep breath, and mumbles mantra-like words. I smell camphor and incense. He dips a bundle of leaves into water and sprinkles me: scents of lemongrass, mango, and betel. Another round of circular hand motions.

I grab his scarf and pull him towards me.

"What the hell are you doing?"

Shankar says, "Oja."

"I can see the animal now," the oja exclaims.

"Get out, you quack doctor, fake magician."

The oja turns away and makes a portentous announcement: a close relative has practiced witchcraft, and I'm suffering because of it. A rooster has been sacrificed. That's the animal he sees. Does the family have reason to suspect anyone?

Papa asks me: "Have you seen Auntie Ranee doing anything peculiar with roosters during your visits to her since Uncle Ram's death?"

Visits that Papa had frowned upon and Mama encouraged.

"I saw her once taking a black rooster to the Hanuman shrine in her garden. I thought it was just another offering to the monkey god, an improvement on the banana and coconut Auntie usually gives him."

"Don't talk like that about Hanuman," Papa says.

"What's the big deal? Catholics offer flowers and candles. Hindu women pour milk and water on Shiva's lingam during the Shivratri festival. It's all the same superstitious nonsense: candles and flowers for Christ, milk for Shiva's penis, and roosters for Hanuman's stomach."

Shankar smiles. I release the oja's scarf.

"Why would Auntie Ranee want to harm me?" I ask the oja. "I'm on her side."

He does not dispute that. "Witchcraft by amateurs can work like a boomerang: it can boomerang back to hurt the inexperienced practitioner, or boomerang sideways and harm those who are close or related to the intended target. You're a sideways victim, your father was the main target."

The taxi is back. The tall neighbor walks up to us.

"Io, how come you, a Creole adopted by a Telugu Catholic family, got a female name from Greek mythology? Are you the princess seduced by Jupiter?" My questions puzzle him. With two or three years of primary school, the poor fellow probably never heard of Jupiter and Greek mythology. I don't expect an answer.

"I'll pray to the Virgin Mary for him, Mr. Bhushan. We all need to pray."

Papa thanks him.

"Don't waste your time praying, Io."

He ignores me and hugs Papa. "If you want me to, I'll speak to the sacristan of the church. He can perform an exorcism. Too much reading has worn out his brain."

The taxi passes Mare d'Albert, about five miles from Mon Désert. Across the harvested cane fields, mounds of stones bull-dozed out of the soil by the sugar estates and shaped into pyramids stare at me.

Napoleon rides in on his white horse, resplendent in red-and-gold uniform, and declaims, "Soldats, du haut de ces pyramides quarante siècles vous contemplent."

I grab Papa's felt hat and put it on my head. "Let's march on to victory."

There are no mameluke warriors to vanquish.

We leave the sunny south and drive to the Plateau. Sugarcane fields and mango trees flush with blossoms become sparse. Eucalyptus trees disappear, tea plantations and fir come into view, covered with a shroud of mist and fog. I ask Shankar for pen and paper.

"Do you remember what the oja chanted? I'll write it down for you."

No Beverly Hills mansion this time. We walk straight into the doctor's office.

"You look better, Vishnu."

"I've deplumed the rooster. You should join the conclave of goons, Doctor."

Another medical certificate, another month of school leave, more tablets.

The trees stir, birds shriek. I hear the vegetable seller on his bicycle shouting "Brède cresson! Margoze!" Watercress, bitter melon!

I ask Mama to cook me dal puris.

I'm glad Shankar brought back the books I threw away. I devour them.

I sneak into Papa's clutter while he's teaching at school and unearth Zola's Thérèse Raquin *with its sulfurous book cover, and Somerset Maugham's* Of Human Bondage. *He inveighs against immorality in films but relishes the passions in the classics.*

Mama offers Shankar and me parsadee, sweets for celebratory Hindu prayers.

"Why are you in brown today?" I ask Mama.

"I promised Saint Anthony in church that if you get better, I would wear brown every Sunday till you turn eighteen."

"Did you go to the mosque and ask Allah to intercede? When are you going to wear green?"

Mama laughs in a way I haven't seen in a long, long time. "Don't be ridiculous. They wouldn't let a woman in."

Dr. Curé visits at home.

"I have some catching up to do at school."

"Spend some time at the beach to get used to sunlight again."

"He should go to the cinema for relaxation," he tells Papa, who looks dismayed.

ON MY FIRST day back to school, some kids on the bus asked questions about the rooster sacrificed at Hanuman's altar. The oja must have spread the rumor, my father speculated. The story was now embellished with a counterclaim— that Papa had met the Tamil mystic to discuss supernatural ways to accelerate Uncle Ram's demise. In those days, there were still people for whom there was no such thing as a natural death. No matter if one is an alcoholic and can therefore succumb to liver cirrhosis: death has to be caused by some supernatural intervention or the machinations of a longanis hired and paid to invoke spirits.

WHEN PAPA'S CASE against Auntie Ranee came up for a hearing—nine months after the goonda sabha—I went

to the Mahébourg District Court. My father caused a sen-
sation. Having learnt that his lawyer, stuck pleading at
another district court, was going to be late, he asked the
judge for permission to start, and quoted extensively from
the Napoleonic Code to support his claim. The audience,
mostly retirees of Indian and African origin, was thrilled
when he scored points against Auntie's lawyer, a prominent member of the Franco-Mauritian upper class. My
father lectured him on the subtle meanings of an archaic
French word in the Code. Even some of my classmates'
parents were talking about the self-taught laborer turned
schoolteacher who humiliated a barrister! Though all the
goonda uncles testified against him regarding the parentage
of Uncle Ram, my father won the case.

Auntie Ranee sought advice from a nephew who had
just returned from England after graduating from one of
London's Inns of Court. *Bhushan v. Bhushan* would be the
first case this barrister would litigate in his career—pro
bono. Auntie Ranee and the nephew lost two rounds of
appeals: the Intermediate Court and the Superior Court
upheld the District Court's judgment. Three years after
the initial district court judgment, the case landed on the
docket of the Supreme Court. Auntie's tenacious nephew
recruited a QC—Queen's Counsel, a senior barrister recognized by the bar for his mastery of the law—to join him.
Unfortunately for my father, his lawyer died soon after, taking to his grave the French tradition of green-robed avoué
plaidant on the island. He scrambled to secure a lawyer
who had to be briefed from scratch. The Supreme Court
quashed the verdict of the District, Intermediate, and Supe-

rior Courts. In their ruling, they dug up an 1866 judgment
issued by a French court in Toulouse that established the
doctrine of tacit renunciation of rights. By remaining silent
and not claiming his rights to his father's land for so many
years, my father was deemed to have renounced them.

In late 1964, Papa had moved back to Mahébourg.
While the *Bhushan v. Bhushan* case meandered through the
courts, I slowly recouped the academic ground lost through
my extended absence.

I submitted a poem to the school magazine:

THE PRAYER ROOM
Multi-armed Hindu goddesses with ample bosoms
embrace Kufic verses
on sumptuous silk.
A red and lapis lazuli icon
jeers a sober menorah,
and is mocked in turn by
ritual masks from the Congo.
A Bible, a Koran, and a Bhagavad Gita
lean on each other.

When everyone is asleep,
do the gods fight or make love?

The editor rejected it. "I love it, but it will likely offend
the religious sensibilities of many parents." I surmised I
would have better luck with a French poem. Next day, I
went to my French teacher, Daniel Koenig, and asked him
to recommend the following to the editor:

LUMIÈRE
Enfant de l'agonie qui brise mon âme,
Mon coeur, révolté, me revendique, me réclame—
Moi, vile vomissure de mes vices,
Enfer où les fluides pourries de l'obsession
Dansent l'indécence.

Coeur qu'enflamme une frénésie salvatrice
Délire du Moi en fervente ébullition
Extase de l'être trempé au feu expiatoire.

Incandescence.

Active in the Catholic Church and nephew of a prominent politician, Daniel became my favorite teacher the day
I argued against the doctrine of Papal infallibility in class:
he told me I would make an infallible pope were I a Catholic. About the poem, he was gentle. " 'Agony's child . . .
revolt of the heart . . . the vile vomit of your vices and the
rotten fluids of obsession . . . delirium of the self.' Vishnu,
these are well-chosen, strong words." The lanky descendant of settlers from Alsace-Lorraine paused, took a Gau-
loise from its pack, and assumed an ironic, jesuitic tone:
"I see the ghost of Baudelaire over your shoulders, advis-
ing you to broaden your experience and develop your own
voice before you submit poems about agonizing souls and
salvation. Baudelaire loved, caught syphilis, suffered. You
have to live some more, Vishnu. At the same time, I can
imagine him admiring your efforts and offering you his
helping hand on the hard climb to Parnassus."

The following month, my poem appeared in the magazine. I took up debating to overcome my shyness. Mama asked Shankar if my more extroverted ways were the long-term side effects of Dr. Curé's medicine.

ON THE DAY the judgment in favor of Auntie Ranee was rendered, the Oxbridge A-level examinations results were announced: I was fourth in the National Scholarship Competition. Shankar joined us for dinner.

Papa congratulated me. "We have to focus on your university admission and scholarship now. You know I lost the case."

"The goonda uncles think you are taking the case to the Privy Council in London," I said.

"The Supreme Court says I should have filed twenty years earlier, but I couldn't afford the legal fees then."

"You can make that point at the Privy Council," I said.

"Where will I get the money for an expensive British barrister? The local lawyers have eaten up my savings."

Papa sighed. "You and Mama never wanted me to win. But no matter. We have to celebrate your achievements now. We are all proud of you. Aren't we, Mama?"

My mother's face sparkled. As she served her crab curry, she said, "Who knows? Maybe you'll be a famous lawyer someday."

Papa could not resist. "Maître Vishnu Bhushan, QC, advocate for Shiv Bhushan in *Bhushan v. Bhushan* at the Privy Council."

· · ·

EIGHT YEARS AFTER my Oxbridge results, the day after
I earned my doctorate at Harvard, I wrote Shankar a letter:

> You wrote that Papa and Auntie Ranee have
> fully reconciled. This is wonderful. Maria was
> with me at the graduation ceremony. Not the
> Maria who sang to me after the Conclave of
> Goons but the woman I'm going to marry. She is
> not exactly what Uncle Ram would have wished:
> she's neither English nor European à la Brigitte
> Bardot or Sophia Loren—but she comes pretty
> close to his criterion of "defiling the purity of
> Hindu blood." She's American and, like him,
> a non-believer. I've told her about my nervous
> breakdown, my adventures with Natalie Wood,
> the oja and the black rooster. She knows how Dr.
> Curé (Dr. Seegobin?), Papa and Mama spared me
> a lifetime at the lunatic asylum and saved me from
> the stigma of madness. I've asked her to do the
> same if ever I behave strangely: don't ever take me
> to a mental hospital.
>
> I sometimes wonder if Mama and Papa feel
> bad, that they may have driven me to that state.
> In truth, I'm forever grateful to Papa for insisting
> that I be treated at home, insisting that there be no
> mention of "nervous breakdown" in my school or
> medical records.
>
> When I was in Mauritius, I blamed the whole
> thing on him. I've had other thoughts since. A
> sudden growth spurt with all kinds of hormonal
> imbalances may have caused it too. Maybe you

were right—I needed sex and should have listened
to you and gone to Rekha's. Maybe in the society
we had at the time, Dr. Curé couldn't say sexual
repression caused my breakdown. How could I
have sex? Too young to have a girlfriend, Papa and
Mama said. Too young, the priests, the imams and
the pandits would say. What they didn't know, or
didn't want to hear, is that at every opportunity,
the stronger guys groped and caressed a classmate,
the Adonis in our class—the dainty boy with the
soft face, smooth skin, and rounded derrière who
reminded them of the girls they couldn't touch.

P.S: Did you hear that Natalie Wood drowned
last week? I was melancholic all day.

Shankar replied by sending me a copy of the oja's incan-
tation as I had written it down:

Alpha Omega Swaha
Paternum Nobiscum Christum
Allah Akbar Mashallah Subhanallah
Jadoogar Agram Bagram
Lingam Yoni Spiritus Concupiscentia
Chatvari arya satyani
Om Shantee Shantee Shantee

Sanskrit, Latin, and Arabic words from Hindu, Bud-
dhist, Christian, and Muslim prayers mixed with words
denoting sexual organs. An interpretation of the oja's chant
by a delirious adolescent, part sacrilege, part ecumenism.

XI

A Safe Place

He lent us his Kama Sutra and *The Perfumed Garden,*
our private tutor in maths,
guaranteeing top marks in exams—
a genius in the eyes of our parents

until his unmarried sister got pregnant.

At the market, beach, and barbershops,
at church, mosque, and temple,
the townsfolk dissected the news:
her lover was unknown, she an orphan,
her brother an alcoholic.

Our parents got us a sober tutor
who disapproved of *Lady Chatterley's Lover.*

Tamasha

Though a quarrel in the streets is a thing to be hated, the energies displayed in it are fine. The commonest Man shows a grace in his quarrel.
—JOHN KEATS, LETTER TO GEORGE AND GEORGIANA KEATS, MARCH 19, 1819

As I walked left into Colony Street, about five minutes from the Catholic church in Mahébourg, I saw a crowd gathered in a circle in front of our house. On the outer fringes, men had put their shopping baskets on the asphalt. From the verandas and windows of the surrounding houses, women and children stretched to watch whatever event was unfolding at the center. As I got closer, I noticed the younger men were on the inside of the circle. A gambling match, I thought, but immediately realized that would not attract so much interest, especially from women and children. There was no festival, religious or otherwise, that Sunday. And the days of cockfighting were long since gone, even in remote villages. It was election season in Mauritius, but there were neither loudspeakers and microphones nor orators.

"Vishnu, vin guette tamasha," someone shouted to me. Come see the tamasha!

Tamasha: a Hindi word I often heard in Bombay movies, a word that had become part of the Kreol language on the island. A word whose meaning encompasses song and dance, fun and excitement, as well as commotion and drama.

I wondered once again why my father, a schoolteacher who enjoyed reading his books and newspapers quietly in his room, had chosen to live in such a noisy neighborhood. That afternoon, he had gone with my mother to the market.

Just as I was about to reach the perimeter, the circle swelled outwards, with people shouting, "Watch out! They're going to hurl it!"

Some twenty-five feet away, Kalipa, barrel-chested and wearing the red shirt of the Labour Party, moved towards Fringant, lean and supple and wearing the blue shirt of the PMSD, the Parti Mauricien Social Démocrate. Two brothers in their thirties, both fishermen. Each held a harpoon pointed at the other's stomach.

I thought of *Moby-Dick,* which we read the previous year in secondary school, of Queequeg the Polynesian and Ahab's harpoon crew. Indeed, Kalipa, a Creole, could pass for a Polynesian. Fringant, had he been a shade or two lighter, could have passed for a mulatto in the complex color scheme of Mauritius.

"Éta gogot, to marche ek sa pilon-là," Kalipa said to Fringant, expressing his disgust at his brother's support of Gaëtan Duval, the supposedly gay politician. Duval, the Lord Byron of Mauritian politics, whom I would meet fifteen years later in Washington at a Mauritian embassy reception, resplendent in a satiny pink shirt with ruffles, kissing the women's hands and generating envy among the men. Duval, the leader whose pedigreed horses stole the show at his funeral.

"Vini, liki to mama, mo paré pou toi," said Fringant, egging on his brother to fight.

In 1967, genitalia-rich profanities like *gogot* and *liki to mama* were common currency in our neighborhood, uttered so loudly in the streets that they penetrated our walls.

In the crowd, I recognized neighbors, hardworking Creole fishermen whose livelihood was earned at the mercy of the vagaries of sea and weather. Among them were two who had suffered a beating at the hands of the belligerent brothers a few months earlier at the débarcadère, the historic fishermen's wharf. They had been showing off, to a gawking crowd, a wounded yellow-nosed albatross they had captured in the high seas, each stretching wide the giant white-and-black wings of the bird; in its helpless posture and suffering, it looked like Christ on the cross. Fringant and Kalipa smashed their noses and teeth and took the bleeding bird to the parish priest, asking him to drive it to the nearest veterinarian, fifteen miles away.

I also spotted the neighbor who, it was rumored, had raped his concubine's daughter, and the soft-spoken carpenter vilified by his mother-in-law for being a hunchbacked dwarf. "You ugly frog! I know you've spent a fortune on sorcerers to seduce my daughter." It was on a market day and on a street corner that the mother-in-law yelled the accusation.

Supporters of both political parties, clad in red or blue shirts, were at the Kalipa-versus-Fringant event. Someone shouted, "This is Muhammad Ali versus Sonny Liston"; whistles followed. "Cain and Abel," said an old man standing next to me. His remark got no response. Part of me was puzzled that so many men were leaning on their bicycles, waiting for the outcome of the confrontation instead of intervening to stop it or riding to the police station, about half a mile away, to ask for help. The other part of me was a sixteen-year-old who wanted to stay and enjoy the tamasha.

The two brothers put down their harpoons, took off their shirts with a flourish, and cast them on the pavement. Their chests glistened in the sun.

I moved towards the inner circle, close enough to Kalipa and Fringant to see their rib cages moving up and down as they breathed. My heart beat faster. At first it was in anticipation of their next move. Then it was unease. A devilish trembling of my knees. When they picked up the harpoons, I got scared. One miscalculation by Kalipa or Fringant and a harpoon would skewer my entrails. Or the groin of the guy next to me. I turned and tried to walk back to the gate of our house, but there was no turning back. Behind me were sweaty and sinewy men reeking of rum who wouldn't budge; they were here for the tamasha and didn't want their show disturbed. I felt like an early Christian trapped in the pit of the Colosseum, forced to watch the gladiators kill each other. Except this was no Hollywood film or novel. It was the real thing.

As the tension grew, the crowd turned quiet. The scent of papayas from our yard wafted on the wind. Kalipa's shorts exposed calves as thick as Fringant's thighs. Fringant taunted his brother by shuffling his feet rapidly, as if he really were in a boxing ring. In a split second, Kalipa aimed and flung his harpoon. Fringant ducked. The harpoon landed at their father's feet just as he rounded the street corner.

The crowd gasped.

Tonton George ignored the harpoon and walked straight to his sons.

He pointed to the shirts on the asphalt. The sons bent to pick them up.

Men grabbed their bicycles, and within a few minutes the crowd was gone.

When I reached our gate, I breathed a heavy sigh of relief and vowed to myself never to venture that close to a fight.

EARLIER THAT MORNING, on my way to the seaside, both brothers had said hello to me from the bar owned by the Chinese shopkeeper Chung Fat, three minutes' walk from our house. Like many of the patrons, they dropped in on their way back from Mass. They stood at opposite ends of the veranda, Kalipa, glass in hand, chatting with Chung Fat, and Fringant pouring a drink for Tonton George. They were dressed in their Sunday best—white shirts, black trousers. No red, no blue.

THE DAY BEFORE Kalipa flung his harpoon at his brother Fringant and missed, they attended a political meeting at Ville Noire, a coastal hamlet adjoining Mahébourg. Like many of the youngsters there, I went for the entertainment that such a gathering provided and to revel in the oratory of Harold Walter. A Labour Party member, Walter represented our district at the Colonial Legislature. A political meeting was a fun place to hang out. There was no TV at home, and though I enjoyed the two- or three-movie matinees on weekends, my meager pocket money or the rupee or two I sometimes filched from my father's pocket could stretch only so far. Going out with girls? Like my classmates, I saw petting and sex in the movies but could only dream and grind my teeth in frustration; parents didn't let their daughters go out alone after school. Like Warren Beatty and Natalie Wood in *Splendor in the Grass,* we read the Romantic poets in school. Unlike them, we couldn't indulge in actual romance. Unless we craved a good thrashing from the girl's father or uncles.

I didn't have the right to vote, but, strange as it may sound, I had caught the political fever sweeping the country. So had most of my classmates.

It was hard to resist the lure of posters glued to electrical and telephone poles, on shopfronts and walls that announced:

> *Grand Meeting*
> *à la Ville Noire*
> *Ténors du Parti Travailliste*
> *Honorable Harold Walter*
> *Honorable Jay Narain Roy*
> *Honorable Iqbal Mohamed*
> *Honorable Ah-Chuen*

When I arrived, the crowd could barely fit into the makeshift soccer field where the meeting was being held. It was half a mile from the water's edge. The sultry sea breeze blew in the stink of the nearby abattoir, the slaughterhouse. After the initial assault on the nostrils, I got used to the porcine smell, like everyone else. I spotted people from the nearby villages whom I usually ran into at the Mahébourg bazaar. Even the charcoal vendor, who never left his store by the southern side of the bazaar, near the Mahé Cinema, was there. Loudspeakers blared music at the four corners of the field, while the organizers waited for all the orators to show up on an improvised wooden platform decorated with red ribbons and flags.

Red-shirted Kalipa stood in the front row. Like a bouncer in a nightclub, he would handle hecklers who got too close to the speakers.

Blue-shirted Fringant, with other PMSD supporters, were at the far end.

A stout man with a square jaw and intense eyes, Walter thanked those who had elected him in 1964 and spoke about his contribution to the welfare of his constituents. After all these years, I've forgotten what he boasted about, but I remember the heated moments that followed.

A blue-shirted heckler burst forth. "You voted for birth control. You're against the Catholic Church!"

Another blue shirt shouted, "Baby murderer! Immoral pagan!"

Walter, a Protestant, took them on. "Immoral? Is it immoral to have two or three well-fed children instead of many you can't feed? Is it immoral to be able to provide an education to your kids?"

Some Labour Party supporters turned to the blue-shirted hecklers and screamed:

"Shut up, you morons!"

"Go home!"

Walter resumed: "Nobody is forcing you to use contraceptives. If you want more children, have them. Use the rhythm method if you want. A Labour government will finance all genuine family planning organizations."

Then he added, "But I'm not here to talk about myself or birth control today. We are here to talk about independence. The independence of Mauritius. Independence is inevitable, whether Duval and the PMSD like it or not."

The red shirts, mostly Hindus and a few Creoles, clapped their hands.

"Causer, frère! L'indépendans nous ouler!" Say it, brother! We want independence!

Kalipa and I exchanged smiles.

By that time Fringant had moved closer to the speakers' platform. He saw us but didn't smile.

Walter's sonorous voice went on: "The British prime minister has said the wind of change is blowing through Africa. But Duval doesn't hear it. Duval doesn't feel it. Duval doesn't taste it. How can he? He's in the pay of the white sugar barons who want to keep their privileges."

The blue shirts, largely Creoles and a sprinkling of Hindus, were for the most part quiet. Fringant frowned. One blue soul brandished a poster of a skeletal child with an empty bowl; the caption read INDEPENDENCE = FAMINE. Other posters read:

DOWN WITH INDEPENDENCE!

WE WANT INTEGRATION WITH ENGLAND!

A blue shirt screamed, "Long live Duval, lé roi Creole!"

Walter was a Creole like Duval, but lighter-skinned and therefore assumed by quite a few to be a mulatto.

His voice turned pugnacious. "Duval king of the Creoles? How can he be when the sugar barons are his paymasters? Have you forgotten how the sugar estates exploited your slave ancestors? My Creole brothers, vote for independence, for your dignity, for freedom."

Walter sized up the crowd.

"They talk about Hindu hegemony. They tell you after independence the Hindu majority will dominate the minorities. Don't let the fat cats who own the Parti Mauricien divide you! Creoles and Hindus share a common destiny—we are brothers in suffering."

Walter paused. Then he thundered, "It's time for our freedom. Freedom now! Independence now!"

Walter had fired up the red shirts. The wind carried the applause beyond the Ville Noire bridge to Mahébourg, I was told later by the blacksmith hammering away by his forge at the edge of the bridge, as his sooty assistant pumped the bellows.

Throughout the meeting, Kalipa and Fringant had their ears glued to the orators and stayed quiet. When the meeting was over, Kalipa shook Walter's hands. They chatted for a while and hugged each other as they took leave.

Most of the crowd, including the blue shirts, was good-humored when they dispersed. However, with their clenched jaws and frowning eyebrows, Fringant and a few of the younger blue shirts didn't look happy.

WHEN MY PARENTS returned home from the market and I told them about the Kalipa-Fringant tamasha, Mama's perennial worried look turned into one of alarm.

"Oh, my God! I hope nothing happened to you," she said as she touched my cheekbones and lips. She was checking whether I had sustained any blows! "Couldn't you just stay home after we left?"

"They won't do anything to him. It's between two brothers," Papa said. "That's the way they settle their political differences. Tomorrow they'll be hugging each other."

"I don't like politics," Mama said.

"Papa, we should leave this place," I said.

"We've had this conversation before, and you know the answer," Papa said.

"You expect me to study with all that fighting and noise? I can't win that university scholarship living here."

"Vishnu, you're at the best secondary school in the country. At your age, I labored in the sugarcane fields. Instead of secondary school, I had to take a correspondence course years later."

"I know. And you walked three miles every day to your primary school."

He went on: "You have good genes. I passed the entrance exams to the Teachers Training College with higher scores than the guys who went to secondary school. You have it in you, Vishnu, believe me!"

"You lived in quiet Ferney," Mama said. "Here we have to put up with drunks gambling at our doorstep and stray dogs barking all night."

"Papa, we wake up to the tune of *gogot;* I come back from school, it's a chorus of *liki to mama;* in the evening, I start my homework and it's a concert of *fallou to mama.* On the weekend, the whole neighborhood is drinking the night away and dancing the séga."

Mama handed me sweets she'd bought at the market and shook her head. "You can't win with the old man," she said, and went to the kitchen. "I'm getting dinner ready."

"Remember Disraeli?" Papa said.

"You mean the clown who was jeered in the House of Commons for wearing multicolored trousers?"

"Vishnu, don't make fun of me!" Papa said. "You know very well what I'm driving at."

I knew what was coming, for Papa had shown me the course materials from his correspondence school, Wolsey Hall, Oxford. On the word "Oxford" he would linger.

"Disraeli, the first Jew to be Britain's prime minister. What did he say when the establishment scoffed at him?"

I didn't want to answer.

Papa went on: "'The secret of success is constancy to purpose.' Bear Disraeli's words in mind and you'll make it."

"Why don't we move to the Quartier neighborhood, where we used to live with Uncle Ram?" I said.

"You know very well that I offered to buy Uncle's house after he died, but Auntie Ranee got a better offer. I don't have the money for that neighborhood. Have some patience. Two more years here and off you go to England!"

"Aren't you afraid of the violence? We Hindus are outnumbered by Creoles here."

"Their fear of independence is temporary. Once they realize we depend on each other, the violence will pass."

"In the meantime, we stay here and get harpooned!" I said.

"They won't harm us. You forgot what happened in 1965?"

. . .

I HADN'T FORGOTTEN what happened in 1965. In early May, I woke up one morning to find a policeman on the veranda. He was addressing my parents: "Don't worry, we've posted riot police in front of your gate and on the street. This will dissuade anyone from attacking your house."

After he left, I asked my father what had happened.

"A white man driving through Trois Boutiques has been killed by Hindus there and some Creoles are seeking revenge. Creoles and whites are allies now."

Trois Boutiques, five miles away, a village with a Hindu majority. Mostly sugarcane laborers and planters, and vegetable growers. A village so somnolent that some of my classmates had never heard of it.

Mama was shaking. She could hardly breathe as she spoke: "We're one of the few Hindu families in the neighborhood."

Papa shook his head and said, "Hindus and Creoles killing each other! This has never happened in Mauritius. It must be the politicians stirring trouble."

"I don't like politics," Mama said.

I raised my arms to open the window. I wanted to see the riot police.

"Don't," said my father.

We had breakfast with the doors and windows closed. It was eerie. Mama always opened the doors and windows at dawn, when she got up to pray outdoors to the Sun God, and they stayed open until sunset. Everyone kept doors and windows open; theft was never a problem, even though the neighborhood was rough. That early morning, however, life was different. The habitual sounds of daily existence were missing. We didn't hear, even in muffled tones, the bicycle bells ringing on their way to the bazaar, the milkman squeezing his bulb horn to announce his arrival, or the fishermen greeting one another after spending the night at sea. The silence was menacing.

By the time the church bell struck ten, I could hear some of the familiar sounds returning to the street. Shoes and flip-flops hitting the asphalt, mingled with conversation. The itinerant fruit seller shouting, *"Goyaves de Chine! Jamblons!"* We opened the windows.

The helmets of the riot police gleamed in the sunshine. It was the first time I saw fully armed police that close. I often walked by the sleepy police station on my way to Papa's sugarcane fields: the guys in there were not armed; they looked like boxers in khaki uniforms, boxers condemned to a life of paperwork. They often smiled and said hello, and when they patrolled the streets, their only weapon was a baton. The men standing stern in front of our house that day looked like they had parachuted out of a World War II movie, with their boots and rifles.

Papa asked one of them if it was okay for us to walk around.

"The situation is quiet now; but stay alert," he replied.

"Let's check out the bazaar," Papa said to me.

We passed by the bar. Chung Fat was sweeping peanut shells and bread crumbs off the veranda floor, getting it ready for his lunchtime customers.

On the way, we saw small groups, not more than four

at a time, talking softly, whispering almost. The air was heavy with disquiet and suspicion.

We reached the house of a police superintendent, a Hindu acquaintance of my father's. The windowpanes had been shattered. A smashed television set lay on the floor of the veranda.

"That's a warning, Pa. They want us to decamp," I said.

My father didn't respond, but his nervous tic flared up. He kept turning his head to the left and blinking his eyes. He went to knock on the door but was stopped by a policeman who told him that the occupants had left.

Another quarter-mile walk and it was evident that the other Hindu families in the vicinity had also vacated their homes.

At the bazaar, we heard that Creole families in the Trois Boutiques area had moved out of their homes. Some Hindus claimed that the white man killed in Trois Boutiques had been delivering arms to the Creole election agents of the Parti Mauricien. "They want Hindus and Creoles to fight and kill each other so they can convince the British that Mauritius is not ready for independence" was their refrain. Creoles said that Hindus were storing arms in their baïtkas and temples; Hindus said that Creoles were hiding guns in churches. News reached the bazaar that the riot police had rounded up all the adult Hindu males of Trois Boutiques and herded them into the village soccer stadium. When we left, I was dizzy with the flood of rumors jumbled with information, and asked Papa to buy me two tablets of aspirin.

"Too many hotheads on both sides," my father said to me as we walked home. "The truth is slippery."

As we neared the district court building on Maurice Street, a tall wiry fellow named César advanced towards us. I never figured out how he earned his living. A Creole, he stayed in a comfortable bungalow near the beach; he dressed smart, and I sometimes saw him coming out of Pac Soo with a shopping bag. At that time, Pac Soo was the only Chinese retailer in Mahébourg that stocked the fancy goods affluent Franco-Mauritians from the sugar estates sought: French wines and cheese, Scotch, Gauloises cigarettes, magazines like *Paris Match,* crystal glasses. Some said César was an election agent of the Parti Mauricien; others described him as a tapeur—a goon—of the party. In those days, most parties had their tapeurs who acted as bodyguards to party officials but could also be relied on to execute assignments requiring strong arms. In a respectful but firm voice, César told Papa that we should leave our house if we care about our safety. He was gone in less than a minute.

I felt my pulse racing and my heartbeat quicken. I wanted to ask Papa about his plans but felt too weak to do so. Maybe I had ambivalent feelings. I was angry at him for moving us into such a neighborhood. At the same time, I felt sorry for him: he would lose much of his hard-earned money if he had to sell the house at a distressed price, and he would feel humiliated by the move. He remained quiet.

When we reached Chung Fat's bar, two men came out to greet us—Kalipa and Fringant, both of whom supported the PMSD at the time. I felt my sweat go cold. They are here to enforce César's wishes, I thought.

Papa didn't wait for them to speak. "So you want me to leave," he said.

"Mr. Bhushan, César talks from his derrière," Kalipa said, using the relatively mild, almost polite, word for *backside*. I expected him to use the Kreol equivalent for ass or asshole.

"Don't worry, Mr. Bhushan, we won't touch you and your family," Fringant said. "You were our teacher—how can we forget that?"

"Stay put, but don't leave the lights on at night," Kalipa added as he waved good-bye to us.

That evening, we heard on the radio that British troops were being dispatched from Aden to the island to quell any further disturbances.

"Not just any British troops," Papa said when he heard the news. "The Coldstream Guards," he emphasized.

His mood changed. The two brothers had assured him that we would be safe. But the arrival of the Coldstream Guards gave him an extra measure of reassurance, and Papa the schoolteacher launched into yet another history lesson.

"The Coldstream Guards is the oldest English regiment serving continuously in the British Army. They fought against Louis XIV in Flanders. Crack troops guarding the monarchs of England."

On Saturday May 15, the Coldstream Guards were deployed throughout the island. Three of them replaced the riot police stationed in front of our house and at the crossroads. When my father learnt from one of them that their commander was a Major Willoughby, he embarked on speculation.

"What a coincidence!" he said. "He's probably a descendant of Captain Nesbit Willoughby, the commander of the British frigates who fought the French off our coast in 1810.

Imagine! His ancestor lay wounded and was treated at the Château Gheude, here in Mahébourg."

"I hope Major Willoughby will take some time off to visit the château and have a conversation with his ancestor's ghost," I said.

At that moment, I was irreverent and cheeky, an adolescent chafing at what I thought was pedantic. Decades later, I read the official history of the Coldstream Guards and found that my father was right about the lineage of the two Willoughbys. In another time, another place, where he had a university education, he would have been a professor or historian.

The next day, Sunday, Papa and I went to check work done in Mama's sugarcane field, Carreau Cocos, thus named because in the middle of her two acres grew towering coconut trees, so tall they were visible a mile away. The island's airport was close, part of its boundaries skirting Carreau Cocos. At the time, the landing strip was small. On the tarmac, we saw a plane bearing the Royal Air Force insignia.

"This must be the Argosy aircraft that flew the Coldstream Guards," Papa said. "It's powered by four Rolls-Royce engines."

My father's knowledge of military transport aircraft surprised me. He had never talked about engines or airplanes.

He then confided, "Before I was a teacher, I was an inventory clerk at the airport during its construction. It was right after World War II. My boss was an Englishman. When he left, he asked me to join him in England. Sometimes when I come here and see an airplane, I ask myself how my life would have been if I had accepted his offer."

. . .

FOR THE FIRST *three weeks . . . the Platoons patrolled on foot and in vehicles round the villages and likely trouble-spots . . . almost invariably they were well received, though on a few occasions they were not made so welcome, but they were never attacked and never had to fire a shot . . . By the end of the month the situation had eased . . . on 12 June the Queen's Birthday Parade was held in Port Louis . . . Thereafter patrols decreased . . . For the rest it was training, competitions, sport and entertainment and most hospitable the people were. It was a sad Company that finally flew away from the island and back to Aden on 18 July.*

Thus wrote the Coldstream Guard historian. A different sadness pervaded Mauritian homes. The air we now breathed tasted sour. The unspoken question in people's minds was "Will Hindus and Creoles ever see each other the same way again?" For almost a year my friends didn't feel comfortable or safe to walk to our home; I had to meet them near the church and escort them.

TWO YEARS BEFORE these 1965 riots, my father was, for a brief period, headmaster of Trois Boutiques primary school. As he waited for the Mahébourg bus in the afternoon, some of the villagers would talk to him, and once in a while he would tell me about it. They asked about their children's progress but would quickly veer to politics and what they read in the newspapers. Not unusual in a country where politics has been the national pastime for as long as I can remember.

My father had related one such conversation that took place in November 1963.

"Mr. Bhushan, some supporters of the Parti Mauricien have insulted us at the Champ de Mars," said one villager. "They called Hindus 'Malbars coolie,' like in the old days. Why isn't the government doing something about it?"

"They screamed, 'Malbars nou pas ouler, envelopés nou pas ouler,'" said another. "They don't want Malbars, they don't want Hindu women enveloped in saris. We are the majority in this country. How dare they talk like that?"

Not to be outdone in venting grievances, a third villager added, "Remember Jules Koenig, Duval's mentor? Remember what he said about giving Hindus the right to vote? 'It's giving a monkey a razor.'"

Jules Koenig, uncle of my favorite French teacher, who once described him as someone from la vieille France, the France of the old days. A figure worthy of a Shakespearean or Corneillian tragedy: assaulted in the 1930s as a young barrister taking up the cause of Indian and Creole workers, he ended his political career by returning to the fold, fighting to maintain the privileges of the sugar barons.

A fourth villager added, "Now their propaganda is 'After independence, Hindus will force everyone to wear the dhoti. Shiploads of dhotis will set sail from India.'"

Papa wasn't surprised when someone asked, "Mr. Bhushan, are they blind? Can't they see we all wear European clothes? I don't even know how to put a dhoti on."

As I tried to make sense of the Trois Boutiques Hindu riots and the Creole riposte in Mahébourg, I remembered César, Fringant, and Kalipa, their blue shirts fluttering in the wind, boarding the "Special Route" bus that took them to the Champ de Mars demonstration of "malbars nou pas ouler, envelopés nou pas ouler" fame.

WHEN, TWO YEARS after the 1965 Hindu-Creole riots, Kalipa and Fringant faced each other with harpoons in front of our house, Kalipa had discarded his blue shirt for a red one. Unlike his brother, he had switched political allegiance from the Parti Mauricien to the Labour Party and canvassed hard for independence. In August 1967, the pro-independence coalition won the elections.

A few months later, around the time the shop windows started displaying Christmas toys and New Year's firecrackers, Mama and I were relaxing on the veranda when we saw Papa walking to the gate, flanked by Kalipa and Fringant. I was mystified. Mama's face turned pale. Had Papa suffered a malaise at the bazaar and they were escorting him home? Or was there something more sinister?

Before we could run down the steps and ask if anything was wrong, Papa said, "The seas are rough, and Kalipa and Fringant need work. I told them to fix the gables."

I knew their father, Tonton George, was a carpenter who enjoyed a reputation for refined workmanship. His clientele included the sugar barons who owned beach houses in nearby Blue Bay. But neither Mama nor I had ever heard of the sons doing construction work. Besides, the gable repairs could probably wait another six months.

Their survey of the repairs to be done and their negotiations didn't take long. After they left, I told Papa, "I hope Tonton George's construction skills have rubbed off on them."

"This is a special time of the year, and they need the money," Papa said.

Over the Christmas holidays, Kalipa and Fringant worked on the gables, and I would bring them sardine-and-tomato sandwiches that Mama made for them. On the second or third day, as they washed their hands at the out-door tap, they asked me to join them for a chat at lunch. We sat on tree stumps. I realized that, in the four years I'd been living in the neighborhood, this was the first time I was having an extended conversation with adult neighbors. They asked me about school and my favorite movies, and I asked about fishing in the high seas.

"Come with us one day," Kalipa said. "You've been to Île de la Passe?"

"Papa won't let me."

"You're sixteen or seventeen and you've not been there? You can see that islet from your roof," Kalipa said, staring at me in disbelief.

"Mr. Bhushan is afraid his only child will drown," said Fringant.

"Right. Whenever I ask my father to let me go, he reminds me of the night you two went missing in the storm, when the whole neighborhood waited by the shore till dawn for you. I remember all the lanterns flickering in the wind. Everyone worried that you had drowned."

Kalipa shook his head. "They make you read crap about Napoleon and how his fleet defeated the Royal Navy at Île de la Passe, and you haven't set foot there!"

Soon after they completed the repairs, in early January 1968, the brothers had a belated Christmas present for me: a trip to Île de la Passe, on a day my parents were out of town. The occasion presented itself when the latter went to a wedding in Cap Malheureux, the northernmost village in Mauritius, almost fifty miles away by bus. That Sunday, I met the two brothers at their home. "We'll leave in the afternoon and come back late in the evening, so you can see the high and the low tides," Kalipa said.

Their house was made of corrugated iron sheets that had turned reddish brown from rust. All doors and windows were open for maximum ventilation, and I could see their three rooms. One had a double bed, which I assumed was Kalipa's and his wife's. Adjacent to it, a room with a crib and a single bed for their two kids, who were gamboling on the street, there being no yard to play in. On the wall hung a picture of brown-robed Saint Anthony of Padua cradling a chubby child Jesus with lilies in his hands. And at the far end, a room with two mattresses on the floor, where Fringant and Tonton George were getting dressed. No living room or veranda.

Kalipa's wife asked me into the kitchen, a shack outside the house. With apprehension on her face, she opened the three aluminum food containers on the table. Macaroni, fried mullet, and rougaille of prawns. I inhaled the tangy aroma of seafood cooked with cayenne pepper and tomato. "That's the kind of meal Mama makes on festive occasions," I said.

Her eyes brightened. "I can see you'll enjoy your picnic," she said as she closed the containers and put them in a basket.

Though I was curious about the Île de la Passe, it was with some trepidation that I stepped inside their pirogue, a narrow boat built from wooden planks. No life jacket or life buoy in sight. The brothers punted the boat out of the shallow water with push poles, then unfurled the cotton sails. The pirogue felt unsteady, and I held on to the gunwale, but the brothers looked comfortable and smiled at me. Fringant noticed that I was eyeing the diesel motor on board. "No need for that today," he said. "We have fair winds."

The brothers tried to make conversation, but it took me a few minutes to relax and overcome my worry that the boat would capsize. The wind blowing on my face took the sting out of the brutal summer heat. I looked behind me. The sight of Mahébourg and the coastline receding was, for reasons I couldn't fathom, calming. I looked up. The confidence of the birds soaring over the neighboring islets was inspiring and made me question my fear of the water. Fringant and Kalipa showed me the areas with the highest fish catches, where they cast their nets.

After we disembarked on the Île de la Passe, I saw a different Kalipa and Fringant. They spoke of French corsairs who raided the ships of the British East India Company off the coast of Mauritius. They morphed into unofficial guides proud to show off their knowledge of the remains of the French garrison. "Do you hear the cannons firing and exploding? Do you see the blood of British and French soldiers turning the sea red-purple?" Kalipa said. He spoke of "our" lost strategic importance: "When Ferdinand de Lesseps built the Suez Canal, ships bypassed us on their way to India and China, and we were no longer the Star and Key of the Indian Ocean," he said. Fringant was more down-to-earth. He showed me the powder house that stored wooden barrels of gunpowder, now overrun with shrubs growing in the cracks of its walls, and the graffiti of regimental flags soldiers had carved on the sides of the storehouse. Both, however, had a similar fascination with the hot-shot furnace. Their eyes glowed when they explained how iron cannonballs were heated red-hot before being launched to blast and set fire to enemy warships.

By the time we sat at the corner of the battery wall and the storehouse, and Fringant opened the picnic basket, the sky had turned a reddish-orange hue and the sun was dipping behind the Mahébourg coastline. The sea around the islet was calm, and we were the only ones there. Kalipa took out a bottle of A-1 Rhum de Prestige. With twigs, sticks, straw, and leaves that Fringant and I gathered, we built a campfire. Not long after, the brothers transformed the emptied food containers into improvised ravvan, percussion instruments to accompany "Noir noir noir do mama, guette couma faire noir" and "Lotte côté Montagne Chamarel." The light of the campfire softened their features, and the way they interpreted these songs, with their hypnotic rhythms and jagged edges, revealed to me the richness of the séga. It was no longer simply a song to dance to, one that disturbed my weekend study. In Kalipa's and Fringant's resonant voices I heard more than two centuries of suffering and resilience compressed into a two- or three-minute melody. In that islet surrounded by the endless expanse of sea and sky, the brothers transported me to the days of Maroon slaves fleeing oppression to find joy in music and sex in the ravines near Chamarel.

On the way back to Mahébourg, it was dark, but now I wasn't afraid. I trusted the two brothers to bring me home safely, and I enjoyed the sea.

Fringant pointed out the treacherous spot where they

had nearly lost their lives in a storm. "Now that we're almost home, I'm telling you. Didn't want to alarm you when we were sailing to Île de la Passe." I recalled that dawn when all the neighbors had gathered on the beach, apprehensive because the brothers had not returned.

Ten minutes from the coastline, they questioned me about my plans for the future. I told them I was studying hard for the university scholarship.

"You'll be the first one from the neighborhood to win that scholarship," Kalipa said. "Mahébourg will be proud!"

"Everyone here is rooting for you. Bets have already been placed," Fringant added.

"You'll go beyond the seas to bigger and better things," Kalipa said.

The neighborhood appeared to me in a new light. *They consider me one of their own. I'm their horse in the race.* I had wanted to move away, but now I had to question whatever I believed about the neighborhood. The racket in the streets, the outbursts of violence, were suddenly irrelevant. I smiled, but I didn't know what to say to Fringant and Kalipa. Sure, my goal was to thrive among the elite. I was flattered, but what if I let them down? More than a thousand students were taking the A-levels and competing for four scholarships.

Kalipa patted me on the shoulder. "Whatever you do in the future, avoid politics," he said. "Politics in this country, it's a predator. It devours you."

"You're not an election agent anymore? You were so into politics, you were about to kill each other over Gaëtan Duval once," I said.

Kalipa lit a Matelot and inhaled. "Duval's party couldn't

buy my vote with promises of jobs and rum. Duval can't stop history. Vive l'indépendans!"

"Elections are over," Fringant said. "Time to move on."

Kalipa took the cigarette out of his mouth, blew the smoke through his nose, and said, "You voted dumb."

My eyes flitted from Kalipa to Fringant.

In the glow of the hurricane lamp, I saw Fringant frown, but his voice remained calm: "Your friend Harold Walter talks big. He babbles about the winds of change. I know about winds, and I can tell him they don't blow the same for all."

"It's the same fucking wind," Kalipa said.

"It's not the same for us, on our peanut shell of a boat, and for the big shot on his giant yacht. Some will sail smoothly with the winds of change, some will withstand them, and others will be swept away."

Kalipa ground his barely consumed cigarette on the floor of the boat.

BARELY TWO WEEKS after the peanut shell boat conversation, in late January 1968, Creole-Muslim riots broke out in the capital. They made the 1965 Hindu-Creole riots look like a barbecue on the beach.

The talk among my friends: "Will Kalipa and Fringant get involved?"

"They're fed up with politics," I tell them.

"Are they fed up with knives and harpoons?" was the rejoinder.

More than thirty dead and hundreds wounded, compared with three dead and a dozen wounded in Trois Boutiques–Mahébourg three years earlier.

With a total population of 790,000, thirty dead is no small number.

Again, the lines between rumor and fact blur.

"The official figures lie," a neighbor told Mama at the time. "Three of my cousins have been missing for two weeks. Bodies have been dumped in the sea. More than two hundred have been killed, believe me!"

The neighbor also said that the Muslim "Istanbul" gangs and the Creole "Texas" gangs, fighting for control of drugs and prostitution, started the battle after some Muslim women had been molested at the Venus Cinema. Fringant gave me a different version: "The match was lit when a Muslim pimp killed a Creole whore who stopped working for him."

WOMEN RAPED.

Houses looted and torched.

Molotov cocktails hurled.

Hundreds displaced. Mixed neighborhoods denatured into exclusively Creole or Muslim neighborhoods. Plaine Verte becomes a Muslim fortress, Roche Bois a Creole citadel.

Penises inspected at improvised neighborhood checkpoints. Muslim males are circumcised; Creoles are not. Woe betide if you have the wrong penis!

Dried blood on the ground.

A hundred and forty British troops dispatched from Singapore in three Hercules aircraft—the King's Shropshire Light Infantry.

"These soldiers don't have the pedigree of the Cold-stream Guards," Papa said. "They'll take longer to quell the riots."

HMS *Euryalus,* a Royal Navy vessel, arrived to guard the island's gasoline storage depot.

Three Sioux helicopters flew into the capital.

In Mahébourg, we were all anxious—our family, the neighbors, Hindus, Muslims, Creole, Chinese, everyone. The miracle: the riots are confined to Port Louis and its environs.

ABIDING BY THE election results, the British announced that they'd transfer power to Mauritians on March 12, 1968. Kalipa had no doubt the riots had been fomented to show Britain that Mauritius was not ready for independence: "Politicians who owned metal-making factories in Port Louis supplied the knives and sabers, my father told me and Fringant. He warned us not to get involved."

MARCH 12, 1968. Independence was proclaimed and celebrated at the Champ de Mars, in Port Louis. The oldest racetrack in the Southern Hemisphere, the parade ground of the sugar magnates and their thoroughbred horses, was, for the day, the place where more than a hundred thousand descendants of slaves and coolies saw the Union Jack pulled down and the national flag raised.

Duval called on his supporters to boycott the celebrations by staying home but promised not to organize counterdemonstrations.

No boatload of dhotis sailed into Port Louis Harbour.

We were watching the flag-raising ceremony on our new TV when we heard laughter from the street, followed by hand clapping. I ran to the veranda and looked. The neighbors were out, some grinning, some chuckling, others giggling, quite a few nonplussed and speechless. Walking towards our house was Tonton George, wearing a dhoti! He was smiling and waving at the onlookers, basking in the acclaim of some, daring those who disapproved. His was not your run-of-the-mill dhoti that Gandhi wore to identify with the Indian peasantry. No. Tonton George's was a red dhoti complemented by a blue blazer. A white rosebud in the lapel of the blazer softened the look. I had never seen, in Mauritius or in the Bombay movies, anyone look so dapper in a dhoti. It was a dhoti worn with aristocratic flair.

A Creole fisherman in a bastion of the Parti Mauricien showing up in the dreaded dhoti. This was a coup de théâtre—panache of the highest order.

Fringant and Kalipa stood in front of Chung Fat's bar. Were they here to protect their father in case matters turned awry, or to admire his audacity? I asked myself.

I opened the door of the veranda as Tonton George entered the gate.

My father, dressed as usual in his suit and tie, came out and extended his hand. Tonton George did not shake it. Instead, he joined his palms together in front of his chest, fingers pointing up, and uttered the Hindu greeting "Namasté."

"We must celebrate!" he added.

"Mauritian rum or Scotch whisky?" Papa said as they embraced.

XIII

Reincarnation

1968

The shop opposite the pharmacy
smells of resin and sawdust.
The muscular carpenter
planes, assembles, varnishes
the coffins, which his plump wife
displays with dignity.

As we pass by, Mama asks Papa:
"Do you wish to be buried in a dhoti?"
"I love my suit and tie.
I don't want to be Gandhi in his loincloth."

"But you got married in a dhoti."
"If that's your wish, dress me in a dhoti.
But place a suit next to me.
If I wake up, I'll put it on."

XIV

The Man with the Glass Eye

Never seen in our seaside town,
he knocked on the open tin gate
and walked towards the veranda,
palms joined at his chest.

We put our books aside.

"Daya karo malik, daya karo malik," he said.
Hindi words I didn't understand.

He bowed,
handed my father a piece of paper.
It looked official.

"How much will the new eye cost?" Papa said.

"Expensive—two hundred rupees.
More durable, more comfortable.
God will pay you back a thousandfold,
malik."

He removed his right eye,
a brown marble,

placed it in Papa's hands.
It threatened to slide through his fingers.

From his coat pocket Papa took out a fifty-rupee note.
Mama walked in.
"The prescription is from Dr. Curé," Papa said.
"We need to save money
for Vishnu's education," she said,

and stared at the stranger's empty socket.

XV

Six Pounds of Fish

1969

On the morning of my interview with the Scholarship Committee, Papa insisted on accompanying me to the Mahébourg bus terminal, a five-minute walk from home, by the seaside. It was unseasonably gusty and the whistling of the winds through the filao trees on the beach was particularly shrill. Though the previous evening he had coached me through a mock interview, our conversation was punctuated by awkward silences, which had grown more frequent ever since I'd sided against him at the family intervention Papa sneeringly dubbed "the conclave of goons."

When we reached the terminal, Papa said, "This is an important day. I know you're disappointed that you didn't make it to the top two and that your name won't be inscribed in the Royal College Laureates' Hall. But you've graduated, came out a brilliant fourth, and a Commonwealth Scholarship will be yours after this interview."

Historically, the top two students in the Arts-and-Humanities track and two in the Science track at the Oxbridge A-levels were automatically awarded scholarships financed by the Government of Mauritius to attend universities of their choice, and the next ten obtained scholarships financed by the Commonwealth to attend universities in the United Kingdom.

"I'm over it now, Papa. Too busy to wallow in disappointment," I said. A month had elapsed since publication of the results, and I was working as a secondary school teacher.

"That's the right attitude, Vishnu. Best to let go of unpleasant things of the past."

For the first time since the conclave, Papa shook my hands. "We should spend more time together."

I nodded, but it was a weak nod.

Papa strengthened his grip. "You'll be off to England before you know it."

The bus driver started the engine.

"Time for you to go. Good luck! All the Bhushans are thinking of you and wish you well."

As I waved good-bye from my seat, images of the Bhushan clan ran through my mind. A clan that had so far produced two primary school teachers, including my father; a railway stationmaster; one discharged policeman, who found redemption as an industrious sugarcane laborer and success as a planter; a tailor whose activities as a foreign exchange counterfeiter would come to light ten years later when he was caught and sentenced to five years in jail; and a few self-styled "small proprietors." "Small proprietor": a fancy phrase for laborers who over time acquired small plots of land to grow sugarcane and vegetables, and who were eager for their children to get an education that would land them white-collar jobs.

.   .   .

WHEN I GOT off the bus in Port Louis, the salty breeze filled my nostrils with the smell of algae. It was around ten o'clock, and I had about an hour to spare. I had read in the newspapers that the era of the passenger ship was soon to vanish from Mauritius: the *Ferdinand de Lesseps,* starship of the fabled French shipping line Messageries Maritimes, was anchored in the harbor and was to embark passengers on its last voyage to Marseilles. So I walked to the harbor. Most of the other passengers, preoccupied with tasks to accomplish or errands to run, hurried in other directions, along the bustling streets that led to government or business offices, the bazaar, the hospital, or the Champ de Mars racecourse, at the foot of the hills overlooking the city.

On the way, I silently rehearsed the interview: What did you learn from your extracurricular activities or community service? What is the most pressing problem facing Mauritius? Why do you want to study law and economics? What do you plan to do after you graduate? What are your strengths and weaknesses? What real or fictional person has influenced you most?

When I saw the *Ferdinand de Lesseps,* I remembered my secondary school teachers telling me how they were both elated and anxious when they boarded this ship or its sister ships, the *Pierre Loti* and the *Jean Laborde,* how exotic they found the ports of call—Port Said and the Suez Canal— and how sad they felt in Marseilles as they parted company with other young passengers taking the train to different destinations for university study, mostly in the cities and provinces of England and France. I imagined the ships carrying the hopes and dreams of previous generations, and thought of my own dreams of going to Oxford or Cambridge, and my heart swelled.

For a few minutes, I gazed at the vessel's promenade deck from afar, then proceeded to the Hotel du Gouvernement. A stately plantation-style mansion that faced Port Louis Harbour, it housed the offices of the speaker of Parliament and members of the cabinet. Leading to it was a boulevard lined with flamboyant trees and statues of eighteenth-century French governors of the island. A statue of round-faced, dour Queen Victoria welcomed visitors at the wide entrance. I went through security with surprising ease: the policemen who waved me in were polite, even deferential.

I entered the interview room, ready to be tested.

The Scholarship Committee, comprising seven members, was chaired by a retired senior Member of Parliament, Sir Pralad. He had the reputation of being "un homme cultivé," the descendant of Indian coolies who had grown into a connoisseur of opera, poetry, and art and who moved with ease in high society. He defied Hindu convention and the hermetically closed Franco-Mauritian community by living with a local white woman who was an accomplished writer.

"Coming home with a foreign wife, that's easy—every other Mauritian returning from Europe or India with a medical degree is doing it," Jeewan the barber said of Sir Pralad when I went for my pre-interview haircut. "But a local white mistress, a poet: what a prize! Imagine the pissed-off white men in the sugar estates turning red like a carrot!" The clients in the barbershop concurred.

During a school visit to Parliament a few years earlier, Sir Pralad had impressed me and my classmates. He had presided over the Parliamentary proceedings with gravitas, and so his first question to me was odd:

"Vishnu, where do you live?"

A question for first and second graders, at an interview for a coveted university scholarship. Sir Pralad could read the answer on the second line of the Scholarship application form, but I could ill afford to offend him. I gave him the address in Mahébourg and told him that our house was at a street corner, walking distance from the sea, the District Court, and the bazaar.

"Can you describe your house and its surroundings?" Sir Pralad asked.

I looked at the other members of the committee. Their eyes were blank.

"My parents' house is located in a neighborhood of fishermen, and the surroundings reflect their economic status. Our house is quite sturdy and built of wood, with four rooms and a veranda, a small yard with mango and papaya trees. Our neighbors' houses are smaller. Many of them need repairs and a coat of paint."

I paused for a reaction. There was none.

I continued. "The neighborhood retail shop and bar is very close, about two minutes' walk from our house. One can see the butter-colored bell tower of the Catholic church."

Another pause. No reaction.

To give a distinctive flavor to my reply, I said that the previous owner of our house had affixed a nameplate that read CITY OF BOMBAY on the front door, but my father, thinking it was presumptuous to give the name of a large Indian city to his modest house, had removed it.

Sir Pralad nodded his head but said nothing.

None of the intelligent questions I had prepared for came up. Instead he was subjecting me to the humiliation of having to answer such basic stuff! The other committee members were impassive.

The sole foreigner on the committee, the head of the local British Council, finally asked the one relevant question: "Why do you want to study economics and law?" The others half-closed their eyes, as if they wanted to avoid the burden that my answer—any answer—would impose on them.

"Economics and law are useful tools for problem solving in a range of situations. In government, knowledge of these subjects can—"

"You can stop here," Sir Pralad said. "We'll let you know our decision in a month, after all candidates have been interviewed."

At home in the evening, I told Papa what had happened. "They must think your results speak for themselves and there was no need to test you. The interview was mere formality. Let's wait," he said.

Two days later, a classmate told me that he'd been selected. He was not among the top ten in the National Scholarship Competition.

"Papa, what's going on? Decisions were going to be made in a month."

My father was relaxing in his armchair. He straightened his back, thought for a few seconds, and got up. He put his arm around my shoulders.

"There's more than one scholarship to be awarded, Vishnu. They can't ignore the fact that you came in fourth."

My father's words were clear. But the tremor in his voice was not convincing.

My rejection letter arrived a month later, and my first impulse was to crush it into a ball. I controlled my anger and showed the letter to my father.

"Those who thought Mauritius was granted independence prematurely by the British were right," Papa said.

Over the next week, my father voiced to friends and family his view that the way my case was handled was yet another proof that the new rulers of Mauritius were not different from their counterparts in Africa and Asia. "Nepotism and corruption," he said.

With his meager teacher's salary, and his savings depleted by the Supreme Court case, he could not finance my university studies.

SO WHEN, TWO months later, in June, I was awarded a French scholarship and was told I would be attending the University of Paris or Nice, the family as well as the clan were happy. The interview at the French embassy was unmemorable: the questions were more intelligent than those asked by Sir Pralad, but they didn't tax me; they were manageable. To prepare for my trip to France, I read books on etiquette, having heard the French are quite particular about le savoir vivre. ("Wipe your mouth before raising the wine glass to your lips," one book said. "The sight of food stains on the rim is unpleasant for your dinner companions.")

I went to pick up my French visa on a sunny afternoon in late August.

"Il y a eu un pépin à propos de votre dossier," said the young Cultural Attaché with a crew-cut. There had been a bureaucratic foul-up. A serious and unforeseen problem with my file. "Neither Paris nor Nice got your documents."

"How can that happen?" I asked.

"I don't have the answer to that question. Only the Ministry would know."

He offered a consolation prize: Go to the University of Madagascar. An institution that did not have the reputation of a French university. Furthermore, I had read that young Malagasies were grumbling about President Tsiranana's subservience to France and that a coup d'état was brewing there.

I went to the Ministry and knocked on the door of the top civil servant. His secretary came out and told me that her boss and two other Ministry officials had gone to the Hotel du Gouvernement for a meeting with the minister, a meeting that would last all afternoon. When I told her the purpose of my visit, she took me to another official. "We cannot fix a problem caused by the embassy. We did our paperwork and submitted the file to them for action," he said.

I walked back to the embassy and related what I was told to the Cultural Attaché. "Monsieur, who or what caused the pépin does not matter to me. I would appreciate your fixing the problem."

"That's not within our jurisdiction," he said. "The Ministry is responsible."

The sun, now a bright orange, was heading down

towards the sea; dusk was approaching. I rushed to the Ministry before the offices closed, for another try. I asked the secretary who had helped earlier to refer me to a more senior officer. The official she took me to looked up from the stack of papers he was leafing through, took off his spectacles, and rubbed his eyes. He was nasty.

"You've already got an answer from my colleague. Why are you wasting our time? Only the French embassy can unblock the situation."

I was upset but didn't know what to do, where to seek advice. Our town was a fishing town with only one university graduate. Papa reacted the way he always did when he was furious and felt he would lose his temper: he quietly left the house and walked towards the Pointe des Régates beach, facing Grand Port. The sight of the Mouchoir Rouge, an islet half a mile from the beach, with its red-roofed bungalow, always soothed him. Mama got worried when after more than two hours he hadn't come back.

"Vishnu, you have to go get him." My mother took my hands in hers and continued, "Beta, you must overcome your anger towards him. The court case is over, and in time Papa and your Auntie will be reconciled. You have to reconcile as well."

I found him at his usual spot, the foot of the monument commemorating the Battle of Grand Port. "The only naval victory scored by Napoleon's fleet against the British. Inscribed in the Arc de Triomphe," he would tell visiting relatives or friends, as if he had won the battle himself.

"I suppose Mama sent you," he said as he rose. "I needed time to think. We can't allow all your hard work to go to waste."

"Who cares?"

"It's not the time to give up. We're proud of you."

"Maybe I should join the Young Communist League. They offer scholarships to the Soviet Union and Czechoslovakia."

He put his hands on my shoulders and straightened my frame. "Vishnu, tomorrow we are seeing the minister."

"You made an appointment?"

"We don't need one. We're going to his home."

WE LEFT MAHÉBOURG by bus at five in the morning to catch the minister at his residence in the cool Central Haut Plateau before he left for his office in hot, dusty Port Louis. The Plateau—with towns named Curepipe, Rose Hill, Floréal, and Quatre Bornes—was where the merchant and ruling classes lived. On the bus, Papa was back to his usual taciturn self. He was in no mood to waste his day's leave from work.

The minister, Honorable Bara Thakoor, received us in his living room. The furniture was ornate, what the magazines I'd seen at the Carnegie Library called Victorian-style furniture—a secretary bookcase, Chippendale back chairs, and a Victorian writing desk. I had no notion whether they were original or copies, or if they belonged in a living room. They must have been imported. Papa and I sat on oval-back armchairs, Honorable Thakoor on a wing chair. On the wall, there was a photo of him as a student in London, standing under a YOUNG LABOUR banner with Clement Attlee, the post–World War II British prime minister.

Honorable Bara Thakoor was a short man. Small may

be more accurate, as he had no physical presence. "Inco-lore, inodore, et sans saveur" is how my secondary school French teacher would have described him. Colorless, odorless, and tasteless. Not ugly, for ugliness would have given him some "couleur et saveur." Just unimpressive, far from the articulate type I had expected to see in a bar-rister trained at one of London's Inns of Court. To me, these institutions brought to mind alumni like Gandhi and Nehru, the leaders of independent India, and many British prime ministers.

My father had told me that the minister had been a col-league of his at the primary school. Dr. Maurice Curé, the labor leader and politician, spotting a man who he thought would contribute to the uplift of the country's poor, had organized a national fund drive to finance Thakoor's legal studies in England. The same elderly Dr. Curé who treated me for free when, six weeks after my premature birth, my mother had taken me for consultation because my chances of survival looked dire.

Earlier in his career, Honorable Thakoor had crossed the floor; that is, he had defected from the opposition to join the ruling party, "for the good of the country." So he had told a boisterous seaside meeting attended by thou-sands of his constituents. Many had cheered; many had booed; few had been indifferent. A week later, he had been rewarded with a ministerial post.

For the meeting with Honorable Thakoor, my father had put on his best suit. Unlike the newly minted, university-educated professionals, he believed in dress-ing up every day. That meant suit, tie, and felt hat, winter or summer. He was especially proud of his hat. A present from an Englishman he had met and befriended during his weekly walks to Blue Bay, it gave him the sense of belonging to the gentlemanly class. My father was schooled in the old colonial manners. Like many of his generation, he ended his letters to his superiors with "I have the honor to be, Sir, Your Faithful and Most Obedient Servant."

After he took off his hat, he addressed the minister. From his days as the minister's colleague, Papa knew the minister would speak in either English or the local Kreol, for his French was only adequate. So Papa chose to speak in French: his English was good, but he had mastered Molière's tongue. Though he was a supplicant, he was not going to let a London-educated barrister intimidate him.

My father handed him a copy of my Oxbridge results and explained the situation.

"Monsieur le Ministre, not only has my son been denied a Commonwealth Scholarship, but he's been robbed of the French scholarship awarded to him a few months later."

Papa had brought with him, besides the award letter from the French embassy, a newspaper that carried the names of the top-scoring students. During those early post-independence days, all the newspapers listed them. These published lists boosted family pride. They gave the parents bragging rights with relatives and friends; in town and on the bus; at weddings and funerals. He handed these to the minister.

"Why should someone who came out fourth in the nation, with excellent grades, be denied the chance to attend a top university? Monsieur le Ministre, it is unfair that inferior students with rich parents are getting the prestigious scholarships."

The minister nodded, though whether to mark his agreement or his neutrality, I couldn't say.

My father continued: "The information we have is that my son's scholarship has been 'given' to the niece of one of your colleagues in the cabinet. She didn't even rank in the top twenty. Her parents can afford the university expenses."

The minister turned to me. I took the opportunity to reinforce my case. I told him how, two weeks before my scheduled departure to France, the French Cultural Attaché had informed me of a "pépin," how I had knocked on the doors of government bureaucrats as I tried to dig deeper, and how Ministry officials and the French Cultural Attaché blamed each other for the problem.

Honorable Thakoor looked baffled.

"Shiv, I can't understand why he's been treated this way. This is unacceptable. Come see me at the office in two days."

Papa picked up his hat.

"Very smart hat," said Honorable Thakoor as he shook Papa's hand. "Bates of Jermyn Street?"

Papa smiled and nodded. "Yes."

On the way back home, Papa stopped in the village of Rose Belle and took me to a man I had often seen at political rallies: the election agent of another member of the cabinet, Minister Pierre Legrand. My father must have assessed the situation as desperate, to resort to such a meeting. Election agents were individuals, with varying degrees of honesty and reliability, paid by politicians to collect intelligence, mobilize votes, ensure that transportation is available on Election Day for the party supporters, and if necessary win the voters with rum and promises of public sector jobs. They were referred to in the local vernacular as *bachara,* the "politician's tout." Men who, in the normal run of things, were deemed "pollution" by Papa.

"The academic year in France starts in mid–September. We have only two weeks, and I don't want you to miss that," Papa said. "I've racked my brains thinking who to turn to. The agent was my student at primary school." He didn't say his name.

In the 1960s and '70s, teachers were revered like the gurus of ancient India. Even by election agents.

Once again, Papa explained the situation. The agent expressed concern. "Pas traka, Missié Bhushan. I'm here to help, and my minister is always at the service of the people. I'll be at your house early tomorrow morning."

Shaking my hand, the agent added, "I'll take you to Minister Legrand. He'll fix it."

As we boarded the bus for home, my father told me we'd better enlist the support of Honorable Iqbal Mohamed, who in Parliament represented Ferney, the village where many Bhushans grew up. Ferney was a bastion of the ruling party. Honorable Mohamed was another former colleague of my father's who had left the teaching profession for politics. He played a prominent role in the major Muslim religious organizations, much as Honorable Thakoor played in organizations of the Hindu faith. He was a backbencher, not a member of the cabinet.

Honorable Mohamed must have seen us from his window: before we knocked, he opened the door and embraced my father. Greeting us inside was an imposing tapestry on the wall that featured Mecca, with the black cubic Kaaba, Islam's holiest shrine. As for the furniture, he shared my father's spartan tastes—it was utilitarian, not decorative. On a sideboard was a photo of Honorable Mohamed, palms joined in the namasté gesture, with Prime Minister Nehru. Smart, I thought, for him to display that photo; Hindus formed the majority in his electoral constituency.

He served us tea and inquired about various members of the Bhushan clan. When Papa explained the reason for our visit, he muttered something about being frustrated by the actions of some of his Parliamentary colleagues, excused himself to write a letter to Honorable Thakoor, which he showed me. When I saw the letter, on Legislative Assembly letterhead with the country's coat of arms, I felt my heart beat faster.

> I urge your serious and urgent consideration of
> Vishnu Bhushan's case. In addition to his superb
> academic results, he has considerable personal
> qualities, exceptional maturity, a gentlemanly
> manner, a clever sense of humor not only
> about the world but also about himself. He is a
> purposeful young man with a deep interest in the
> economic and social problems of our country.

My friends were reading and hearing gossip about our post-independence rulers, and I was sitting in their living rooms and getting gushing letters of recommendation! Honorable Mohamed also wrote that my father was a strong supporter of the ruling Labour Party—a questionable statement.

When I finished reading, Honorable Mohamed said,

"Vishnu, with your father's genes, I expect you to go very far. Did you know that he topped our class at the Teachers Training College? Bara Thakoor and I trailed behind."

This was the first time I had heard about Papa's ranking.

Honorable Mohamed handed the letter to my father and hugged him tight. "Shiv, you should have joined us and run for office. You were stubborn and didn't listen to me!"

At the door, Honorable Mohamed's son handed us a bag of lychees. "From our orchard," he said.

On the bus, I asked Papa, "How come you never told me about being top of your class?"

"That was such a long time ago."

"But you did tell me how you got higher scores than the other applicants in your entrance exams."

"What's the point of boasting?"

Papa then reminisced about his younger brother who joined the British colonial army to escape poverty and was blown up in Palestine in the last year of the British Mandate. "He was the hot-blooded one in the family. He didn't care for education."

"Maybe he was right," I said. "Look at what's happening. Aren't you sick of these politicians and their pimps?"

"We have to be optimistic. You'll get that scholarship. We just have to fight for it."

Back home in Mahébourg, Mama looked at us, exhausted from the day's travels and meetings, our oily skin made shinier by the day's sweat. She dared not ask what happened, so I told her. She reacted with her usual worried look.

"Son, it will be all right. God helps those who work hard."

AFTER DINNER, MAMA asked me into the kitchen. "Vishnu, I know you have a lot on your mind. But you have to help Papa."

"I'm the one who needs help."

"The judgment against him includes paying Auntie's legal fees. He's got the money, but he has too much pride to face Auntie's attorney."

"So he wants me to deliver the cash?"

"He hasn't said that."

I remembered Mama's words about reconciliation. I took a deep breath and exhaled. "I'll go to him and offer to do it."

THE FOLLOWING MORNING at six, the agent showed up in a taxi. Papa handed me a sealed envelope marked "Maître Robert Foiret, Attorney-at-Law," and a wad of banknotes to cover taxi and other "expenses." Until then, we had traveled by taxi only when someone was too ill to take the bus.

"Minister Legrand likes a special kind of fish. Let's go to the bazaar," the agent said.

When we arrived at the market, the agent didn't proceed to the fish section right away. Instead, he walked up to the sellers of Indian pastry and savories in front of the corrugated iron building. The flaky crust of the samosas and the smoke from the piping hot dal puris beckoned to my taste buds. But I had to stay by the agent as he greeted everyone with a namasté and chatted about the latest political news.

He then strolled through the main section of the bazaar, addressing the vegetable and fruit sellers by name. The sweet scent of red lychees and the fragrance of green mangoes were soon swept away by aromas of cardamon and coriander, saffron and turmeric, from the spice stalls. In this section, we came by a stall owned by the son of a Hindu priest. He sold goods used in religious rituals—incense sticks, threads for initiation ceremonies, betel leaves, sandalwood, clay lamps, statuettes of gods and goddesses. The agent noticed a calendar that had Jesus, Buddha, and Gandhi appearing next to Hindu gods and goddesses. "Next year, you'll have to add Chacha on that calendar," the agent said. I wasn't sure if he was joking or serious. Chacha was the Prime Minister's sobriquet.

I thought we were ready to move on to the fish section, but as we reached the western end of the bazaar, the agent took me outside, some twenty yards away, to a small building where beef was carved and sold. I had never been inside. Hindus, for whom the cow is sacred, didn't loiter here. The butchers were all Muslim, and the agent switched to the greeting "Salaam alaikum." He then turned right, to another small building for pork, anathema to Muslims; the butchers here were Creole, and he pumped hands and switched to Kreol, saying, "Bonjour, ki nouvel?" By then I was convinced the agent had higher ambitions—he would one day run for political office himself. He may even become minister.

When we hit the fish stalls, I was curious about the special fish the agent was seeking. He inspected each stall.

"They don't have it. The taxi will take us to the Port
Louis bazaar, then we'll backtrack to the minister's house
in the Plateau," he said.

In Port Louis, we walked straight to the fish section.
I concluded that the agent didn't know many people here
and that the capital was not his boss's electoral district.
After checking a few of the stalls, he found what Minister Legrand liked: a fish I had never seen, whose name
I had never heard, selling for seven rupees per pound.
The Mahébourg bazaar carried fish with prices per pound
ranging from one rupee, for the proletarian corne, to 1.70
rupees, for the aristocratic capitaine or guele pavé. The
agent bought a six-pounder.

"I give you discount," the fishmonger said. "You have
it for forty rupees."

I thought of my monthly teacher's salary, 160 rupees.

When we arrived at Honorable Legrand's residence, it
was around nine. The gardener was trimming the roses;
the driver was shining the ministerial Jaguar. I thought we
would enter through the veranda to deliver the precious
package to the minister, and I was shocked when the agent
motioned me to accompany him to the back of the house.
At home and in the circles I moved in, only family and very
close friends entered through the back. The minister's wife,
still in her peignoir and baring her ample cleavage, opened
the kitchen door to usher us in.

"We've brought you Pierre's favorite," the agent said as
he opened the newspaper wrapping to reveal the red-and-
white fish. The agent referred to the minister by first name,
as one would family and friends.

"Magnifique. Grand merci," she said, with an English accent. "Pierre will see you at his office."

Before we drove back to the capital, I gave myself a minute to take in the luxurious kitchen—the sort I had seen only in movies. Instead of the logs, twigs, and pookni (a piece of metal pipe used to blow the fire) we had at home, here were electric countertops; instead of a plywood table on which lay the family's enamel teacups, glasses, and plastic plates were kitchen cabinets holding real china. A refrigerator. A floor of real marble. I was getting a foretaste of the luxury that, hopefully, would come after a good university education.

Unlike Honorables Thakoor and Mohamed, who as descendants of Indian coolies had experienced privations in youth, Honorable Pierre Legrand was a child of privilege. He was a big donor to the Catholic Church. A mulatto who could pass for a white person, he had been decorated for bravery during World War II and subsequently knighted by the Queen. He had met his wife in London during the Second World War. Prior to his entry into politics, he had a thriving law practice. Yes, he, too, was an alumnus of the Inns of Court.

At the Hotel du Gouvernement, Honorable Legrand's office wall was adorned with a photo of him in a Royal Air Force pilot's uniform, next to a bomber aircraft. He was a big man with the looks of a movie star. A lady-killer.

After I was introduced by the agent, Minister Legrand began with a warning.

"I want to make one thing clear: when you leave this office, remember that the fish you brought home was meant for Madame. I did not ask for it and you did not give it to me."

He looked me in the eye. I turned to the agent, who shook his head to confirm the gravity of Honorable Legrand's words. Fishy business it sure was. My blood boiled as I imagined him savoring the fancy fish with his wife later that evening, followed by a night of voracious lovemaking, while Papa and I were trying to figure out how to get my scholarship back.

The minister gave me more than a few seconds to digest his point, and then I presented my case. When I finished, he said that he would contact the French embassy to see if they could do something. His face was blank, his voice unconvincing. I asked for his phone number so that I could check the outcome. He pointed to the agent: "I'll let him know what they say."

I never heard from the agent.

From the historic grandeur of the Hotel du Gouvernement, I proceeded to the attorneys' chambers, walking distance from the Supreme Court. It was an oppressive building: low ceilings, stuffy hallway, and piles of law books about to crash on you at any moment; febrile, anxious faces in the waiting room. Maître Foiret, a portly, bald man, wore a sad face when he took the envelope of cash. "It's a pity so many families are torn apart by such cases. I told your father to accept a compromise, but he wouldn't listen. Il est tenace et coriace." Tenacious and hard as leather.

It had been a depressing morning. By the time lunch was over, I had a headache. Thinking some levity might help, I took the bus to Curepipe to chat with Voltaire, a primary school classmate who had excelled academically but didn't go on to secondary school. He became a tailor's apprentice to help his father, a night watchman, make ends meet. I had used my first two months' salary as a teacher as down payment on a new suit, in anticipation of the social life at university. The day I selected the fabric, my father came with me. He agreed with Voltaire's recommendation that I go with the luxurious Dormeuil wool. "After seven years at that snobbish school, it's time Vishnu gets some stylish clothes," Voltaire had said. It was now time to try on the suit to ensure a proper fit.

Voltaire had an endless store of jokes that derided the pretense of the various communities on the island. Himself a Creole with unmistakable African features, he poked fun at the Creoles' living beyond their means and mimicking the lifestyle of the whites; immediately after, he would regale us with stories ridiculing the Indians' reluctance to spend the slightest cent; and he did not spare the whites for their delusions that they were still French. At a time when political correctness was unknown, he entertained everyone with his colorful, sometimes bombastic portrayal of ethnic stereotypes.

That day, however, I found his stories boring. Trite. Cheap.

"You fucking Malabar," Voltaire said. "You come here to talk, and now you show me a face that looks like an asshole."

He had addressed me with the derogatory word for Indians. I shouted back "Mazambique," the pejorative word for Creoles, but couldn't complete my sentence. I was ashamed and shocked at the word I had used.

Voltaire left his sewing table.

"Something the matter, Vishnu? All the years I've known you, you've been so controlled, so cool."

I avoided his eyes and turned my head towards the half-finished jackets hanging on mannequins.

"Let me go next door and get you something to drink. It will calm you down."

Life was proving more complicated than I'd ever envisioned; my hopes were being dashed to pieces. Memories of my mental breakdown after the conclave came back, more vivid, and I was afraid I would suffer a relapse.

When Voltaire returned with a cup of tea, I told him about the meetings with the Honorables Thakoor, Mohamed, and Legrand, and about the ministerial fish.

"Things have a way of working themselves out," he said.

I wondered if Voltaire, in the workplace for more than five years, had acquired a kind of wisdom not available to those of us immersed in books. Tailoring had brought him into contact with people from various walks of life.

He added that Minister Mohamed's strong letter of recommendation would surely carry weight. "They have to please Muslim politicians; Muslims make up the swing vote."

I was barely out the door when he asked, "Why don't you try Gérard the longanis?"

"A longanis? You believe in sorcery?"

"Gérard is not illiterate and beggarly like the others, and he doesn't smell of salted fish. You must meet him. He carries his stuff in a leather satchel, not a two-rupee vacoas basket. He's traveled overseas, to the sacred forests of Madagascar to study with a famous ombiasi."

Voltaire put his hands on my shoulders and lowered his voice. "To thank me for an outfit I made for him, he invited me to a midnight séance at the Ville Noire cemetery. His style and words were grandiose. As soon as he pushed open the iron gate, he reached into his satchel. Out came a spice jar whose contents he sprinkled on the soil. 'Cloves to repel the forces of the enemy,' Gérard said. He squeezed some lemons. The waves howled at the full moon as he hurled the spent lemons towards the seashore. When we reached the Crucifix, he took out a framed picture of Saint George slaying the dragon, which he placed at the foot. He knelt, lit a candle on each side of Saint George— one red, one white—and prayed in some kind of Latin. He then walked towards a gravestone capped by a cross. He garlanded the cross with a rosary and string of flowers and chanted, 'Grand Shetani of Makonde, we invoke you tonight and beg you to accept this most humble offering from Mr. Richard Sooklall.' He plunged his hand in the satchel again and took out two bottles. He circled the tomb, pouring down liquid. 'On this ground hallowed by the blood of the goat, I implore you, Invulnerable Lord of the Orient and the Occident, to punish the illicit lover of Mr. Sooklall's wife. Great Archangel, make his tongue blister, his private parts limp, and, O Supreme Spirit, infect his brains with maggots.' With arms outstretched like a soaring bat, he continued: 'As the imam, bishop, and swami of Mosavy and Fanafody Gasy, I remain eternally bound to you.' "

"The watchman slept through all this?"

Voltaire raised his voice back to its usual volume. "Vishnu, imagine, just imagine, the power of Saint George,

Satan, and the Spirit of the Sacred Forests combined! Would the watchman dare challenge that?"

"And I bet your Catholic heart kept its regular beat all night?"

"To fortify myself, I drank a few pegs of rum before I left home. Under the stars, the angels and cherubs on the richer tombs looked serene. I expected the smell of corpses and dug earth. Instead, the flowers left by the bereaved released their fragrance. It was so peaceful."

WHEN I REACHED home, Fringant and Kalipa were at the street corner near our house, seated on two stones, their usual place in the late afternoon. I remembered clearly how, four years earlier, in front of our gate, they had confronted each other with harpoons over their support of rival politicians, and how, two Christmases back, Papa had given them a roof repair job to help them ride over a difficult period when rough seas prevented them from fishing. Since then, they had taken a liking to me and regularly asked me about "your progress in life."

"We heard you were at the bazaar today shopping for rare fish with the agent," Fringant said. "Everything okay?"

"Everything's fine," I said and opened the gate.

"Remember the days we were agents part-time? We know how the system works," Fringant said.

Kalipa got up, walked over to me, and puffed out his chest. "If some politician is messing with you, let us know. We'll show up at his place with our harpoon and settle the matter."

I told my father about the brothers' offer.

"We don't do things this way," he said.

I didn't mention Voltaire's séance.

FOR THE SECOND meeting with Minister Thakoor, my father decided that the stakes were high enough for him to take another day's leave. Papa had never taken leave before, though he had often complained of illness.

With his suit, tie, and felt hat, going through security at the Hotel du Gouvernement was not difficult.

In his office that late afternoon, Honorable Thakoor had a hard countenance. This was difficult for me to comprehend.

Papa began. "You remember, Monsieur le Ministre, in 1952 we and Honorable Mohamed were working at Ferney Primary School. He has asked me to give you this letter of recommendation."

The minister grabbed it with his tiny hand, looked at the envelope, marked FOR OFFICIAL BUSINESS, and with a matching tiny voice said, "This letter is not worth a nail."

Without opening the envelope, he tore it to shreds.

Though of North Indian ancestry, my father had the swarthy complexion of a South Indian, unlike most of the Bhushan clan. That armed him with an advantage in tense social situations: one could never see him blush. As Honorable Thakoor threw the bits of paper into the wastepaper basket, I looked at Papa. His ears and face had turned reddish! His otherwise calm demeanor made it difficult for me to figure out his feelings: was it disappointment with the crass behavior of an ex-colleague, or anger?

"Surely you can do something for us, Monsieur le

Ministre. Your ministry has jurisdiction over scholarship awards."

"These days, if you do something for someone, you get pilloried for it. The decision has been taken."

He turned to me.

"You better go to the ministry and fill in the paper-work for Madagascar. It is not so bad."

Papa put his hat back on, did not say good-bye, and went home.

I walked to the ministry, determined to put up one more fight. I remembered a teacher at my secondary school quoting some professor—something along the lines of "We sometimes blame politicians for decisions and actions that entrenched civil servants take." With these words in my ears, I knocked on the door of the second in command, Kamban Pillay, and barged in.

As a senior functionary, Pillay was part of the emerging middle class of Indian origin. No mere clerk, he was clearly conscious of the status that a degree from the London School of Economics conferred on him. He rose from his chair with the solemnity of a pope about to deliver a statement ex cathedra.

Somehow he knew why I was in his office. Before I could open my mouth, he called the third in command, Yash Bissoon, and, pointing at me as if he'd just thrown the remnants of his lunch to a stray cur, said to Bissoon, "He's not satisfied with Madagascar. Oliver Twist asking for more!"

They shared a hearty laugh.

Bissoon patted me on the shoulder. "You should consider yourself lucky you're getting this scholarship."

"Why didn't you study there? Why didn't you send Miss Sharmila there?"

I could not believe I had blurted this out, yet I was glad I did. Miss Sharmila was the minister's niece Papa had alluded to during his first meeting with Minister Thakoor.

"You'll get a good job when you graduate. In this country, we give equal weight to degrees, regardless of the universities that confer them," Pillay said.

Bissoon handed me the Madagascar papers.

When I walked out, Cousin Shankar was standing at the gate. I suggested we stroll along the harbor and Albion Docks. People were spilling out of offices, grabbing the evening newspapers from the tobacco kiosks, and rushing to catch their buses home. The harbor looked different from the day I had my first scholarship interview. The majestic *Ferdinand de Lesseps* was gone, and drab Japanese fishing trawlers dominated the horizon.

I persuaded Shankar to join me for dinner and drinks at the A-1 Restaurant Bar. The A-1 was a notch above the harbor bars patronized by foreign sailors; it hosted no hookers and witnessed no brawls. It attracted young men who had just joined the lower-middle echelon of the workforce, older bus and taxi drivers, and a smattering of secondary school students whose parents were liberal with pocket money. The background music reflected its broad clientele: Enrico Macias and Edith Piaf, the Beatles and Elvis, Hindi film songs and the local séga. Though its Chinese meefoon noodle enjoyed some renown, I went there on Fridays for its boeuf aux petits pois. My paycheck during the preceding few months empowered me to defy the Hindu dietary taboo against beef.

Dusk stretched into evening. We talked and talked, ate and ate. We kept ordering pegs of rum. My recollection of what was said is foggy, though we must have spent some time on my ongoing Kafkaesque travails. Suddenly, looking around, we realized we were the only patrons left. I asked for one last peg. The Chinese waiter, worn out, implored us to leave. It was ten.

We looked for a taxi at Victoria Station. The last bus had already left. Empty of its noisy and energetic trains, which had been sold and dispatched to apartheid South Africa a few years earlier, the grayish-black stone building had a ghostly, melancholy charm in the moonlight. It reminded me of Uncle Ram, the railway stationmaster, and his prediction about my studying in England. He had disappeared, and so had his world.

In the taxi, Shankar confided that Papa was worried and had sent him to Port Louis to check if I was okay. When I got home, I slumped into the tottering rattan chair on the veranda. The sea breeze caressed my face and slowly woke me up from the alcohol-induced torpor.

I ambled inside and saw that poor Shankar had some explaining to do. "Couldn't you stop him from drinking so much?" I heard Mama say.

"He's too skinny for that," I said. "He forgot to swallow his Wate-On fattening beverage."

I sat on the chair facing Papa and said, "I can't believe you and those other suckers gave your hard-earned money to this motherfucker Thakoor to finance his law studies!"

I didn't wait for his response; swear words were forbidden in the house. And I rarely used them even with my friends.

I stood up and nearly knocked down the TV in the room, the one luxury item Papa had bought, so we could watch the news. As my mother and Shankar tried to steady me, I raged, "Honorable Bara Thakoor . . . small man . . . small brain . . . small dick."

I broke free and hobbled to the veranda.

I raised my head to the sky just in time to catch shooting stars disappear into the horizon.

"Bara Thakoor, impotent son of a bitch," I shouted.

I waited for more shooting stars. They were gone. Restless, I went back inside. Mama had her perpetual worried look, and Papa quickly, surreptitiously closed and put away a book he held in his hands. Shankar had a smirk, and this drove me mad. I stepped to a window and yanked the draperies from the curtain rod, tearing off the eyelets. I went to the second window and ripped off the curtains with even greater rage. When I turned to the third window, Mama was standing in front of it.

She wasn't there to berate me or to protect her last remaining curtain. Her face was soft, and I broke down in tears.

I bent down and sat at Mama's feet. I was a spent force.

"Ma, I'm sorry. Forgive me. You remember what I told you last week, don't you?"

She caressed my head.

"I told you how refined your taste was; you choose the most exquisite curtains. And now I've ruined them."

I continued.

"Smile, Ma. You have beautiful, well-shaped white teeth. That's the best thing I've got from you. That's what the girls tell me. Look."

I flashed my teeth.

Papa broke his silence. "It's been a rough day, Vishnu. You need to rest."

"I'm staying right here. No sleep tonight."

"Shankar, give me a hand," he said, and they both raised me up from the floor. "They can't put you down, son. You're worth much more than they ever will be."

I shook my head as they brought me to my bed.

"Adversities are temporary, Vishnu. You have it in you to overcome."

At breakfast the next day, my father said nothing about my drunkenness.

Papa rarely solicited my, or even Mama's, opinions. When, on his return from work, he asked "What do we do next?" I just showed him the Madagascar papers.

"I sell my sugarcane to Kissoon Singh, the broker. We'll go see him. He claims to be close to the prime minister."

"Your crop is minuscule. Why should he care?"

"It's not only me. Twenty years ago, I persuaded all your uncles and aunts to sell to him. He knows we can sell directly to the white man's sugar estate or use another broker."

Papa's words were a gentle reminder: he was head of the clan.

Two days later, Papa took leave from work once again. We were in the prime minister's office, waiting for the Father of the Nation.

His chief of staff walked in. After my father thanked him for arranging the meeting, he handed him the newspaper listing the French scholarship awards. "My son's case is simple and straightforward . . ."

The chief of staff cut him short.

"We had to juggle the prime minister's schedule. He can't see you. We are in the midst of organizing National Prayer Day, which comes soon. We are familiar with your case, and we'll get back to you."

The meeting had lasted barely three minutes.

The chief of staff ushered us back into the plush antechamber, where a saffron-robed swami, a Catholic monsignor in black cassock, and an imam in immaculate white were admiring the model of the Legislative Assembly, then under construction. Papa recognized the Hindu priest and made the expected reverential bow. "Namasté, Swamiji."

The chief of staff quickly whisked the ecclesiastics into the prime minister's office.

Papa hugged me.

"How could I be so gullible? I believed in meritocracy. I should have canvassed these carnivores much earlier. From the day your exams results came out."

When he relaxed his embrace, I realized that during the previous two weeks I had spent more time with him than any time before. Here was a man everyone knew as bookish and reserved. Now I saw someone who stood his ground in the corridors of power. But he also had a look of disgust and bitterness that I had never seen.

On the bus, Papa dozed off. I watched the face and body of a man who had been dealt two heavy blows within six months: he lost a court case in which he invested so much time and energy, and now the hopes he had pinned on me had evaporated. He was a man fighting for my future.

All avenues were now exhausted. I sat weighing my prospects. I told myself the program in Madagascar would be a breeze—I'd make the top grades there without too much effort, and use these to win a scholarship to a prestigious American university. I ran my fingers through my hair. I felt it had turned gray.

The bus was packed with secondary school kids doing their usual thing: egging on the driver to race against another bus full of students from a rival school. Like most younger bus drivers, he obliged.

XVI.

Tamby at the Rex Cinema

1969

I went to the Garden of Love,
And saw what I never had seen:
A Chapel was built in the midst,
Where I used to play on the green.

And the gates of this Chapel were shut,
And "Thou shalt not" writ over the door;
So I turn'd to the Garden of Love,
That so many sweet flowers bore.

And I saw it was filled with graves,
And tomb-stones where flowers should be:
And Priests in black gowns were walking their
    rounds,
And binding with briars my joys & desires.
—WILLIAM BLAKE, "THE GARDEN OF LOVE"

By the time I earned my first teacher's paycheck and could afford my first sexual experience, Rekha's had gone out of business. Some said Rekha had moved upscale and had become a procuress for politicians and wealthy businessmen. Others claimed that the police had closed the place because she had dared charge a police inspector, who was visiting from another town, for tasting the charms of one of her newer girls. Cousin Shankar dismissed these as unfounded rumors. "She's just tired and wants a less complicated life."

Five years earlier, I had turned down Shankar's invitation to join him at Rekha's. He thought a visit there would hasten my recovery from my nervous breakdown and invigorate me. "Parents want you to deny your body; if those old trees could castrate you and graft your balls back on your wedding day, they would," he said.

In those five years I had longings. There were one or two girls I saw on my daily bus rides home who stirred dreams of romance. But how could I approach them? A conversation on the bus or at the bus stop would soon reach the ears of the girl's parents or brothers—who would waste no time in teaching me a lesson. Or they would contact my parents, who'd do the thrashing for them. I knew from my female cousins that the girls had yearnings, too. They faced a harsher reality than us boys: it wasn't uncommon for parents to withdraw their daughters from school if they were suspected of having a boyfriend.

Now, when I told Shankar I was ready for sex, he proposed we check out the loka behind the Majestic Cinema, in Port Louis, a stone's throw from the Jardin de la Compagnie des Indes. Every adult around us who mentioned the place had condemned it as worthy of damnation. My father, who never talked to me about sex, had warned me much earlier, the first time I went alone to the capital to watch the horse races: he had heard of prostitutes from the loka drugging the son of a leading politician with potions the day before he sat for his A-levels.

We arrived in the capital in the late afternoon, after two sweaty hours on the road, with a bus change in Curepipe. To cool down, we sat for a while in the Jardin de la Compagnie under the watchful eyes of Rémy Ollier and Adrien d'Epinay, the former a staunch defender of the descendants of slaves, the latter the leading champion of the Franco-Mauritian anti-abolitionists. The discordance of having these two within yards of each other didn't occur to me then, and I didn't question why my country celebrated the memory of an advocate of slavery in such a peaceful garden. What I saw were two statues contemplating what I was about to do. We let our bodies relax to the sound of water jetting out of the fountains, in the shade of the banyan trees, with their languorous tresses. Though we were in the city center, we were protected from its noises and smells.

Half an hour later, we walked to the Majestic Cinema. On my left, sunset shone a coppery light on the yellow walls of the Natural History Museum and caressed the leaves of the tall palm trees with a shimmer.

Behind the cinema, a different world awaited us. The alley was lined with wooden shacks with low doors and dark curtains. I imagined they all shared a courtyard at the back. I heard groaning and laughter.

A woman came out of one shack, wearing a rather ordinary blue skirt and white blouse, not the figure-enhancing clothes that I associated with women who work in a loka. Her garb had seen better days.

"Vini mo garson," she said.

I didn't respond to her request to come in. I recoiled at the strong smell of cigarette emanating from her bright red lips.

"Vini mo garson, pas per," she said. She must have sensed my anxiety, for now she was asking me not to be afraid. She stepped forward, grabbed my arm, and tried to drag me inside. I pulled back and was surprised at her strength. It all happened so fast. Shankar darted towards her and yanked her hands off my arm.

We hastened back to the Jardin de la Compagnie. I was perspiring.

"That was a narrow escape," I told Shankar. "What a pitiful woman!"

"She's desperate for clients. Rekha's was classier," Shankar said.

The incident disquieted me for many days, but the stirrings of conscience were not vigorous enough to chase away the craving for sex.

A month later, in the late afternoon, Shankar showed up in a car with a friend at the steering wheel. "We're going to find some fine women in the city," his friend said. Since this guy had a car, I reckoned he must be acquainted with a better class of women.

When we arrived in Port Louis, Shankar's friend drove past the Police Line Barracks and towards the Civil Hospital. He stopped by a few retail shops along the way and asked the guys sipping rum at the bar if they knew a Jean-Philippe. Nobody claimed to know him. Their faces gave away that they did know but didn't trust us. A few minutes later, we reached a street corner where an elderly couple sat at their doorsteps enjoying the evening breeze. Shankar's friend asked them about Jean-Philippe. Their faces were blank, and the man frowned. "Why don't you go back to your neighborhood?"

We drove away.

"Maybe the Creoles here think we're Muslims," I said. "Creoles and Muslims were killing each other in this city two years ago. Let's go back."

I was uncomfortable, fearful even, and wanted to return to Mahébourg. We were in another ward of Port Louis that I didn't recognize; at some point Shankar's friend had negotiated two women for the three of us.

Guided by the two women, we drove to a wooded area outside the city, then walked down a ravine. The warm breeze intensified the grassy and woody scents. I was nervous and thought, *What if this is a trap? What if their brothers or husbands are hiding behind the trees, ready to rob us or slice us with sabers?* There was no conversation; we didn't even ask each other's names. I could hear the crackling of the grasshoppers and the rustling of the leaves.

By the time we reached the bottom of the ravine, no stranger had materialized. I felt reassured. Since I was the virgin, Shankar and his friend gave me first choice. Both women were young, dark, with shiny skin and frizzy hair. Their makeup was subdued, nonexistent almost; it seemed like they had left home in the middle of some chore like ironing clothes or sweeping the floor. One wore Bien-Être lavender eau de cologne; the other the Bien-Être natural cologne. I knew because Bien-Être was a popular brand on the island. I selected the woman who, in the moonlight, appeared the friendliest, the warmest. The one with the lavender cologne.

Down on the grass, she lifted her skirt and took off her panties. The moon shone on her thighs and on her pubic hair, which glistened. I kissed her; she turned her lips away. I fumbled with the buttons of her blouse and she firmly warded off my hands. She went straight to my erect penis and took it in her hands. Why she inserted it inside her with such verve but denied me the taste of her lips and breasts baffled me. No kiss, no foreplay, just my member hitting a moist membrane, followed by a thrusting of her hips, and an ejaculation. Neither of us moaned as in the films. No singing bells rang in my ears. Here I was with a young woman on the slopes of a ravine, under a moonlit sky with scintillating stars, the stuff of romantic poetry, and yet the sex, my first, was most unpoetic.

When I returned home, my mother was at the door. I had an uneasy intimation that she had been waiting for me, waiting to detect the smell of grass, soil, and lavender that clung to my messed-up clothes. I was relieved when all she said was "You're late, Vishnu. I'll make you some warm milk."

TWO OR THREE weeks later, around Easter, I heard a bizarre conversation in the staff room of the Mauritius College Secondary School, where I had taken a temporary teaching job after completing my A-levels; I expected that within a year I would secure a scholarship to attend university overseas.

"How often do you have sex?"

"Twice a week, on average."

"That's all? You've been married only a year. I thought it takes longer for the fire to die out."

"By the time you get home from work, you're exhausted, no energy left. You do it on the weekends."

A moment of awkward silence.

"Why do you ask?"

"You haven't noticed the strain in my walk? I've been to the doctor for pain in my testicles. He advised sex."

The married man burst into laughter. "You have the monk's disease, caused by backing up of sperm. We're all monks on this island until we get married. Unless you're white or Creole—then you can have a girlfriend." A graduate of St. Andrews who had previously told us how he and his classmates prevailed over the Scottish cold with booze and sex, he continued, "Masturbate more often or have your parents arrange a marriage. With your University of London degree, you're a good catch. Your parents-in-law may even throw a new car or a beach bungalow into the bargain." He walked out of the teachers' staff room and hurried to the end of the hallway, to the classroom where his students were waiting.

Kumar, the other teacher in the staff room, had been silent. He rose from the sofa where he had been sipping his tea. "You should never ask someone about his sex life in public. Next you'll be asking him if his wife was a virgin when they met." He patted the shoulders of the man with the monk's disease and smiled. "I have the solution for you. Come with me this Saturday."

He then gave me a wink.

Kumar confounded the stereotype of a smallish subservient Hindu. Standing at more than six feet, in a country where the average male was five feet six, with military shoulders and deportment, he was the scion of one of the few low-caste Hindus who were landed gentry. With more than four hundred acres of land, at least twenty rental houses and a fleet of a dozen cars and lorries to their name, his clan commanded respect, even of the sugar estate whites.

Of the four teachers in the staff room that day, I was the youngest, and the only one who was not a university graduate and had not traveled overseas. As a novice in teaching as well as life experience, I didn't feel I belonged to this informal club of graduates. But Kumar's wink changed that; I read his gesture as an invitation to join.

Kumar had already helped me a few days earlier, with a teaching tip. Quite a few of the students played truant on Thursday and Friday afternoons and flocked to the Novelty Cinema, which was separated from the school by a bamboo hedge. "You can't change these kids' behavior; that's probably the only pleasure they have in their life. Incorporate the movies in your English composition classes. Have them write about their favorite film scenes instead of some boring topic like overpopulation or a picnic under the filao trees."

The day after the wink, I told Kumar about my night in the ravine. He laughed but quickly switched to a serious tone, as if to punish himself for laughing. "Women who do it for money often avoid kissing, for fear of getting emotional. But the ones with experience know how to handle a kiss." He had guessed why I approached him. He asked me to meet him at his home in Quatre Bornes on Saturday. "I'll rent a beach bungalow for the day."

On Saturday, after lunch and tea at his house, we went

to Port Louis in his Citroën DS21. Once in the capital, he drove straight to the Rex Cinema and, from his driver's seat, asked for Tamby. Everyone on the steps in front of the cinema—the old guys playing dominoes, the seller of sweets and samosas, the loiterers—seemed to know the man. They hollered his name and he showed up in minutes. He was dressed like a civil servant in the colonial days, on his way to work in the summer—beige cotton pants, white shirt, brown tie and dress shoes. He waved to Kumar and got into the car.

"Tamby, you should get a phone. Your business will boom."

"Mr. Kumar, I'm no aristocrat. You know very well it takes more than a year to get a phone line."

"At least put your name on the waiting list. I'll call my friends at the Ministry of Telecom to speed things up."

Tamby shook his head. "Okay. But I prefer you help me with a more important matter. It's about my son. He needs private tuition. He failed all his exams."

"Send him to me on Sunday afternoons. I'll coach him in maths and physics. No charge."

"I'll bring him to you. What woman do you want today? The one you had last week isn't available right now." Tamby sneezed and continued, "By the way, she said you treated her nicely."

"Today we need someone special for my young friend here."

"His first time?"

"You could say that."

I turned my head to Tamby in the back seat, his legs spread wide as one would at home on a sofa. Against his dark South Indian skin, his teeth gleamed yellow as he smiled and extended his hand.

"Vishnu," I said as I shook it.

A few minutes later, around three, we made four stops in the outskirts of the capital. At each, Tamby got out of the car, knocked, and went inside a house, then came out with a woman who stood at the gate for a few minutes, waiting for Kumar's approval. The houses were not humble abodes. They looked like homes of middle-class Mauritian families—shopkeepers, schoolteachers, nurses, policemen—with yards where kids were shouting, boys spinning tops or kicking soccer balls, and girls playing hopscotch. Kumar asked for my opinion each time, and we agreed on the women from the first and fourth houses Tamby took us to.

He introduced them as they joined us in the car. "Hey, mister, the leather smells new; it's a fancy car," said Gauri, with light brown skin, big eyes and long black hair tied in a ponytail. Next came Yasmin, fair with almond-shaped eyes and sporting what we at the time called a Mireille Mathieu haircut, short hair shaped like a bowl around the face and tapering to an oval at the nape of the neck.

We dropped Tamby back at Rex. I moved to the back seat next to Yasmin, and Gauri took the front passenger seat. We drove on to Pointe aux Sables, twenty minutes away. On the way, Gauri was loquacious. She talked about the cars she liked ("expensive ones I'll never be able to afford: Jaguar, Rover, and your Citroën," she told Kumar), the men she disliked ("those with oily hair and mustaches" and "those who are rough in bed"), and her dream (going to France and "getting married to a Frenchman who won't

care about my past"). Kumar responded with positive, optimistic remarks: "Don't underestimate yourself. You may
get a Jaguar one day." "Where there's a will, there's a way."

Yasmin was quiet. I tried to coax her into conversation
by asking about her likes and dislikes, but she answered
in monosyllables. *Maybe a broken heart,* I said to myself. A
husband who left her. She was beautiful, taller, and more
arresting in her looks than Gauri. She had sensual lips, and
her tight blue dress revealed a small waist and medium-size
breasts and hips. She wore a pendant with Arabic calligra-
phy, which I assumed was the holy phrase "Allahu akbar."

"Nice campement, mister. You have good taste," said
Gauri as we entered the bungalow in Pointe aux Sables. For
sure it was well-appointed for the occasion: two bedrooms,
king beds with fresh linens, hot showers, which were a
luxury to me, and a bar stocked with whisky, rum, Coke,
and lemonade.

Gauri and Yasmin went to the showers. "I bring my
own," Gauri said as she took a Lux soap bar out of her
handbag.

"Go with Gauri; she'll be more fun!" Kumar said, as if
he were a grand expert.

When Gauri returned, the ponytail was gone. She
swirled her flowing hair like a playful stallion flinging
his mane, wiggled her derrière, and rubbed it against my
crotch. I noticed Ganesh, the Hindu elephant god, on her
neck pendant. He looked playful: the god of auspicious
events, the remover of obstacles, was smiling! What followed was a dream come true, a dream I fancy would have
been realized years earlier had I been in America or Europe
and had a girlfriend: exhilarating sex that left me with a

memory that has never waltzed away. We started slowly, with a kiss on the lips, a flick of the tongue on the neck and nipples, and she was pure joy and wild abandon. Whenever I allow myself to think of Gauri, the scent of her body sails through my mind, carrying with it echoes of a rose garden in the sunlight.

Kumar warned me not to get too involved. "Gauri is nice, but she can trap you," he said—exactly the word Auntie Ranee had used in Madame Lolo a few years earlier to describe Karan's woman. "You've read too many Romantic writers. Too much Zola and his Nana." I smiled at his lumping Zola the naturalist with the Romantics.

On Saturdays over the next few months, unless we had a wedding or funeral to attend, we would meet Tamby in front of the Rex. His filles de joie hailed from all communities except the white community, and all religions— Hindu, Muslim, Catholic. There were poor women and middle-class ones, some with little education, but most with five or more years of secondary school. Some hurried home after the sex, some stayed for food, drinks, and conversation.

Every weekend, Kumar drove the women and me to rental campements by the beach on different parts of the island. Belle Mare, Grand Baie, Trou aux Biches, Tamarin, Le Morne, Cap Malheureux, Baie du Tombeau. Over these beach towns and villages, not yet frequented by tourists in designer swimwear or snorkeling gear, hovered a faint bouquet of delicious sin.

In the car, Kumar spoke glowingly about Calcutta, where he'd studied, and how he crisscrossed India. Around the time I heard of my French scholarship award, in June, I sensed a growing restlessness in him. "It's so quiet here. I miss the noise of Indian cities, I even miss the dust," he said one Saturday. The following week, in the staff room, he was more prolix: "You have no idea what it is to hang out at the College Street Coffee House in Calcutta, and who you can run into there. Satyajit Ray, Aparna Sen. You can discuss poetry, movies, world politics. Life is so small here, Vishnu."

Coupled with his restlessness was the increasing amount of alcohol he now drank on our Saturday outings. Gauri noticed it and told him, "Mister, you should get married—it will make you more responsible." Kumar responded with a dispirited face. She turned to me: "You should talk to your friend before the whisky sends him to hospital with delirium." Before I could say anything, Kumar had a rejoinder: "This place is a prison; whisky is freedom."

Two weeks later, Tamby took us to Rose Hill, in the center of the island, to the house of a mulatto woman who was so stunning that we couldn't believe she was in the trade. "Tamby, she can get any man she wants," Kumar said in Bhojpuri, an Indian language she wouldn't understand. Tamby smiled, shook his head, and left to visit his cousin nearby. We had barely started the drive to Pointe aux Sables, where a bungalow was waiting for us, when I saw Kumar's countenance change as he looked in the rearview mirror. He was pale and he bit his lip.

"Foutou! I have to make a detour," he said.

"Why are you swearing?" the woman asked.

Kumar didn't reply. He took the first left that presented itself, then another left, and raced for half a mile. The woman and I turned behind to see if anyone was following us.

"My asshole of an uncle was behind us. I can't risk going that way again," he said. "I'll drop you back at your house."

"Don't you want to have a good time, guys?" she said. "Why don't you drive in the other direction, to the south. Le Chaland Hotel is a lovely place."

I told Kumar in Bhojpuri, "It sure looks delightful, but it's too close to Mahébourg and Mon Désert. My folks may see us."

We were at her door. "Can't risk it, mademoiselle," he said as he handed her an envelope.

She opened it. "You're generous," she said, and blew us a kiss.

We drove away.

"Why did you let such a beauty go? We could have driven east to Belle Mare," I said.

"Vishnu, that asshole is going to ask me who that mulattress was. He's going to tell my parents and blame them for the way they brought me up." Kumar was shaking. "He is a bigot, as much a bigot as the higher-caste Hindus who look down on him. I'll have to tell him that the woman is your friend. I hope you don't mind."

"Mind? I should be thankful for all that you've done for me," I said.

I wasn't worried about word getting back to my parents, relatives, or neighbors: Kumar's uncle would think twice before leaking information to the outside world about a family member cavorting with me and a mulattress, the more so because of his clan's high standing in Mauritian society.

Since the rent for the bungalow was already paid, we ended up in Pointe aux Sables to chill out. We sat on the veranda. The late-afternoon sun was mild, the wind balmy yet strong enough that multicolored kites were flying in the clear blue sky. We started with a bottle of Scotch to accompany the prawns with oyster sauce we picked up at Lotus Bleu, in Rose Hill, then, to do justice to the copious Chinese restaurant portions, we moved downscale to a bottle of rum. Kumar repeatedly congratulated me for the French scholarship. "You'll realize how lucky you are when you land there. No one telling you what to do. You'll get a girlfriend and have sex without paying for it," he said. "You'll fall in love." I repeatedly thanked him for Gauri and the others and insisted that he take my money; he repeatedly refused my contribution, even for the drinks or food or petrol for the car. After more rounds of drinks, of mutual congratulations and thanks, our eyes dim and our voices a slur, Kumar offered a toast: "To Vishnu, to freedom—freedom to be yourself, freedom to make your own fucking mistakes." His hand trembled, he slumped on his chair, and his glass smashed on the cement floor.

My eyes opened to a golden sunset. Kumar was standing with the car keys in his hand. "We overdid it today," he said. "We better get going." How he drove to Mahébourg and back to his house in Quatre Bornes—fifty-five miles in all—in that half-drunken state remains a mystery to me.

We didn't go anywhere the next two weekends. Kumar looked like a chastened man. In the staff room, he kept to himself and read the newspapers. I wondered if his uncle had caused trouble for him or if the alcohol binge had unsettled him, making him apprehend a deeper problem. The colleague with the monk's disease speculated that Kumar was being pushed into an arranged marriage by his parents and uncles. I didn't press for any explanation. My departure overseas was approaching and soon I'd be busy with formalities such as getting a French visa.

"Let's go out once before you travel," he told me. We were getting close to the August school holidays.

Tamby took us near the Civil Hospital. The house, surrounded by a five-foot whitewashed stone wall, had a narrow gate with an intricately wrought metal grille, carrying a design that looked like tendrils of vine. A huge lychee tree rose above the wall. Clearly not a poor family's home.

We were greeted by a woman in her early twenties, with a cat's gray eyes, who held a copy of *Paris Match* in her hand. She wore a blue polka-dot skirt and a cream-white turtleneck sweater that accentuated her breasts. I peered beyond the veranda into the rooms behind, and saw shelves of books.

"She can't go anywhere with you," Tamby said. "You'll have to stay here."

Kumar and I looked at each other. To me, there was nothing threatening about the house, no foreboding of danger. The presence of books, the woman's coiffed hair, and the subtlety of her perfume made me comfortable with staying. But Kumar's face registered first a whisper, then a suspicion of something amiss, something improper. I held my tongue.

"Let me show you to the bedroom," the woman said.

Tamby would have left by then, but he stayed with us. We went behind, past the veranda. There was a dark reddish-brown poster bed with transparent curtains. The height of luxury and style, I thought. I suspected the wood was mahogany or keruing from Indonesia. The only similar bed I'd seen before was in the Mahébourg National History Museum, the bed that belonged to a French governor of the island.

In a corner, behind a partially open drape that trailed the floor, I spotted a porcelain sink, but not at waist level; it was on the floor.

"Don't gape like that, Vishnu," Kumar said. "It's a bidet. To wash after."

He turned to Tamby: "Classy stuff."

"I better leave you now," Tamby said.

As Tamby turned towards the veranda, we heard a groan. "Shireen, where are you?" It was an old man's voice, not mournful but dolorous, a voice that sought appeasement.

Shireen rushed towards the voice and carefully opened a door. We fixed our eyes on the room. A man in his fifties was sitting in bed, his shoulders and back against the headboard. His legs ended in amputation stumps. A wheelchair lay by the bedside. He motioned us to come in. We approached but stayed by the door. "You don't have to worry about anything," he said. "I called because I needed my tablets."

After giving him some tablets and refilling his glass of water, Shireen came out and closed the door.

Kumar took Tamby and me aside. "Tamby, how can I get it up with her after seeing the poor man? This is sad."

"This is the first time the old man interrupts. Shireen is my most sought-after woman, the most expensive, the most intellectual."

"Vishnu, can you get it up?" Kumar said.

I was tongue-tied. I shook my head.

Shireen walked towards us, poised and dignified. "What's the problem?"

"I'll be with you in a minute," Tamby said.

His words didn't register.

She faced Kumar and me. "Pull yourself together, messieurs, my time is as precious as yours. I have a father to support."

She picked a book from a shelf.

"We all deserve a comfortable life, don't we?" she said, and headed to the garden.

In the car, Kumar took Tamby to task. "You can't put your clients in such situations. What's the story with Shireen and her father?"

"Mr. Kumar, if God meant me to ask such questions, he would have made me a priest or a social worker. I know my place in this world. I'm here to find women for you, not to dig into family problems."

We dropped Tamby at the Rex, and that was our final Saturday outing.

TWO MONTHS LATER, I left Mauritius for university studies. In my third year in the United States, during our courtship, my future wife Maria and I went to the Smithsonian for an exhibition of Utamaro's paintings. The world of Gauri and Shireen was far removed from the glamorized palaces of pleasure depicted by the Japanese painter of the Edo period, with their geishas walking about in the richest silks and brocades against a backdrop of cherry blossoms or participating in elaborate tea ceremonies. Nonetheless, the sight of these women called to mind the difference Kumar made in my life.

At dinner that evening, I asked Maria, who was writing a thesis on Japanese art, "Were Japanese adolescents in Utamaro's time expected to repress their sexual desires?"

"I'm not researching that subject," she replied. "Why do you ask?"

I told her about Kumar and my initiation, sparing her the graphic details.

She squeezed my hands. "You had no options," she said.

I was relieved. I expected a lecture on morality; instead I got love and understanding.

When I returned home to Mauritius with Maria after six years abroad, we went to see Kumar. I had heard that he got married, ran successfully for political office and was a junior member of the cabinet. That didn't surprise me, given his charisma and the fact that over the years he had provided free tuition to hundreds of poor kids. A housemaid answered my knock on the door; I caught a whiff of burning sandalwood and ghee emanating from inside. I told her who we were, and she came back after transmitting my message.

"Sir, he can't see you now. He's in the middle of a religious ceremony."

"When can we meet him?"

"He didn't say, sir."

As we left, Maria said, "That's a strange friend."

Unlike her, I wasn't upset. "Some friendships last, some don't," I said.

Seven years earlier, Kumar had performed his role as a mentor to me, and after I left he moved on with what Mauritius had to offer him. He was now a married elected politician, dutifully performing the rituals of a Hindu life. He now had other obligations, other duties.

XVII

Sookwaar Hands

1971

"You don't want to spend the night in New York. It's too dangerous," the Canadian told me.

Sitting next to me on the London–New York flight, crammed with noisy students returning from summer holiday, he was unable to sleep. He had the craggy face of movie villain Jack Palance, and the frame, height, and enforcer eyes of Clint Eastwood. He spoke to me about his hitchhiking across California, his work as a lumberjack in Alberta, but mostly about New York. He described how, on a trip to the city, he manhandled two thugs who thought they could intimidate him with their Colt revolvers. He told me about the prostitutes and pimps pestering him in Times Square, and the story of Kitty Genovese's murder in Queens and how more than thirty neighbors heard her screams and never called the police.

When I boarded the plane in London, I was excited by the prospect of roaming around New York for a few days. But now, as the pilot announced our arrival at JFK in thirty minutes, the veins at my temple were pulsing and my heart was pounding—not with excitement but with anxiety, even fear.

"Proceed straight to Connecticut. It's much more civilized," the Canadian said.

I hadn't intended to be in the United States that early in August 1971. The Tuckers, my host family in Connecticut, expected me the following week, under a program run by an international students' organization. But the immigration officer at Heathrow denied me a two-week visa, allowing me to stay in England for only a week. I was reluctant to show up at the Tuckers' early. From recent Royal College alumni returning from university studies abroad, I had heard that in Europe and America you don't just drop in at someone's house, even if you are a close relative; it has to be arranged in advance. And you certainly don't hang around for a week longer than arranged.

What shall I do? New York sounds like hell, and I don't know anybody in America.

When I walked out of the international terminal, the doors opened automatically. I went back inside, and this time I stepped out slowly, deliberately. *America, land of wonders!*

Three hours later at the Windsor Locks airport, in Connecticut ("the Gateway to New England," proclaimed the brochure), I was checking billboards. They showed pictures of hotels, but no rates. I picked the one that looked the cheapest—one floor, nondescript facade, no lobby, no lawn. A "motel," which I assumed was an American abbreviation for mini-hotel. I reckoned that calling the Tuckers after two or three days here would be reasonable; they would regard me as a well-bred young man who hadn't imposed on them right upon arrival in the United States.

This would be the first time in my life that I set foot in

a hotel. In Mauritius, I had looked longingly at Le Chaland Hotel, where airline pilots and hostesses stayed, and where one of Tamby's women had wanted to go. In London, I passed by the Savoy on my way to the apartment where Marx had lived in Soho, but the Rolls-Royces and Bentleys dissuaded me from venturing into the lobby.

Exhausted and sticky from lugging two suitcases from terminal to terminal, I went straight to the shower after check-in. The water pressure, amplified and pumped up to a degree I had never experienced before, turned the banal act of physical cleansing into an aquatic massage. I abandoned myself to the water, body gyrating, eyes closed. *America, land of wonders!* After a few minutes, I opened my eyes and looked down. The water hadn't drained from the bathtub; it was sloshing back and forth with bits of hair and soapy gunk dancing around me.

A week earlier in London, I had luxuriated in a bathtub. Back home, my only cleaning options were showers or water poured from a bucket. My cousin's landlady, pitying my worn-out face after the twelve-hour Mauritius-to-London flight, ran me a bath, showed me the bath plug, and instructed me to pull it out after I was done. So, on my first day in the States, faced with watery slime, I bent down and looked for the bath plug. Not seeing any, I knelt and groped through the length and breadth of the tub, and the perimeter, feeling for rubber or metal components with some sort of chain attached. Nothing remotely resembling the London bath plug. I felt a round metallic protuberance at the head of the tub. Eureka! I pulled it, pushed it, turned and twisted it left and right, forward and backward, all to no avail. Watching Hollywood movies and reading American history hadn't prepared me for this. By the time I came to this realization, I was dirtier than when I started, and all but craved the rustic water bucket. I rinsed my body and got out.

I switched on the radio next to the bed. "And now it's time for an American classic, Gershwin's *Rhapsody in Blue,*" the voice said.

I sat down on the bed. I couldn't call for help. The cute receptionist in hot pants at the front desk would think, *He came in wearing a suit, looked so sophisticated. He doesn't know how to use a bathtub!*

I went back to the bathtub and tried again. In went my hands and fingers, waddling through the slimy pond. No results.

The grime of the past is not washing away. It's clinging to me.

But this last thought was a fleeting one. I was too young to have accumulated so much grime, I told myself. Besides, one shouldn't look for a metaphor in everything.

As I washed up in the sink, I recalled my mother's hands holding mine. Though she made delicate embroidery after she got married, years of chopping, collecting, and carrying sugarcane leaves for cow fodder in early life had hardened her palms, knuckles, and fingers.

"Sookwaar hands," she said, pressing the flesh on my soft hands. "You're all books, Vishnu. You've never worked with your hands. Papa made sure of that."

I smiled.

Mama continued. "You should get used to some manual work; you never know what life may bring you."

Papa countered, "I don't want Vishnu to be a drone like

the rest of us. The Bhushans have endured the drudgery of manual labor long enough."

Mama sighed, "Vishnu, you must have been a Brahman or a maharaja in your last life."

Sookwaar, a Hindi word that means delicate and carried among family and friends connotations of effortless well-being. Confronted with the memory of that word in the motel room, I wondered if coming to America was a smart move. I had left behind a generous French government scholarship that took me from a life in Mauritius that straddled the working class and the lower middle class to an upper-class lifestyle at the University of Madagascar. My dorm room, which overlooked a lake, was cleaned daily by a man whose wife did my laundry; he was glad for the extra income and wept when I gave him most of my clothes upon leaving. On the weekends, I dined at gourmet restaurants with names like Éléphant Rose and La Marmite Enchantée. I wanted the prestige and the challenge of an elite American school. But would I survive here?

Survive? That's not why I came to America. I came here to thrive!

I leafed through my five hundred dollars in American Express traveler's checks and wondered if that would last me until early September, when Yale University would give me my stipend. Staying at the motel even for one or two days and restaurant dining would eat into what I had saved from my French scholarship money in Madagascar. Second thoughts crept through my mind about appearing impolite or ill-bred to the Tuckers. I called them and explained the problem I'd had with the British immigration officer.

"We'll be there in an hour," Mrs. Madeline Tucker said, in a voice that sounded rather young.

I wondered if I should tell the receptionist about the clogged tub. I decided that silence is golden.

UPON MY ARRIVAL at the Tuckers' house in Farmington, Connecticut, Bill, the teenage son, showed me around the house. In the bathroom, I spotted what looked like a bath plug but could discern nothing detachable as on the English one. "This is a pop-up plug," Bill explained. "You move this handle on the tub up and down to open and close the drain." I ran the water and tested the mechanism. Twice. My American education had begun.

After dinner—barbecued chicken, corn on the cob, and mashed potatoes drowning in gravy, all bland to my taste buds, fluent in curries, French garlic, and Creole rougailles—we moved to the TV room. Mrs. Tucker, her hair in curlers, laid a huge basket of string beans at her husband John's feet and plopped down on a recliner. The daughter, Kate, a junior at Emory, joined Bill and me on the couch. While we watched Thomas More clash with Henry VIII over the latter's divorce from Catherine of Aragon, Mr. Tucker was stringing beans. I couldn't believe it.

My attention shifted to poor Mr. Tucker. He lifted his head and caught me staring at him. "I know what you're thinking, Vishnu. In your country, this is women's work, and you're feeling sorry for me," he said with a smile.

"Oh, no! You're more dexterous than my mother at it, and Mama is regarded as the best in the Bhushan clan," I said.

Mrs. Tucker got up and stretched her arms towards the ceiling. "You have a way with words, Vishnu. It must be that British education you got on your island," she said, and went to the kitchen. She returned with a bucket of okra, which she put at Mr. Tucker's feet. "Our friends from Tennessee ship these to us, and John cuts them before we freeze them."

Mr. Tucker looked at me with benevolent eyes. "General Electric sends me to India and Africa regularly, and I know that men there don't string beans. You don't have to worry. We won't ask you to do kitchen work."

I looked at my sookwaar hands and remembered Mama's words about getting used to manual labor.

On Saturday, the Tuckers took me to a football game. Having gone to Wembley for a soccer game during my week in England, I found the Hartford stadium rather small, and the game dull. The constant movement of the soccer players dribbling and kicking the ball had been energizing; here, the football players stopped playing every now and then and gathered in a circle, where they appeared to whisper to one another before they resumed. Soccer improvisation was more exciting than the American huddle. At halftime, the crowd got excited over the beauty pageant. The guy sitting on the bench in front of me got up and turned, beer can in hand, half his shirt hanging over his jeans.

"Where are you from? India or Pakistan?" he said.

"Neither. I'm from Mauritius."

"Mo . . . Mori . . . Where is that?"

"It's an island in the Indian Ocean."

"So it's part of India."

"No, it is off the coast of South Africa, twenty-five hundred miles from Cape Town."

"Africa," he said and paused for a moment. He gulped down some beer. "What kind of government do you have there? Tribal government?"

His questions disconcerted me. *What do they teach about Africa in schools?* I asked myself. I remained calm and replied, "It's a Parliamentary democracy, based on the British system. You have a president, we have a prime minister."

The man took a bewildered swig. He squinted his eyes, strained to formulate a question, failed, and took his seat.

The crowd cheered as another beauty contestant flaunted her assets on the field.

Bill nudged my elbow. "Next time say you're from India. Mauritius is way too complicated. Too many syllables; people like him can't handle it."

Mrs. Tucker's face was red. "This man is ignorant. Let's move to another seat," she said.

Mrs. Tucker had barely got up when the man was back on his feet, this time with a fully formed question. "Who civilized your people?"

I sprang up and faced him. For the first time in my life, I felt my national honor at stake. The honor of a nation only three years old, but my nation nonetheless. In my Oxbridge A-level high school course, two years earlier, I had written a paper on the difference between the words *civilization* and *culture,* and I still remembered the OED definition of *civilization.* I summoned up my courage.

"Do you know the meaning of the word *civilize*?" I asked him.

He was taken aback. He didn't reply.

"English is your mother tongue, isn't it?"

His face was blank.

I looked him straight in the eye. "Civilize: bring out of barbarism, enlighten, refine. While your ancestors were barbarians living in caves, my ancestors were building cities. We had a written language; we were producing literature."

Two guys sitting next to him forced him down to his seat. His beer can fell from his hands and rattled down the rows.

I looked around. The white people were red with embarrassment, the Tuckers being the reddest. The Black Americans smiled. A young man with a huge Afro hairdo raised his hand in a Black Panther salute and said, "Right on, brother."

The crowd cheered as the loudspeaker blared the name of Miss Hartford 1971.

OVER THE NEXT two weeks, before they drove me to the Yale University campus, the Tuckers exposed me to the whole gamut of American culture and way of life, from what they called lowbrow to highbrow. Lowbrow: lunch at Kentucky Fried Chicken and a visit to the local police station, where the sheriff showed me the short-term detention center where they lock people up for one or two nights before they are arraigned in court. Middlebrow: miniature golf followed by a tour of Mark Twain's folly of a house in Hartford, which drove him to near bankruptcy. High-brow: a visit to the Mystic Seaport residence of a classical music radio announcer who was probably in his sixties or seventies. "You'll see some Andrew Wyeth paintings at his home," Mrs. Tucker told me before we left. I remembered seeing a photo of Wyeth's *Christina's World* at the American Cultural Center in Madagascar.

Standing by a piano in his white linen suit and white wing-tip shoes, with Wyeth art on the walls behind him, the radio announcer was an aesthete who could have walked right out of Oscar Wilde's writings. He played two rare records of Caruso—first time I heard of him—and delighted the Tuckers with stories of the tenor's live performances. Unfortunately for me, the conversation was not about books, and they used a lexicon alien to me. They talked about arias, cadenzas, coloratura—words I had never heard or even read.

I was relieved when we moved to the veranda, which overlooked the sea. The old fishing schooners, the rigged ships, and the smaller boats made me nostalgic for Mahébourg, my hometown by the beach. I thought of my parents, relatives, and friends and the fishermen who were my neighbors. I pictured them going about their daily activities.

A uniformed butler served us a lobster lunch as a warm breeze blew over the veranda.

"You've been very quiet, young man," the announcer said to me as the butler walked back to the kitchen. "Are you familiar with American music?"

"Quite! I love Elvis Presley. Also, two years ago the American embassy arranged a performance by Buddy Guy on the beach, not far from our house."

"Elvis will be forgotten by the time you're my age," he said. He raised his head and scanned the vessels on the water. "Buddy Guy—he's a brilliant blues guitarist who'll stand the test of time."

He got up, went inside, and called the butler. "Play it loud so we can hear in the veranda," he said.

When he came back to the veranda, he sat next to me. "You're going to hear George Gershwin's *Rhapsody in Blue,* a concerto that combines classical piano with jazz. It has ragtime and Charleston jazz rhythms."

I didn't tell him that I was a complete ignoramus when it came to concertos, ragtime, and Charleston jazz.

"Listen to the opening clarinet glissando."

Another word I had never heard. I thought of the French word *glisser,* meaning to slide, to glide along. "The music glides," I said.

The aesthete's face brightened. "You've got it, young man! It glides. Listen till the very end and you'll know why *Rhapsody in Blue* is a kaleidoscope of America, a musical reflection of our melting pot."

He patted me on the shoulder and returned to his seat.

I tackled my lobster with gusto. From the corner of my eye, I caught the butler's smile of approval as he served a second helping of bread roll.

WHEN I ARRIVED at Yale University in September 1971, I had to report to the financial aid officer, who would inform me what job I had to do as part of my work-study aid package.

"Take this form to the manager of the Commons dining room. You'll be working there."

The manager was a huge man whose stentorian voice intimidated me as he issued commands left and right. His girth didn't impede his movements. He was a nimble, Black

American version of President Taft, down to the three-piece suit and pocket watch. I must say I was impressed and pleased by the sight of a Black man giving orders to white people. A month earlier in London, I had seen for the first time white men driving buses and taxis, digging soil and fixing rooftops, and how weird it felt—you wouldn't see whites in Mauritius doing these jobs.

"Let me show you around the kitchen so you get an idea of what's involved," the manager said. For the next fifteen minutes, he showed me giant freezers, meat mincers, meat slicers, bone-sawing machines, baking ovens, chopping blocks, fryers, and the assembly line for washing dishes, among other contrivances. They all seemed to be spewing steam or some kind of vapor. At the end of the tour, the various pieces of equipment were all jumbled up in my mind, pieces of shiny metal indistinguishable one from the other. The closest thing to this kitchen that I had seen back home was a sugar mill. This was an industrial operation, with noises and smells to kill one's appetite. The sight of the heavy sweat dripping from those manning the machines was another antidote to a good appetite. No aromas of Mama's kitchen here!

At home, the stove was just a few bricks arranged in such a way that my mother could insert some dry wood logs, which she would light with a match and blow with the pookni. I never used that rudimentary stove, but I stood next to it whenever I smelled that Mama's rotis and parathas were ready, so I could have a taste before dinner.

"Can you be here tomorrow morning?" the manager asked.

"What would I be doing?"

"We'll start you off on the dishwashing line."

I had been hoping for a clerical job, where my hands wouldn't get dirty. My sookwaar hands.

"Would you have a vacancy for a cashier, sir?" I asked.

"You're a healthy, able-bodied young man; you don't need a desk job," the manager said. "I take it you'll be here tomorrow at 6 a.m."

I nodded. A nod that could mean either yes or no.

On my way to Main Street to buy some discounted clothes at the Army-Navy store, I thought, *I must find another job.*

But the university was giving me a scholarship, and the job was to supplement my stipend. I knew I should be grateful to them and not sound like Oliver Twist asking for more. Yale owed me nothing: I wasn't American; I was an unknown student from an unknown country whom they selected over hundreds of deserving students from Asia, Africa, and so many poor nations. Nonetheless, it was hard to digest the thought, the notion of doing manual work. The whole purpose of my seeking a university education was to avoid the backbreaking work that my ancestors from India and my parents had to endure in the sugarcane plantations. Laborers toiled in the fields hoping to save enough for their children to get an education that would secure them an office job. Papa always said, "Better be a maharaja than his valet!"

I spent the evening not on the books and articles assigned for next day's classes but on developing a strategy. The Tuckers had told me about gurus from India who milked gullible young Americans with yoga and diluted Eastern mysticism. The son, Bill, showed me posters of a pear-shaped Indian teenager addressing college crowds and he advised me, surely in jest, to consider being a yogi as a part-time occupation. "You are way more handsome than this guy," he said. "The girls will flock to you."

As I sat on the dorm bed, I cursed myself for not having listened to my father. He'd tried to initiate me to yoga, but I was recalcitrant to any form of physical exertion. As for yoga's spiritual discipline, my atheism couldn't stomach it, and Papa, caring more about my grades than my religious devotion, didn't insist. Now, in New Haven, there was no way I could master the various physical forms of yoga in a week or two.

"The philosophical wisdom is what Americans hunger for," Bill had said. "The contortions, that's not for everyone. It's the spiritual message that Americans want to hear."

I could fake the spiritual part: I knew by heart the Vedic hymns sung at home and at weddings and funerals, and my knowledge of the Hindu Scriptures was relatively extensive. Before we left for the airport, my father had given me *Saints and Sages,* a book by his spiritual master in India, Swami Sivananda, whom he had never met but with whom he corresponded. That day, Papa also gifted me vibhuti. "Sent by the swami from his ashram in Rishikesh, at the foothills of the Himalayas," Papa said proudly. I could apply that sacred ash on my forehead in the manner of the Indian gurus! Better still, I knew how to differentiate myself: the Indian gurus in America based their message on the god Vishnu and his avatar Krishna; I would ground mine on the all-encompassing god Shiva, the Supreme Yogi, the Lord of the Dance of Creation, the destroyer of demons, the god who is half woman, the god worshipped by Vishnu and the other gods. I would disabuse Americans of the notion that Shiva was only the god of destruction. While the other gurus would be singing "Hare Rama, Hare Krishna," I would chant the mantra "Om Namah Shivaya."

That was my niche!

I'd teach the Americans the joys of massaging the feet of the great Swami Vishnu Bhushan!

The yogi-guru fantasy ended when I realized that I wouldn't be able to sustain the untruth for long. Papa and Mama were hovering over my shoulders, unseen but watchful, and their soundless voices would prick my conscience. Sooner or later, I was afraid, the truth would spill out of my guts.

I also had to face the fact that I didn't sound like an Indian. I looked like one, but I didn't have an Indian accent, not even a British one. In the four weeks I had been in the United States, not a single person had recognized it. In Mauritius, I spoke to my classmates in Kreol, read the daily newspapers and counted in French, studied chemistry and history in English, and greeted grandfathers and grandmothers in the countryside in faltering Bhojpuri. After all, my ancestors had left India more than a century ago.

There was no way out of this predicament. I reviewed all that I had seen and heard since I landed in America. I delved into the American psyche, more specifically the American psyche on campus. Protests against the Vietnam War were raging throughout the country, and Yale was regarded as a left-wing, virtually pinko school. More than a few white Americans were feeling guilty not only about the war but also about the way they treated other cultures. The previous year, Yale welcomed a huge rally supporting

Black Panther leader Bobby Seale, jailed on suspicion of murder; Yale president Kingman Brewster Jr. said he didn't believe Black revolutionaries could get a fair trial anywhere in America. At a New Haven café I overheard undergraduates wondering why Yale didn't have what its smaller rival nearby, Wesleyan University, offered: a Malcolm X House, courses on American Indian music, and a highly-rated classical Indian music program, with some of the top exponents of the art hailing from India. Clearly, sensitivity to other, diverse cultures was important.

The next morning, I was at the financial aid office. After thanking the financial aid officer profusely for giving me the "opportunity of a lifetime," I told her that it would be very difficult for me to perform the tasks the dining room manager had in mind for me.

"You see, madam, I've never done kitchen work before. My parents didn't want me to."

"Oh! Why?"

"Well, in our culture men don't wash dishes."

She turned red but didn't say anything.

"I've never seen my father wash a glass. He didn't even take the dishes to the kitchen. My mother wouldn't let him."

Mystified, she asked me a question I thought I had already addressed. "Your mother never asked you to help in the kitchen?" she said.

"Never, madam. The first time I boiled water, it was in the school chemistry lab."

She shifted in her chair. "We haven't had a case like this before," she said.

"You know, I can help professors in the French department grade student papers. I've looked at the textbooks for sophomores and juniors; they are elementary, the kind of material we read in primary school at home. Even the model GRE exams in French don't look that difficult."

I paused to let the information sink in.

"I just completed a year of law at the French university in Madagascar. I came in first in the exams. I also taught French literature to third-year students in secondary school for a year."

I handed her a photocopy of the first-year syllabus at the Université Charles de Gaulle, a translation, and the letter from the dean congratulating me on my results.

She pored over the syllabus and read some parts of the translation aloud.

"Vishnu, let me check with the French department. I'll give you a call in the next two days."

On my way back to the dorm, in Memorial Quadrangle, I ran into Janet Peters, a fellow student I had met on my first day on campus. She was from New York City, taller than me, and she worshipped Gloria Steinem. I told Janet about my conversation with the financial aid officer, in a tone that reflected the matter-of-fact nature of the episode for me. She had a grin of a smile.

"You know what we call this in New York City? Chutzpah!" she said.

She bent her neck, moved her face closer, looked into my eyes, and licked her lips, à la Lolita.

The smile evaporated. "Good-bye," Janet said.

Two days later, as I was grabbing my books for class, the resident adviser knocked on my door and asked me to pick up the dorm phone at the end of the hallway.

"Vishnu, Professor Norman Ghita, who's blind, needs

a reader. Call his office to arrange for an interview," the financial aid officer said.

For the next two years, until my graduation, I got paid for reading the philosophers of the French Enlightenment, the lascivious but thought-provoking works of the Marquis de Sade, and, occasionally, some student papers written in French.

I worked at the professor's home, sometimes late into the evening, for twenty to thirty hours a week. Watching Professor Ghita operate his bulky braille typewriter was a revelation. His fingers moved across the keys and pressed on the carriage return lever and the space bar like a pianist or an organist at his instrument. When I told him I'd never even heard of such a machine, he asked me to draw near, took my hand, and ran it over the raised braille dots impressed into the paper.

His constant reworking of the same sentence was my first brush with serious writing. "Clarity, Vishnu, clarity above all is what we should seek," he said when I told him I didn't see much difference between the fourth and fifth versions. One evening, he came back from a much anticipated lecture by the visiting Jürgen Habermas and looked unhappy. "Why can't these German philosophers speak clearly?" he said. He asked me to pull Diderot's *Jacques le Fataliste* from the bookshelf. I read the first paragraph aloud until he interrupted me. "Maybe it's because of his cleft palate. I shouldn't be so harsh." Four decades later, I've forgotten Jacques's picaresque journey and amorous adventures, but I can still evoke the first sentence of the blind professor's introduction to that work, so often had he revised it: "Qui est donc ce philosophe qui a osé mettre au centre de son roman l'histoire infernale de Mme. de la Pommeraye et le Marquis des Arcis, histoire d'une vengeance aussi raffinée que machiavélique."

The job came with an unexpected bonus. Professor Ghita, a Romanian Jew with a Princeton education, whose parents fled from the Nazis, a proud Marxist who enjoyed close friendships with the French leftist intelligentsia, introduced me to the finest of French wines.

He started with a Pouilly-Fumé. Three or four weeks later, he poured a Pouilly-Fuissé.

"Do you like this one better than what you had last time?" he said at the end of the dinner, as his wife put a record on the turntable.

"They both taste good," I said.

"You mean you don't taste any difference?"

"They are both Pouilly. I suspect the Pouilly-Fumé smells or tastes like tobacco," I said.

Professor Ghita smiled and gave me his hand. As I walked him down the steps to the basement where I read to him, he said, "Pouilly-Fumé is from sauvignon blanc grapes, grown in the Loire, Pouilly-Fuissé from chardonnay grapes in Burgundy. Different terroirs, different grapes, hence different aromas, different tastes. *Fumé* means flinty aromas, a smoky bouquet. C'est un vin sec et parfumé. Le Pouilly-Fuissé est un vin minéral, puissant et structuré. We'll have to expand your wine vocabulary and refine your palate. Next time, we'll do a Sancerre, a sauvignon with more depth and texture."

He had me over for lunch or dinner every month. The university was paying me the minimum wage, $1.60 per hour. The pleasure and thrill of tasting new wines and

eating homemade French food, on top of the intellectual stimulation of the work, kept me from looking for a
higher-paying job.

For my first New Year's Eve in America, the professor and his wife invited me to dinner. Their son Ira was
back home from Stanford, where he was a sophomore. Two
friends of the family, a professor in the music department
and his lover, joined us.

"A Saint-Émilion to accompany the steak," Professor
Ghita said as he uncorked the bottle of wine.

After the glasses were full, the music professor took the
bottle in his hand, read the label, and turned to me. "Not
any Saint-Émilion. A grand cru, Vishnu. Among the best,"
he said.

That day, away from home, I missed my parents and
Cousin Shankar. I thought of Kalipa and Fringant, and
how on New Year's Day the rum would be flowing in their
home and in the neighborhood. The sadness, however, was
accompanied by the joy of being with Professor Ghita and
his wife in their warm dining room, watching the blanket
of snow outside. I knew how lucky I was to be Professor
Ghita's reader.

When I left the professor's home, he said, "Next New
Year's Eve, we'll celebrate with a premier cru. The very
best."

AS THE SUMMER of 1972 approached, students with
connections trumpeted the summer jobs they had landed
in investment banking. "Morgan Guaranty Trust, 23 Wall
Street," said one. These students had been extolling the

virtues of a simple hippie life during the academic year—with some flowers in their hair, anti-war T-shirts, and unwashed jeans—while keeping a well-stocked refrigerator in their dorm room and a fancy car on campus. The less fortunate ones would be selling ice cream at Dairy Queen or flipping burgers or touting the benefits of various lawn mowers to clients in suburbia.

Most of the professors planned to spend the summer out of town. Professor Ghita would be in Paris. With apprehension, I looked again at my soft hands. I heard Mama's admonition pitted against Papa's warning about drones being exploited by the upper class. Unwilling to be a drone, I searched all the notice boards on campus, even in those departments where I had never set foot. I combed the hallways and the library, foraged and ferreted out information on summer jobs. When I told my residence hall mates about my application to a summer program combining morning political science classes at a university in Washington, D.C., with a congressional internship in the afternoon, they were supportive but skeptical about my chances of success.

"You've been in this country a little less than a year. The program staff will wonder how you can assist a congressman in his work."

"You're not a U.S. citizen and don't have a green card. That could be a problem."

A few were unkind. "You should try manual work. You're being pretentious, elitist, just wanting to use your brain." Hearing children of the elite scoff at elitist dreams was the height of dramatic irony. That made me more resolute.

A few years earlier, in secondary school, one of my

teachers, Georgie Espitalier-Noël, speaking of his student days at Oxford, had mentioned an American student who in his written examinations purposely slipped in a reference to an American poet little known in Britain. At the orals, the Oxford don, who had never heard of the latter, fell in the student's trap and asked about the poet. The American expounded at length on the subject, and earned a first-class honours. I learnt from Georgie's anecdote. As part of the summer program application, I submitted a comparative analysis of the newly drafted Mauritian and Madagascar constitutions—totally unfamiliar territory to American academics at the time.

The university in Washington admitted me with a full scholarship.

MY ROOMMATE IN the Washington summer program, Tim, was born and attended college in Tallahassee, Florida. White, clean-cut, well-shaven, he wore a seersucker suit to class and addressed people as "sir" or "ma'am," a far cry from my long-haired Yale classmates, many of whom, to my initial consternation, addressed the dean and professors by first name. A well-bred man by Mauritian standards. I let him select which part of the wardrobe he hung his suits in; he had no problem with my having chosen the bed overlooking the lawn. During the second week, after we had settled one evening, Tim on the couch and me on the desk chair, he asked if I had taken any American history courses at Yale.

"No, I'm focusing on economics. No cocktail party education for me. I need a well-paying job when I graduate."

"But surely you know some American history to have gotten into this program," Tim said.

"My secondary school textbook had a chapter on the American Revolution; one on Lincoln, slavery, and the Civil War; and one on FDR and the New Deal. In Mauritius, I learnt a lot from the radio and newspapers. Stuff about the Ku Klux Klan, Martin Luther King, the Black Panthers, and Vietnam."

Tim wasn't impressed. So I added, "Last semester, one of my courses examined the Cold War and McCarthyism."

"What do you think of McCarthyism?"

"The Ku Klux Klan lynched Blacks to death. McCarthyism lynched people's reputations to death," I said.

"That's what they teach you at fancy East Coast colleges and in British textbooks. America needed Senator Joe McCarthy to weed out the Commies from our government."

He rose from the couch and walked towards me. "You mentioned Martin Luther King and the KKK. In the South, the genesis of the Klan is fresh in our memory. Do you know what happened at the end of the Civil War? Blacks were running amok, and we had to protect our women."

"Is that the Confederate chronicle of history?" I asked.

"Look, Vishnu, where I come from, the Civil War is still alive. I go to bed sometimes thinking of Sherman's march through Georgia. You have no idea how barbaric he was, ordering his troops to set Atlanta on fire."

"More than a hundred years have gone by and Sherman's still gnawing your entrails?"

An uneasy silence descended in the room.

Tim walked away and pulled some books out of his satchel. "I have a lot of reading for tomorrow," he said.

Then I surprised myself. "Tim, how would you feel if your sister dated a Black man?"

I didn't know whether he had a sister.

"She's free to do what she wants, but I won't like it," he said.

"How would you feel if your sister dated a man like me?"

He took a deep breath, the kind the doctor asks you to take during the annual physical. It didn't help. As soon as he exhaled, he convulsed with a nervous cough, which lasted for a few seconds. He mumbled some words I couldn't grasp.

That night, almost a year after my arrival in the country, I went to bed asking myself if there was more than one America. Tim's America of racial anxiety felt so different from the America on the Yale campus. Was there an America of the Northeast and one of the South?

We were a week into the program when we heard that burglars had broken into the Democratic Party Headquarters in the Watergate building. Not long after, cash found on the burglars was linked to a slush fund to reelect the president. Most of my classmates thought the break-in had been staged by the Democratic Party to discredit the Nixon administration. When I compared the incident to the Teapot Dome scandal, the professor said, "We have a Ph.D. in American History here." My classmates reacted to the sarcasm with smiles and laughter. The tenor of the class discussions and lectures was clear: the program had a conservative political agenda. At the end of the second week, I decided to spend less time in class and more time as an intern. The Tuckers had written letters on my behalf, and a senator had agreed to take me on, for no pay. The senator's aides were only too happy to have free labor.

At a get-acquainted party for interns at Hawk n' Dove, on Capitol Hill, I spotted a redhead sipping what looked like orange juice. Everyone else, or so it seemed from the boisterous chitchat, had imbibed more than a few beers. I found it odd that an attractive woman like her was standing alone. I looked at her name tag.

"Hi, Nancy, who are you interning for?"

She told me the name of a congressman from Nebraska.

"I must confess that's a part of the U.S. I know nothing about. What is it famous for?"

"Beef, pork, and corn," she said.

"Beef, pork, and corn," I repeated after her. "Beef, pork, and corn. You make it sound so musical."

Maybe I'd had one drink too many when I made that comment, or maybe that was my way of being flirtatious, but it captured her attention. She laughed. I laughed.

She peered at my name tag.

"Vishnu. That's an Indian god, but you don't have an Indian accent. Where are you from?"

I was in a playful mood.

"Why not take a guess?"

"India or Sri Lanka."

"No."

"Nepal."

"No."

"England, then."

By that time, Nancy and I had moved very close to each other.

"Mauritius," I said.

"You're making that up!"

I put my arm around her waist. She backed away.

"You're fast," she said. Her voice expressed surprise, not criticism or anger.

"Do you always drink orange juice?" I said.

"I don't trust what they serve here. This is such a dive bar."

"What else do you drink?" I said.

"In my Aix-en-Provence semester, my host family introduced me to wines. I'm still a novice, though."

"Would you like to go to a French restaurant with me?"

"I can't tonight."

"This weekend?"

As I walked out with Nancy, I saw Tim. It was hard to figure out the look on his face. I wasn't sure if he was distressed for the woman or stunned. He must have watched our guessing game.

It had been more than a year since my last gourmet meal—at La Marmite Enchantée in Madagascar. In America I had relearnt my frugal Mauritian habits. My scholarship and minimum-wage campus job confined my culinary experiences to cafeteria food and pizza, except for the fine wines savored monthly at Professor Ghita's home.

Nancy Hansen and I deserved a gourmet meal.

Around that time, the most-written-about French restaurant in D.C. was Sans Souci. Kissinger was an habitué, and JFK and Lyndon Johnson had eaten there. The waiting list for reservations was long.

"Pourrais-je parler à Monsieur Bernic Gorland, s'il vous plaît?" I said on the phone.

A woman replied that the owner was away.

"Dans ce cas, Monsieur Paul DeLisle s'il vous plaît," I said.

The famed maitre d' was also absent.

I switched to English. "I'm thinking of making a reservation, but I first want to ascertain if you serve a particular wine."

"We have a fine selection, sir."

The names of some vintage wines Professor Ghita had mentioned to me came in handy.

"Do you have Romanée-Conti?" I asked.

"I'll have to check with the sommelier, sir."

"Could you please also ask him if he has Petrus."

She came back a few minutes later. Her tone was different, softer, eager to please. "We'll try to accommodate your tastes as best we can, monsieur. When would you like to come?"

That Saturday, Nancy picked me up on campus. She drove a white Chevy Impala and wore a sleeveless two-tone dress, navy blue and white.

"Where are we going?" she said as I got in.

"Sans Souci, near the White House."

"Is that a joke?"

I shook my head.

"You're serious? How did you manage that? My congressman couldn't get a reservation until next week."

"His staff didn't do proper research," I said.

Sans Souci did not disappoint. The Maharajah-of-Baroda impersonator from Mahébourg would have felt at home. The gold-and-green decor and the airy layout were impressive, the clientele elegant. Nancy's eyes said wow. The warm ambience and the glow on her face kindled my hopes for an evening of romance.

I didn't expect the dinner to be inexpensive, but I had a plan. Go for dessert and coffee in Dupont Circle, where prices were more reasonable. At Sans Souci, I wouldn't let the sommelier pressure me; I believed I knew enough about wine to order a cheaper but equally gratifying alternative to the fancier ones.

As soon as the sommelier started extolling the virtues of his favorite wine, before I could say anything, Nancy spoke. "Let me see if you have any of the Bordeaux wines I tasted in Aix."

Good thing she's a novice, I thought as the sommelier handed her the wine list.

"Vishnu, you should get this Pauillac. I've had it and I love it. It has flavors of cassis, blackberry, and tobacco."

Of the three Pauillac wines, she picked the highest-priced one! It was not the most expensive on the list, but it cost enough for my heart to palpitate.

The sommelier wasted no time. He pounced. "Monsieur would be wise to go with that Pauillac. Madame loves it."

The wine was exquisite. I ordered the cheapest entrée on the menu.

We spoke about Nebraska, the spiraling Watergate scandal, and our personal likes and dislikes. But my palpitation wouldn't stop. My brain was busy calculating and recalculating the cost of the dinner as Nancy waxed eloquent on the wine every time she took a sip. On her second glass, she switched to French: "Un vin racé . . . un nez de fruits noirs mûrs . . . une belle déclinaison de notes de tabac et d'épices . . . une bouche généreuse . . ." A sophisticated wine-tasting vocabulary that a native French connoisseur would commend. The last phrase about "a generous mouth" took my eyes to her full lips; I fantasized a French kiss.

I was relieved when she said she wouldn't have dessert and coffee. "I like the aftertaste of the wine to linger in my mouth until bedtime."

The relief didn't last long. When the bill came, my head and shoulders sagged.

"Is anything wrong?" said Nancy.

"I have a bit of a problem here," I said, straightening my shoulders. "Do you mind paying the tip?"

Nancy was generous. Her tip was bigger than the prevailing standard of fifteen percent.

As we drove back, I was overwhelmed by feelings and thoughts that froze my post-dinner libidinous intentions. Asking a woman to pay, even for a minor share, was a hard humiliation to swallow. Worse was the realization of my stupidity, well beyond the acceptable folly of youth. In my desire to impress, I had lost all sense of proportion. The cash I had left was just enough to pay my Greyhound bus fare to New Haven via New York. What hubris!

I had to find money for my meals for the remaining month of my Washington summer. Having to eat spaghetti with ketchup for days in a row left me despondent.

As I lay my head on the pillow that evening, I wondered what my mother would say. "You can't escape the karmic law, Vishnu. You'll have to pay for your delusions of grandeur." Papa would be more teacherly. "There's always someone more knowledgeable than you. Nancy knew her wines but did not brag." Then he would toss in an English proverb. "A little learning is a dangerous thing, son."

My options were limited. The Tuckers were on holiday in the remote islands of Fiji. On my student visa, I could only work on campus. I tried the library. "We are halfway through the summer and all jobs are taken," said the head librarian.

When I first told my friend Janet at Yale of my summer plans, she had said that a family friend managed the university dining room and that I should call on her upon arrival in D.C. "She might ask you to join her family for coffee or maybe dinner." I hadn't done so.

Like a dog tucking its tail between its hind legs, I trekked to her office.

"You're Vishnu! Why didn't you call earlier?"

I had rehearsed my answer.

"It took me a while to get adjusted to the system here. Now I'm settled and more relaxed. Indeed, I have free time in the evenings and I wonder if you have something for me to do in the dining room."

She had the eyes of a benevolent yet shrewd aunt who could see through me and guess the real reason for my job request.

"We all need some extra cash sometimes," she said. "I have nothing in the dining room, but I could use you in the kitchen."

Had Janet shared with her the story of my chutzpah at Yale? The thought crossed my mind, but I dismissed it. During the past academic year, Janet and I had become good friends, arguing a lot but enjoying the banter. She had asked me to spend a few days with her family in New York on my way back to New Haven.

The kitchen in D.C. was an even bigger industrial operation than the one at Yale. Colossal vats of shiny steel. Mega freezers and mega ovens. The heat of molten metal. I was sweating before I had even touched any equipment, utensils, or plates.

Cold looks greeted me when the manager introduced me to the staff on Monday, and they all returned to their tasks. *No time for social chitchat here,* I thought.

I spent the first week washing dishes. One of my co-workers looked like an aging version of Pelé. Like the Brazilian soccer star, he danced his way in and out of the kitchen, as if he was always dribbling and passing a ball, enjoying life.

"I can see this is new to you," he said, taking a plate from my hand. "Before you put it on the line, you must swipe the heavy food into the garbage. Otherwise there's blockage somewhere."

I looked at his hands as he disposed of the food remnants. They were strong, veiny, muscular. So unlike my sookwaar hands.

"So much food wasted in America," he said.

He had a French accent.

"Are you from Senegal or Côte d'Ivoire?" I asked, naming the most prominent French colonies that had recently attained independence.

"No, Zaire, the former Belgian Congo."

My next question was prompted by his graying hair.

"Are you a doctoral student?"

"I'm a dentist. I'm preparing license exam."

"Can't you work with a dental practice until you get the license?"

"The American Dental Association don't allow. I graduated dentistry from Bruxelles and practiced five years at Kinshasa, but they require American dentistry exams. I must first take TOEFL course to improve my English."

"Why work here?"

He shook his head. "Student visa. Must follow the rules. I don't want deportation to Mobutu's dictatorship. Besides, I don't mind this; in Bruxelles I cleaned toilets to pay my studies."

"Your name?"

"Patrice."

"Like Lumumba?"

"You know Patrice Lumumba?"

Patrice's face changed. It was a grave look. I didn't know whether to continue the conversation or not.

I took a risk. "Didn't Mobutu and the CIA murder him?"

Patrice slapped me hard on my shoulder blade. His face shone. "I think we are on the same wavelength," he said. "And we'll speak French."

I knew that from that moment on, he'd be my friend in the kitchen.

Our job was simple. Mop the floor at the start of the evening shift. Swipe off the sticky and heavy food remnants, put the plates on the line. Repeat that a thousand times, maybe more, maybe less. Mop the floor before we leave. I needed no special skill, but handling so much left-over food that resembled giant rheums and snot made me nauseous.

"Well done," Patrice said as we bade each other good-bye that night.

I was about to step out when I had a thought.

"Patrice, why don't you ask the dean of the dental school for academic credit and exam waivers? Yale gave me a year's credit for my A-levels and a year for my study in Madagascar. I'll be a senior next year."

Patrice looked skeptical.

"In America, everything is negotiable. Students here are not like at home; they knock on their professors' doors and try to negotiate their grades."

After I left the kitchen area, I sensed a strange odor around me. I sniffed my clothes, drenched in perspiration: they stank. I sniffed my hands: they exhaled the odor of fermentation.

In the dorm, I headed straight to the shower. Tim wasn't in.

In the morning, my calves hurt as I stood up to shave. I remembered that I had spent the evening on my feet.

At work the next evening, Patrice was somber.

"The dean said it's not a matter for the university; he can't do anything about the requirements of the American Dental Association; they are inflexible."

"Well, at least you tried," I said.

I told him about my aches and pains. Patrice advised

me to leave my dress shoes in my closet and buy special working or basketball shoes if I planned to continue in the kitchen for some time. He spoke more as a doctor than a dentist: "This isn't interning in the Congress. With dress shoes, the problems will develop—aching muscles, corns, bunions, ankle pain, varicose veins, back pain."

I couldn't afford shoes, not even secondhand ones.

The third evening, Tim was lounging on the couch when I returned to the dorm from work. He wrinkled his nose. I couldn't blame him; I wasn't emitting perfume.

The tedium continued unabated for a whole week, every evening from 6 p.m. till 10 p.m., when the university dining room closed. The only breaks in the routine occurred when the other kitchen staff—the cooks and those handling the massive equipment—walked by, sweaty from the infernal heat. They ignored me but always greeted Patrice. I asked him why. "They think you're uncomfortable working here, so you must be from rich family. A snob. They'll change when they know you better."

On Friday, my Congolese friend brought me what he called a countryside specialty, goat stew and cassava cooked in banana leaves, and asked me to join him and his friends the next evening. We would meet at the basement apartment where he was housesitting in Adams Morgan, a neighborhood not yet gentrified and at the time bordering on the seedy.

On Saturday, I woke up at two in the afternoon. The alarm clock, set for 9 a.m., had rung for so long that it drove Tim to switch it off. He shook me up, but I fell back to sleep. I was physically drained, and stayed in my room.

I read *The Federalist Papers* in preparation for the following week's test but was unable to concentrate. I longed for my weekends in Madagascar, weekends of leisurely ice cream at Blanche Neige and entraîneuses at the nightclub.

When the glow of sunset on the horizon loomed over my window, I decided to go to Patrice's. It was not just the incandescence and warmth of the sunset that changed my mood. I thought of Patrice—cleaning toilets to become a dentist, escaping death in his native land at the hands of Mobutu's henchmen, and still so resilient that he sambaed his way into the kitchen every day. He lived by my mother's words: "You should get used to some manual work; you never know what life may bring you."

Before I walked out the door, I aimed the cologne at my chest, for a double spray to eliminate the kitchen emanations, vestiges of smells that remained despite taking the shower. When I put down the bottle, I noticed changes in my hands: some fingers were scaly from dryness, others had scars. There were lumps on my palm. Would they grow into calluses like my father's or into boils?

The kitchen crew was at Patrice's. Aware of their indifference to me, he introduced everyone. They were all on scholarship. The foreigners were older and were in D.C. to polish their English language skills before starting graduate school in the fall. In the kitchen, Liu Wang, a Taiwanese woman, seemed to specialize in plants used for seasoning. Whenever I turned my neck to the cooking section, she was carrying bunches of different herbs: mint, thyme, rosemary, and others I couldn't identify. Francisco, from El Salvador, worked with the most mechanized components of the culinary enterprise, equipment too heavy to be moved. "I know how to use these fuckers, and I fix them when they break," he said proudly.

Red-haired James, from a mining family in Appalachia, was the meat man. He grilled the steak served on "special treat" days and flipped beef burgers. He puffed up his shirtless white chest and smiled when the others called him "redneck," but he was diffident about his studies. Patrice told me he was in some remedial program that would help him cope with college in the fall. The other American was a Navajo Indian, Sam Bitsui. He had won a scholarship to Dartmouth, in New Hampshire, and was in D.C. to complete a course in calculus that wasn't offered at the high school on his reservation.

"You know a lot about us," said Sam. "What's the deal with you? What brought you to our kitchen halfway through the semester?"

"I blew my entire savings on a single dinner, just to impress an American girl."

Sam wasn't gentle. "That's what happens when you try to ape the white man."

"The rich white man," said James.

"Vishnu, you have big hole in your pocket to fix," Francisco said. "You can't make it washing dishes only. I got some shifts at a fancy restaurant in town; you can replace me at the university kitchen."

"I'll give it a try," I said, and we toasted our agreement with Patrice's Algerian wine. "Seventy-five cents a bottle. That's what the French mixed with their lower-grade Bordeaux and sold as table wine in the colonial days," Patrice had said earlier. It was heady. Not long after, the pots and pans in the apartment mutated into musical instruments. James had barely finished singing "Take Me Home, Country Roads" when everyone clamored for me to sing a Mauritian song. I did my best to emulate Kalipa and Fringant with "Lotte côté montagne chamarel." Patrice tried to understand it.

"Sounds like Haitian Creole," he said. "A somewhat archaic French."

My memory of that alcohol-soaked summer night has gotten hazy, and the only other song that comes to mind is Francisco slurring over Santana's "Oye Como Va."

On Monday evening, after my dishwashing shift, Francisco initiated me to the intricacies of his machines.

"Every piece of equipment here carries a WARNING label," he said. "That means be careful, otherwise you lose fingers or an arm."

He showed me a giant slicer with a sharp blade spinning around. "Blades have to be washed and wiped," he said as he stopped the spinning movement. He then pointed to the prongs holding the machine in place. Then on to the food grinder, which turned regular slabs of meat into hamburger meat. "Turn you into ground meat if you're not careful," Francisco warned. He took out of his wallet a laminated photo of the man who taught him how to operate the equipment: he had one finger missing. Francisco extracted from the grinder what he called a "worm," a giant metallic corkscrew. I could imagine ground meat being produced by the worm spinning at high speeds, but I couldn't imagine myself inserting the worm in or taking it out of the machine without my fingers being chopped. The next piece of equipment, the food chopper, had a blade that spun at five hundred to a thousand revolutions per minute. By then, the fear of losing a finger or a hand prevailed and I decided to stick to the dirty dishes.

Three more weeks of steam, fumes, and food remnants, smelly clothes and painful calves. On evenings when I lifted fifty-pound boxes of meat from the freezer, my back hurt. My face looked oily day and night, with an unwanted sheen. My hands racked up calluses. Patrice and I got free dinner but often ate it standing, sometimes leaning over a garbage can. I had succeeded in avoiding the purgatory of kitchen work at Yale but ended up in hell on a D.C. campus.

Nonetheless, Patrice set a living example of Mama's admonition about working with one's hands. Life did take an unwelcome turn at Sans Souci, and I wasn't prepared for it. Washing dishes isn't what I want to do in life, but that summer it saved me from total, wretched penury. I thought of Uncle Mohan, who, after losing his job in the police force, had to turn to cutting sugarcane in the pitiless sun to feed his family. After working with Liu Wang, James, Francisco, Sam, and Patrice, I could fully grasp and respect manual labor.

As the day of my departure neared, I grew sad at the prospect of leaving them. Patrice's basement apartment had been the venue for more get-togethers where we unwound. The air-conditioning often broke down, but we didn't mind as long as the cheap Algerian wine flowed and the pots and pans provided the instrumental accompaniment to the melting-pot repertoire.

· · ·

AS THE GREYHOUND bus from Washington, D.C., chugged along the New Jersey Turnpike, the Manhattan skyline sprang up into view. The confident soaring of the Chrysler and Empire State buildings to the roof of the sky inspired awe. The tallest building in Mauritius in those days was five or six stories high. At the same time, it was with some dread that I approached the city. Though Janet Peters's brother, Edward, was waiting for me at the bus terminal, the image that rolled in my mind's eye was the Canadian from Alberta a year earlier, and his dire warnings on our flight from London.

The Greyhound Bus Terminal was massive. The odor of urine trapped in the building, overheated by the summer sun, the beer cans and scraps of hot dogs strewn on the floor, and the armed police eyeing everyone were not an invitation to a holiday. I thought of the bus stop back home, overlooking the sea, and the breeze wafting aromas of pastries and savories from the bazaar. There was never a need for police.

Maybe the Canadian was right about New York.

As Edward ushered me outside towards Penn Station, the oppressiveness of the terminal gave way to the dynamism of the street. It was dirty but throbbing with energy. The smell of burnt pretzels and buttery popcorn clashed with that of fried onions from a steak-and-cheese stall. Unruly taxis, all canary yellow, hurled to their destinations.

Our subway train was smeared with graffiti, outside and inside, some political ("Viva Che Guevara," "Get out of Vietnam"), many obscene or indecipherable, and one or two aspiring to art (a multicolored bird flying out of silvery fish). In half an hour we arrived at Stuyvesant Town, a complex of more than thirty high-rise buildings where Janet's parents lived. It was much quieter and cleaner than the Penn Station neighborhood. Lots of brick and concrete, but no trees. Children frolicking in a sandy playground. I made sure not to lose sight of Edward, as the buildings looked identical. People came in and out of their apartments, and I could glimpse into living rooms. Similar doors, similar beige color scheme. The sounds and smells, however, changed as Edward and I took turns carrying my suitcase from one end of the hallway to the other. Tomato-based aromas filling the air to the tune of "That's Amore" in the background were followed by the pungency of goat curry accompanying a reggae beat. A bald man on crutches lumbered out of a door, yelling obscenities at the woman inside. We entered the apartment that was two doors down.

Janet's dad, wearing a yarmulke, read the newspaper while his wife cooked. At dinner, I asked if Jews always served bagels at breakfast, as my D.C. roommate Tim had said. I didn't get an answer. Instead, everyone offered me an alternative history of the bagel. The mother claimed it was brought to America by Polish Jews, Janet said it came from Russia and originally had a wider hole, and the father averred that the most delicious bagels hailed from Lithuania. Edward had no opinion on bagels. "That's our family. Everyone must have a different point of view."

Halfway through dinner, Janet's dad asked, "What do you know about Israel, Vishnu?"

"I've read the Bible, and Janet has told me about her stay in a kibbutz."

"That's a good start."

"I also have an uncle who's buried in Israel."

His attitude changed to one of concern. He put his arm round my shoulders. Janet's mom placed her knife and fork on her plate.

"How did this happen?" she asked.

"He served in the British colonial army during the Jewish and Arab uprisings," I said. "He enlisted to earn a living and see the world."

There was a moment of silence.

"I'd like to visit his grave someday."

"We'll see to it that you go one day," Janet's dad said. "I know how it feels not to know where your kin's resting place is. So many of our people were denied a resting place."

The rest of the evening, Mr. Peters showed me photos on the wall of his uncle, aunt, and cousin who died in Nazi camps, and related how Hitler's troops had destroyed the Jewish heritage in his native country, with the Soviets finishing the job after the war. He told me of his escape from Lithuania. I felt like part of the family as he shared these sad memories with me, a helpless part who could offer little comfort except to listen and express horror at the barbarism of the occupiers.

"We were from a family of rabbinic scholars," he said. "My uncle and cousin must have died within a week of their arrival in the labor camps. They had never lifted a shovel in their lives."

I noticed that Mr. Peters had soft hands, too, softer than mine were now.

"Let's change the subject to something more uplifting," he said. "The Torah and baseball."

I couldn't see any connection between the American

pastime and Moses. As he walked to the overloaded shelves on the wall and pulled out a book, I was afraid he would launch into what Professor Ghita, reflecting on his adolescent years, called "excruciating Talmudic exegesis."

"It's a present," he said as he gave it to me. "Light reading on the way to New Haven." It was Chaim Potok's coming-of-age novel *The Chosen*.

"Dad, you should tell him about Stendhal," Janet said. "Vishnu works for a Jewish professor who teaches French literature."

He went back to the overcrowded bookshelf and took out a photo album. He showed me a photo of an elegant house in Vilnius where the French novelist, who accompanied Napoleon, stayed during the disastrous retreat of the Emperor's Grande Armée from Moscow. "My family lived in the street right behind," he said. I didn't know then that four decades later I would visit Stendhal's house and have a photo taken on its front steps; it had become the proud seat of the French embassy, with a French bookstore on the ground floor. The Peterses' ancestral home, however, was gone to make way for a public park. Dispirited, I sat on a bench in the park. I thought of Napoleon's ragged soldiers struggling to keep warm and stay alive in their bivouacs on Vilnius Town Hall Square, a thousand feet away, and the Nazis marching through the city 130 years later, and mumbled to myself about the good luck of growing up on an island far from the maelstrom of world events.

After dinner, I offered to help in the kitchen. "You wash dishes now?" Janet said with a smile. "You need rest. We have a busy day tomorrow."

The next morning she took me to Greenwich Village.

"A bohemian neighborhood," she said. I expected artists and writers, their gaunt bodies dressed in gypsy clothes. What I saw was shops selling drug paraphernalia and posters, mostly psychedelic. I had seen these in the dorms at Yale—where, at any party worth its name, the standard greeting at the door was the offer of a joint—but the selection in the Village was enormous. The most memorable poster was a black-and-white poster of President Nixon sitting on the toilet, trousers on the floor. I stood there wondering what would happen if the shopkeepers in Mauritius displayed such a poster of their rulers. Freedom of expression that was truly admirable! *America, land of wonders!*

"Let's go see the clowns and musicians in Washington Square," Janet said.

On the way, by Shakespeare's, a pub-restaurant on MacDougal Street, about a dozen people stood, listening to a woman who sang to the accompaniment of a Black male guitarist. Suddenly a young Black man sprung out of nowhere and shouted, "What the fuck are you doing here, playing with a white bitch?" The couple froze. The latecomer strode up to them and punched the guitarist's face. His guitar hit the pavement and his nose bled. The street, so merry with music, turned sad and empty as the couple hurried away.

"Shouldn't we call the police?" I asked Janet, my voice and body shaking. Back home in Mahébourg, I had witnessed more ferocious violence, but it involved fights between bellicose guys who were more or less equally matched or who were drunk. I hadn't seen bullies knocking peaceful people to the street.

"The police have bigger problems to deal with in this

city," Janet replied. "By the time they get here, everyone will be gone."

On the subway train, I told Janet about Tim's views on his sister dating a Black man.

"Is this sexual anxiety vis-à-vis the other race?" I asked.

"It's worse. It's fear and loathing of those they regard as traitors to the race."

In the afternoon, after a pizza lunch where Janet and her brother tried to reassure me that I'd be okay in the city, Edward took me to Lincoln Center and treated me to a musical, "a uniquely American art form." It was *Man of La Mancha*. I had read *Don Quixote* in secondary school, but I had never imagined it other than as a novel or film, never envisioned such a soulful rendering as the one I saw on the stage, its optimism so different from my recollection of the novel as being dark when I read it as an adolescent. When the hero launched into "To dream the impossible dream . . . to reach the unreachable star," I thought he was singing my song, the song of everyone in the audience. I saw a New York different from the one in the morning and different from what the Canadian warned me against. It was a city that spoke to human aspirations, a city of hope against all odds.

"Let's walk to Times Square before it gets dark," Edward told me.

Brimming with the euphoria induced by Don Quixote's immortal quest, I looked at the marquees above the theater entrances. It was a cornucopia. Shakespeare and *Equus*. Eugene O'Neill and Tennessee Williams. Side by side with *Godspell* and *Jesus Christ Superstar* was *Oh! Calcutta!*, its posters showing scenes of total nudity. Once again, true freedom of expression! The Canadian from Alberta was wrong.

"New York City is the center of civilization, not Connecticut," I told Edward.

Edward took a deep breath and exhaled, and we walked some more.

We came upon a theater where the neon lights were in the shape of cabaret nudes. On the front step stood a young Indian with the urbane mustache of Raj Kapoor, the leading Bombay film star. I hadn't expected Indians in the United States to be working at a movie house; I thought of them as graduate students, doctors, engineers.

"First time in New York?" he said.

I nodded yes.

"From India?"

"No. Mauritius."

"I've heard great things about your island. You guys are quite advanced."

I whispered to Edward: "For once, someone is flattering my country!"

I turned to the Indian. "We're kind of . . . westernized. French and English influence. African, too."

"You must be more open-minded than Indians, then," he said.

"I don't know. I haven't met many Indians here."

"I'm Krishna. In America I'm Kris. Since it's your first visit to New York, I have a free movie ticket for you and your American friend. The film started fifteen minutes ago, but you'll still enjoy it. Go in; it will be my pleasure."

He had a refined accent, not the heavy Indian accent of the taxi drivers I met during my week in London.

Edward and I looked at each other. "What do we lose?" we both said, simultaneously, with a shrug.

The film was set in the Roman Empire, possibly in the reign of Caligula or Tiberius. For the next hour, the screen bared carnal permutations and combinations I had never thought of. I had seen the X-rated *Primitive London* and *The Nights of Lucrezia Borgia* at the Odeon Cinema in Mahébourg, but they were children's movies by comparison. To say that I was indifferent or outraged in that Times Square movie house would be a big lie. I was seeing raw, uninhibited sex for the first time. For all our Western influence, premarital sex was taboo in Mauritius. You read *Madame Bovary,* saw Elvis romance Ann-Margret, even bought *Playboy* and *Penthouse* at outrageous prices, but you couldn't touch a girl. Now was time to enjoy.

"Edward, did you see such stuff before?"

"Nope" he said. "Well, some, yes. But some stuff here was pretty far out."

At the door, Kris thanked us and hoped we'd enjoyed the movie. He asked if we were interested in being swingers.

"My wife and I enjoy it, and we have a select circle of friends we share our pleasure with."

He took out his wallet and showed us a picture of his wife—a curvaceous brunette. Then a photo of a blonde, an East Asian, a Black American. "We're all swingers. It would be great to have you join us. You look clean."

There was no man in his portfolio of swingers, which made me suspicious.

"We'll be back," Edward said. "Thanks for the movie."

We walked towards the subway station. "Vishnu, further down the road you'll meet the New York of your

Canadian," Edward said. "That Indian guy has no wife. He's a pimp. The free movie was a bait to lure us in."

Tamby at the Rex Cinema, Kris at the Times Square movie house.

Still, after the confinement of the kitchen in D.C., the beat and rhythm of Times Square were liberating. After a menacing start, I spent daylight in a twentieth-century Athens of playwrights and artists, and nighttime at a modern Sodom and Gomorrah. This city would have satisfied Kumar's craving for the excitement and vibrant cultural life he experienced in Calcutta and his yearning for sexual freedom.

The Tuckers would have seen the day differently: after a highbrow matinee at Lincoln Center, we washed away the culture with lowbrow trash.

WHEN I ARRIVED on campus to start my last year, Professor Ghita was the first person I called. I had no savings left.

"Would you have some extra hours of work for me? I can start tonight."

"What's the rush? You should unwind before the first day of class. Come by—I've brought an excellent Château Haut-Brion from Paris."

The professor of music and his lover were also there. Professor Ghita and his wife spoke about their stimulating summer in Europe. "So refreshing after a year of endless TV drivel from Nixon," he said. His wife talked about how Europeans now loathed America for the continuous napalm bombing of North Vietnam.

As he poured more wine into the music professor's glass, Professor Ghita said, "Vishnu here has just spent some time interning on Capitol Hill."

"How was it?" said the music professor. "In college I went for light manual jobs, moderately demanding ones that would develop my finger muscles. It helps in piano playing."

"Interesting perspective," I said. "The first time I saw a piano, I was eleven, at school. In Mauritius, that's for the super-rich."

Then I told them about my Sans Souci hubris and the karmic price I paid. I spread my hands out, pressing the parts that were now coarser.

"You'll get back your softer hands," Professor Ghita's wife said. "One day, you'll thank Nancy Hansen for the experience."

Professor Ghita frowned. "You're talking like those elites who want to keep people like Vishnu in their place. 'You have to pay your dues,' they say to the immigrants and the poor, 'before you can join our club.' Their kids don't pay the dues; they get well-paid internships on Wall Street or go on culture tours in Tuscany."

NINE MONTHS AFTER Sans Souci, I was in the dean's office.

"One of our trustees has asked us to identify someone they can train and send overseas. He is president of a bank that wants to expand in a big way. After eight years or so, the person selected could well be in the top tier of the bank's management. Does that interest you, Vishnu?" the dean said.

"I'm flattered. Thank you for thinking of me."

"You're graduating with excellent grades. With your language abilities and intercultural skills, you would be a good fit."

When I told Professor Ghita about the prospect, he had a laugh that was part a chuckle of satisfaction, part the sarcasm of a Marxist. "La Haute Finance, hein! Tu vas devenir un grand bonhomme," he said. "I'd be dismayed if you don't turn out at least a millionaire."

A week later, in the early morning, I was at the headquarters of the Bank of Boston. The personnel officer, who had a limp, briefed me about the recruitment process. I would spend the morning in interviews with midlevel technical staff in various departments—accounting, economic research, retail banking, corporate banking—followed by lunch with the Director of Personnel. The staff did not expect me to know the details of banking and specific subject areas. Rather, they were looking "for a certain quality of mind and personality." I didn't know what that meant. When the personnel officer added that these qualities were hard to define, that what they meant varied from company to company, and even department to department, I thought there was no point trying to get a better handle on the term.

By noon, I was interviewing on the fifth floor. The personnel officer who escorted me from floor to floor told me that was a good sign—I was making the grade with tougher and tougher interviewers. Everyone complimented me on my answers; the handshakes were getting firmer. Comments ranged from "You have a unique perspective on what's going on" to "Your economics is sound."

When it was time for lunch, the personnel officer told me that the Senior VP of International Operations had freed himself from another engagement to join the Director of Personnel and me.

The day had unfolded in a way that was almost too good to be true. But now the stakes were getting higher and I felt sweat in my armpits.

Lunch was at Maison Robert. "The epitome of good French cuisine," said the Director of Personnel. As I entered the formal dining room, I now saw—behind the imposing edifice, the charming demeanor of the maître d', and the menu, listing dishes with sophisticated names—a team of unseen and unsung cooks, dishwashers, and floor cleaners whose underpaid work formed the foundation of the business.

The senior VP, a lean man with unusually long sideburns for a banker, ordered the rack of lamb. I craved the calves' brain (Voltaire's mom made a delicious curry from it) but refrained; Americans get queasy when they see brains and innards on dinner plates. I went for the Dover sole.

The senior VP inquired about my Senate internship. The tone was aggressive, bordering on rude. "Did you get to perform any task that went beyond filing and licking envelopes?"

Georgie Espitalier-Noël, my secondary school teacher, came again to the rescue. I could hear him. "Grace under pressure" is how he passed his orals at Oxford.

I managed a faint smile. "The administrative staff tried

to dump the filing and envelope licking on me, but I went to the senator's senior aide and told him about my one year of law studies and that I really wanted to learn how the American system functions. I said I needed more challenging work."

"What did he say?"

"He told me that, for an intern, I was a hell of a ballsy kid."

"And?"

"I apologized and I shut up."

The senior VP was looking at the way I held my knife and fork.

"For how long did you shut up?" he said.

"The next day, he asked me to suggest an assignment that could help his boss. I knew the issue of revenue sharing between the federal government and states was coming up, and I offered to research it."

The senior VP was inscrutable. I answered his questions about the Glass-Steagall Act and the rivalry between American and European multinationals, but I couldn't guess what he thought of me. He turned to the Director of Personnel. "I'll skip the coffee and leave you now. Give me a call when you're done."

Half an hour or so later, the call was made.

"The President wants to see you."

The President's office overlooked Boston Harbor. Unlike those of his subordinates, it had no bookshelves. A few masks hung on the wall—ancient ritual masks from Africa, Brazil, Indonesia. His desk was clear except for a Montblanc pen next to a sheet of white paper. No files or dossiers. No briefcase.

Everyone who had interviewed me so far wore pin-stripe suits, mostly blue. The president dressed in solid charcoal gray. His only concessions to color were his gold cuff links and his red tie.

When he rose to greet me, I felt there was something singular and extraordinary about him. The sobriety of his office suggested that he was someone who went straight to the essence of things, the core of the matter.

He stood behind his desk as he spoke. "Vishnu, you come to us highly recommended. My colleagues think you have the intellect and personality for the job. You obviously can navigate your way pretty well across the world. Tell me something: why do you want this job?"

I had been asked that question so many times since the morning that I made a determined effort to modulate my voice, so as not to sound robotic. I spoke of the intellectual stimulation, the opportunity to grow, to apply what I'd learnt, the wonderful things I had read about the Bank of Boston, and the pleasure of working with smart colleagues, and I emphasized that I was achievement-oriented.

He walked out from behind his desk and sat in the chair next to me.

"Indeed, Vishnu, all these speak in your favor. But why banking in particular? Why not manufacturing—say, like General Motors? Or IBM? Why not academia? Is there something in banking that's especially attractive?"

He paused, giving me a few seconds to think.

"Is it because it's lucrative?" he added.

"As far as money is concerned, as long as I have a spacious house, well furnished, a nice car, and good food, I'll be satisfied."

"So it does not take much to make you happy," the President said.

His countenance changed, from affable and well disposed to solemn.

He continued, "Money drives this business. We have to bring in money, day in and day out. You won't be able to sustain that if you're not driven by the profit motive. Have you given any thought to that?"

"If I do the job right, the money would come in," I said.

"If I don't bring in more money each year, the Board fires me. Bankers don't have the luxury of tenure that your professors have. What motivates you, Vishnu? That's the question you have to ask yourself."

The interview had turned into a lecture. I looked at the masks; they were laughing at my expense. My earlobes were hot. I was tongue-tied.

"We like you, but I'm not sure you're ready for the business world. The profit motive has to be ingrained in you."

"How does that happen?" I asked.

"Go to business school. A good one—Harvard, Stanford, Chicago. For two years you'll bathe in a special atmosphere, where people are not ashamed to talk about money."

He rose, shook my hand, and wished me luck.

In the taxi to Boston's Logan Airport, I looked back on the occasions when the word *profit* was mentioned at home. There were not many, and they usually involved some unethical activity—the shopkeeper diluting rum with water or the goldsmith falsifying scales to increase profits, the sugar estates cooking the books to escape taxes and keep all their profits. When we arrived at the airport, the driver had to wake me up. It had been a tiring day.

As I handed him the fare, the sight and feel of green banknotes in my palm took me back to a book that my father often referred to, especially when he didn't want to buy something Mama or I wanted. It was written by an award-winning American journalist, Louis Fischer— *Gandhi: His Life and Message for the World.* The back cover carried a photo of Gandhi's possessions when he died: a pair of wooden shoes, his spectacles, his dhoti, and the Bhagavad Gita. "Anything else is superfluous," Papa would say.

No wonder I didn't grasp it when the bank president handed me the answer he wanted to hear:

"Why do you want the job? Is it because it's lucrative?"

I let Gandhi win.

I let the opportunity of a lifetime go down the drain.

I let down the neighbors in Mahébourg who regarded me as "their horse in the race."

As I walked to the boarding gate, inchoate thoughts burst forth. Was I at heart a non-materialist? Or did I enjoy the good life that money brings, gourmet food, fine wines, and stylish clothes? Uncle Ram wanted me to emigrate not to become a millionaire but to escape the repressive and hypocritical morality of the island. The caretaker at the Royal College spoke about students who became *"grands bougres,"* big wigs. What did that mean? Making money, wielding power, achieving something special, helping family and country? Maybe I was a bundle of contradictions, with the family's ambivalent attitude towards money hanging over me. When my father and Uncle Ram spoke of their lost heirlooms and possessions in the wake of Cyclone Carol, they never mentioned their monetary value. True, Papa didn't hesitate to sue Auntie Ranee for Uncle Ram's land, and he talked about suing the sugar estate for damages; nonetheless, he admired Gandhi's austerity and gave to the man with the glass eye and other strangers who knocked on the door; he even gave Uncle Mohan money barely a year after the latter had attacked him at the conclave of goons.

Had I really wanted the banking job, or had I made the trip to Boston to figure things out?

All along, I had been trumpeting to myself the motto *Survive? That's not why I came to America. I came here to thrive!*

Now I asked myself whether I fully understood what I meant by "thrive."

The turmoil had begun.

On the plane that would take me back to Yale, I lifted the shade on the window and caught a glimpse of the few people bidding good-bye to loved ones. As I mused over the advice of the bank president and struggled with Gandhi's influence, I thought about the many people who had chartered a bus to see me off at the airport in Mauritius two years earlier—family, friends, and the neighbors, led by the two Creole fishermen, the brothers Fringant and Kalipa. They brightened the departure balcony with colorful balloons that said BON VOYAGE and BONNE CHANCE. They were proud and full of hope. But the moist eyes, theirs and mine, expressed more than sadness at my leaving: there was the fear of the unknown. None of us knew anyone who had been to the United States. Papa hugged me tight and kissed me on my cheeks. Mama sobbed and held my hands and wouldn't let go. Kalipa bowed to her, gently pulled my left hand, and shoved in a vial of the seven-colored earth of Chamarel ("Souvenir of Mauritius" the label read).

"Never forget what's written in the Bible: Don't let your parents down. Don't let your community down," Kalipa said.

Over the aircraft's loudspeaker system, the pilot announced a ten-minute delay in the plane's departure to Windsor Locks. Simon & Garfunkel resumed their song "Look for America."

Acknowledgments

My deepest thanks to:
My parents, Seenarain and Cossilah, who toiled to create for me opportunities they never had.
My uncle Ramnarain, whose nightly utterance inspired the title of this novel.
Yves Léfébure and Daniel Koenig, teachers at the Royal College (Curepipe) Secondary School, who instilled in me a love of literature.
Kimberly Witherspoon and Maria Whelan, my agents, for their unstinting belief in, and advocacy for, this novel.
Robert Bloom, my editor, for his insightful and sharp editing, and his enthusiasm.
Edward P. Jones, for the guidance and wisdom of a guru.
Tim Johnston and Antonya Nelson, for their comments on an earlier draft.
Teachers and fellow writers in the following workshops: Aspen Words, Jenny McKean Moore Workshop at George Washington University, Lighthouse Writers, UNM Summer Writers' Conference in Santa Fe, Summer Literary Seminars (Vilnius and Tbilisi), and Eckerd College Conference: Writers in Paradise.
Last, but not least, my wife Nessa for her encouragement and support on this journey.

The poem "Truants" first appeared in *Crosswinds Poetry Journal*, vol. IV, 2019.
I have quoted from: (a) Edwin G. Davy, "Meteorology in Mauritius" in *Glimpses of Empire, A Corona Anthology*, edited by Anthony Kirk-Greene, I. B. Tauris Publishers, London, New York, 2001, and (b) Richard Crichton, *The Coldstream Guards, 1946–1970,* printed by Richard Clay (The Chaucer Press) Ltd, Bungay, Suffolk, 1972.

About the Author

VINOD BUSJEET was born in Mauritius, a multiracial island in the Indian Ocean. He holds degrees from Wesleyan University, New York University, and Harvard University and spent twenty-nine years in economic development, finance, and diplomacy, holding positions at the World Bank and International Finance Corporation, and as a secondary school teacher in Mauritius. He lives in Washington, D.C., with his wife. This is his first book.